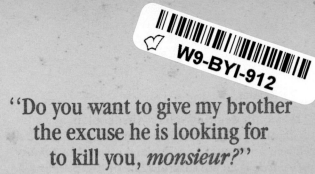

"Do you want to give my brother the excuse he is looking for to kill you, *monsieur?*"

Marie Therese demanded in a low, throbbing voice.

"Non, mademoiselle," Jacques said ruefully. "But what man could have resisted when you flung yourself down on me like that?"

"I did not! You mock me, *monsieur,*" she said, the emotional throb still in her voice. Startled, he saw that her eyes were suspiciously moist, and realized for the first time how vulnerable she was under her tart exterior. He felt a pang of contrition at his plan to deliberately exploit her inexperience and enlist her help.

"No, I do not mock you," he said seriously, catching her hand. "You, *mademoiselle,* are a prize worth any risk."

Dear Reader,

This month we bring you the first book in a delightful trilogy by author Maura Seger. Set in Belle Haven, a fictional New England town, *The Taming of Amelia* is an adventurous tale of two people destined to forge new lives for themselves in the Colonies. It sets the stage for stories of the town's future generations—right up to the present day, with a tie-in book from Silhouette's Intimate Moments line.

Prolific newcomer Kit Gardner is sure to please with *The Stolen Heart,* a high-spirited romance between an aristocratic English girl and the Pinkerton detective whom she thinks is an outlaw.

New to Harlequin Historicals but certainly not to romance, Virginia Nielsen has written a moving story about a privateer and the Creole woman who rescues him in *To Love a Pirate.*

Knight's Lady, Suzanne Barclay's new book, features another of the irresistible Sommerville brothers. Introduced in *Knight Dreams* (HH #141), Gareth is the eldest sibling and heir to a fortune, yet the granddaughter of a lowly goldsmith holds the key to his heart.

Look for all four titles at your favorite bookstore.

Sincerely,

Tracy Farrell
Senior Editor

To Love a Pirate

Virginia Nielsen

Harlequin Books

TORONTO • NEW YORK • LONDON
AMSTERDAM • PARIS • SYDNEY • HAMBURG
STOCKHOLM • ATHENS • TOKYO • MILAN
MADRID • WARSAW • BUDAPEST • AUCKLAND

Harlequin Historicals first edition February 1993

ISBN 0-373-28761-5

TO LOVE A PIRATE

VIRGINIA NIELSEN

is a versatile and prolific writer who was awarded the first RITA by the Romance Writers of America for her contribution to romantic fiction. She has published 250 short stories and thirty-seven books. Born in Idaho, she has lived in several states, including Hawaii, Texas and Louisiana, and has traveled extensively. Currently, she and her husband, Mac, live in Northern California, where they swim almost daily.

To the family and friends of the late
Frances St. Martin Dansereau, of Houma,
who gave so generously of their time and
knowledge of Louisiana tradition and history

Chapter One

Early December, 1814

It was past midnight. The cold mist hanging over the river was more fog than rain. No candlelight was visible through the trees screening the plantation on his right as Jacques Bonnard rode along the deserted levee road, below besieged New Orleans.

His stallion was black as the night, and the swift trot of his hoofbeats was muffled on the wet ground by the rags Jacques had tied over his shod hooves. The animal had the stamina to take Jacques to Jean Lafitte's hideout deep in the bayous of the Mississippi delta by dawn, but his temperament was as skittish as a woman's.

That thought reminded Jacques of the comely barmaid whose eyes had flashed an invitation as she served wine to him and Jean's lawyer in the back room of the blacksmith shop in the rue St. Philippe that he had left earlier. Desire stirred as he remembered the seductive way she had let the fullness of her bosom brush his shoulder when she leaned over to refill his goblet.

He could have spent a most pleasurable night in her bed if the message he carried to Jean were not so important. He wondered if *l'américain,* Livingston, was with her now, exploring those tantalizing hillocks that rose so temptingly from her *décolletage.*

He shrugged ruefully. *C'est la vie, Jacques.*

Suddenly a dark shadow swooped low with a startling whir of wings to pounce on some small creature scurrying across the road. The stallion's ears flattened, and he shied to the left in terror as the great horned owl lifted its wings and was gone with its prey. Jacques cursed as his mount's wrapped hooves slid down the grassy slope of the levee.

In the next instant, he was soaring over his horse's head into the river. Stars exploded behind his eyes as his head struck what must have been a submerged log. Water rushed over his head and into his nose, choking him.

If he lost consciousness, it was only for seconds. But he was helpless against the strong current of the mighty river, raised by recent heavy rains, which was tumbling him over and over as it carried him downstream. He fought it with his considerable strength, clawing his way to the surface to cough up water and fill his tortured lungs with air.

With a tremendous effort of his will, he lifted his head out of the water, dizzily surveying his chances. Blood was trickling into his eyes, making it difficult to see.

A cloud had drifted over the slender moon. There was no sign of his damned horse, which had either drowned or bolted, and he was being swept downstream toward the Gulf with a swiftness he would not have thought possible. It was taking all his strength to keep his head above the swirling muddy water, just hoping the current would carry him to one bank or the other so that he could save himself.

But it did not. The current swept him on like a bobbing cork in the middle of the river. Though groggy, he was aware that loss of blood was gradually weakening him. He had always considered himself invincible, but now it occurred to him that he might drown here alone, and it was an astounding thought.

He might never dally with the buxom barmaid who had fancied him. Never again lock swords with an enemy, or toast victory by rolling the sweet warmth of West Indian rum across his tongue, or know the intense secret pleasure of sliding into a gasping, compliant woman.

And who would mourn him?

The crew of his brigantine would lift a tot of grog, and so would his old friends, Jean and Pierre Lafitte. Somewhere a pretty wench he didn't even remember might cross herself and whisper a prayer. No one else.

So much for Jacques Bonnard, gentleman privateer, rakehell, orphan...

No, by hell! He was not done for yet!

He struggled on, interminably. He lost track of time. He could no longer see. All his senses were concentrated on battling the strength of the current, its tug and direction. At last he divined a curve in the river.... Its current was carrying him toward the opposite bank, and beginning to eddy.

Using his last ounce of strength, he grabbed at the overhanging bushes and dragged himself out of its flow. With his shoulders out of the water, lying in the mud, his legs still feeling the pull of the current, he collapsed. He was scarcely breathing. The sucking, gurgling sound of the river droned in his ears as he closed his eyes and drifted into grayness.

As the rising sun began to color the sky in the east, Marie-Thérèse Dufret galloped south down the levee away from her father's plantation, Petit Bois, the little grove.

She rode furiously, her dark hair streaming behind her, her midnight-blue eyes stormy, her creamy skin flushed a deep rose with anger.

A morning ride on her favorite mare, Beauté, after an early breakfast with Papa was a ritual when they were at the plantation. But this morning she was not riding for enjoyment. To the pounding rhythm of Beauté's stride, she was hearing again the incredible, unforgivable words with which Papa had shattered her complacency.

While Estelle poured their coffee and set the plate of *beignets* before them, Monsieur had asked—idly, Marie-Thérèse had thought—"Which of your admirers do you fancy for a husband?"

"None, Papa. Why should I marry when I have such a lovely home and you and Hébert to look after?"

"Hébert is seventeen. He will go to Paris to study when this damnable war is over and the blockade is lifted."

"But you will still depend on me to manage your households here and in the city."

"You have taken your mother's place with charm and grace, Marie-Thérèse, but you will soon be nineteen. Most of your friends were married or promised at sixteen. Some are already mistresses of great plantations."

She remembered how fondly she had smiled at him. "But I am mistress of the most beautiful plantation on the river! What can a husband give me that I don't already have?"

It was true, she thought, urging Beauté faster to keep up with her riotous thoughts. Since the loss of her mother and Adorée, her older sister, at sea four years before, she had been mistress of Petit Bois and her father's town house, and his many servants. As his social hostess, she had her own unique place in the city's Creole society, with many friends, more invitations than she could accept, and great independence. Her friend Annalise claimed that half the eligible young men in New Orleans were in love with her.

When Marie-Thérèse had voiced the question, "What can marriage give me that I don't already have?" to Annalise, that romantic young lady had retorted, "Love!"

Marie-Thérèse had laughed at her and said, "Only a grand passion could make me give up the life I lead for marriage!"

But to the same question her father had answered, very seriously, "It can give you children. And me grandchildren."

"I do want babies," she'd admitted after taking a thoughtful sip of her café au lait, "but I haven't yet met the man I want for their father."

Papa had not responded to her smile. "The British are coming," he had said quietly. "It is believed that they will try to take New Orleans and then move up the Mississippi to bring America to her knees. Hébert will join the Louisiana Brigade. I must take command of my regiment. Before we risk our lives fighting the army that defeated Napoleon, I want you married to an eligible suitor whose family will care for you if neither of us survive."

"Papa! Is it so serious?" The city had been under British blockade for two years, but they had wanted for little, thanks to the privateers and smugglers like the Lafittes, who brought in all the French luxuries Creole citizens craved. Marie-Thérèse had thought of the war as largely an American quarrel that did not much affect the relaxed and gracious life her father and his friends enjoyed.

"It is becoming very serious," he said. "This is a valuable port for *les américains,* and the British apparently think they can achieve victory in the war by capturing our city." He picked up another sugared *beignet.* "So is it to be Gabriel Duvallier or Etienne Picou?"

Mon Dieu! Marry Gabriel Duvallier? He was a good friend, pleasant to be with for an hour, but he was so stiffly correct in everything he did, and something of a dandy in his attention to his dress. He also had a fondness for writing foolish verses he dedicated to her, which were more often than not an embarrassment.

And Etienne Picou! He was a charming scamp, the darling of every hostess because he was witty and liked to dally in conversation with the ladies, but as a husband she suspected she would not trust him out of her sight for a minute.

"I simply can't imagine being married to either one of them, Papa."

To her utter shock, her father, who had always been so indulgent, who had always treated her as an equal and had usually deferred to her in anything to do with managing the household, said bluntly, "Pick one."

Unwisely, she exclaimed, "But, Papa, I have no wish to be married!"

"I'm sorry, *ma petite,* but if you do not, I shall have to pick one for you. *I* think it should be Gabriel."

Appalled, she said, "I appreciate your concern for my safety, Papa, but I cannot allow you to pick a husband—any husband—for me, just like that!"

Marie-Thérèse glimpsed a look of shock from Estelle and realized belatedly that she was not taking this as a dutiful daughter should. But then, her relationship with her father had changed subtly in the years since he had elevated her position to that of his hostess.

"And why not, pray?" he asked icily. "Have any of your married friends chosen their own husbands? They have accepted the informed advice of their fathers, is it not so? It is the duty of every honorable man to arrange a proper marriage for a beloved daughter. Why should you expect anything less of me?"

She stammered, "B-because you have so often trusted my judgment, Papa. And this is a private matter, one I should like to be allowed to take care of myself in my own good time."

She saw at once that she had gone too far. His face was very red. "You will do as I say, Marie-Thérèse. This discussion is ended." He threw down his serviette and left her. Raging, she called after him that he was cruel and inhuman. Then she slammed down her café au lait and strode out to the stable, where her groom had Beauté saddled and waiting, as usual.

Shame came over her now at the way she had shouted after her father—she, who never raised her voice except in laughter. He had always been so remarkably indulgent with her, and especially so since the tragedy that had lacerated their family. Which was exactly why it was so difficult for her to accept his ultimatum.

But this was such a personal matter! She would *never* accept his choice of a husband. She simply couldn't. What was she going to do?

Angrily she realized that it was not only rage she was feeling; she was aroused in a curious way by the serious talk of an immediate marriage and children, and all that implied. She was very conscious of the feeling of her mare's muscles moving smoothly between her thighs. Oh, her body was ready for marriage! But Gabriel, or Etienne? Never!

In her shame she had slackened her hold on Beauté's reins, and the lathered mare slowed to a walk. Marie-Thérèse let her gaze wander to the river. The water was high this morning, and muddy with the early winter rains. Her anger had cooled, but her wild gallop had done nothing to revive her spirits or settle her mind. She must calm herself and plot how to dissuade *cher* Papa from forcing her into a lifetime with someone she did not love, simply because *les américains* were at war.

She turned Beauté's head, intending to return to Petit Bois, when her eye saw a dark and muddy object at the river's edge that almost stopped her heart. Was that a man's hand lying in the mud?

A corpse, she thought, recoiling. A runaway slave, perhaps, who had drowned trying to cross the river. Was it Gilly, who had run away from Petit Bois last month? Her immediate impulse was to ride back and report it to Papa's overseer. It was well known that the British were inciting the slaves to rebellion, and the number of runaways was increasing. Few managed to survive in the swamps surrounding New Orleans, but if they reached the city they could lose themselves in the throngs of free men and women of color who had poured in from the West Indies.

She doubted that Gilly could have survived for this long. What she saw still had the shape of a man, which meant the corpse was newly dead—or barely alive?

Perhaps she should make sure.

Temporarily distracted from her anger at Papa, she dismounted. She wrapped the reins tightly around her hand and closed her fist on them. Then she led her mare carefully down the slope of the levee. The grass was damp and slippery, and her mount was frightened of the water.

"You can do it, Beauté," she coaxed her reluctant mare. "I'm certainly not going down there alone and find you've run away home without me."

She saw at once that it was not Gilly, or anyone else she recognized. The man was black with mud, but neither his skin nor his clothes were those of a slave. Actually, his clothing must once have been rather fine. Ah, but he was a big man! Even Gilly, a canecutter, had not had shoulders so broad.

The ground around his head was colored by something more than water. Her stomach churned when she realized that it was blood and that it looked surprisingly fresh. *Could he be alive?*

If so, he was in a precarious situation. Although his head and shoulders were out of the water, the current was tugging at his submerged legs, even as it seemed to be alternately pushing him against the bank.

Something in the way he lay with that arm outstretched desperately spoke of complete exhaustion, and of a despair that touched her compassion. It suggested what her mother and sister must have felt on that dreadful day when the pirates seized the ship bringing them home and set them adrift in a small boat.... She choked off the painful memory and studied the unconscious man more closely.

Did he still live? She could not tell. He was deathly still, but his color, although pallid, still suggested someone living in the sun. She pulled up her riding skirt to keep it free of the mud and squatted near his head, listening for the faintest sound of breathing.

Suddenly the hand, almost beneath her, moved convulsively and wrapped its curling fingers around her exposed ankle, tight as a vise. Thrown off balance, Marie-Thérèse screamed and tumbled on her back. Her startled mare echoed her scream with a wild neighing and danced backward, pulling her roughly over the brush at the river's edge and almost wrenching her arm from its socket.

Stunned and bruised, Marie-Thérèse lay on her back, Beauté's reins still wrapped tightly around her fist. It took her a few seconds to realize that the grip she felt on her leg meant that the man she had thought dead still held her ankle in a grasp like steel.

She sat up, brushing the dark, curling strands of hair out of her eyes, and looked down at him. Because she had so tangled her hand in Beauté's reins, her mare had pulled the man completely out of the water. *Mon Dieu,* but he was big!

She bent forward and, with difficulty, unlocked the frozen grip of his fingers, one by one, then gingerly put her hands on his shoulders. The solid feel of his flesh beneath his sodden clothing was faintly surprising, as though she still thought him an apparition. He was definitely real, and very heavy. It took all her strength to roll him over on his side.

It was a strong face she saw, clean-shaven, but with a dark and dangerous look, which was enhanced by a faint saber scar that slanted across one muddy cheek from the corner of his eye to his jaw. Her heart gave a painful leap when she saw the wound on his forehead from which his blood had been oozing into the mud.

Had that terrifying grasp of her ankle been made in the last convulsive throes of death? She thought he was breathing, but barely. He must have collapsed upon reaching the bank. What fortitude it had taken to save himself from drowning after the grievous blow he had received! He must have the strength of two men. Perhaps he was strong enough to survive, if she could get attention to him quickly enough.

With shaking fingers, she undid his cravat, and was relieved to see a faint pulse beating in his throat. She tied the cravat tightly around his head, covering the swollen wound.

"Come, Beauté," she said. "We must go for help."

Her mare did not need encouragement to leap up the slope to the road. Marie-Thérèse mounted and said urgently, "Home, Beauté! We must ride like the wind."

Chapter Two

Marie-Thérèse galloped between moss-hung oaks up the long drive toward Petit Bois, feeling as if every hoofbeat marking a passing second were crucial to the man on the bank. Could he survive until she could get help to him? At the end of the drive the familiar two-story house with the double *galerie* running completely around it was silhouetted against the sun rising over the cypress trees of the swamp, sending long rays of light down each side veranda toward her.

The cluster of buildings around the *grande maison* was like a little village—the stable, with its adjoining forge, the sugarhouse, the slave quarters and beyond them, the swamp.

"Harness the cart, immediately!" she ordered the groom who came trotting out of the stable to help her dismount. Tossing him her reins, she ran up the steps and into the house.

Estelle, the housekeeper, was in the hall. "Ma'mselle?" she asked, but at the same time Marie-Thérèse asked, "Where is *monsieur?*"

"The master ride out to the fields."

"M'sieu Hébert?"

"He takes breakfast."

Marie-Thérèse burst into the dining room. "Hébert!"

Her brother was seated at the long mahogany table, with a plate of eggs and a mug of café au lait before him. The blue damask morning coat he had recently begun affecting accentuated the youthful rosiness of his cheeks. He looked up, lifting his eyebrows in a bored criticism of her unseemly haste.

"What is it, Marie-Thérèse?"

"A man who has met with an accident on the river. He lies half-drowned on the *batture,* about a mile and a half down the levee. Will you take two grooms and go in the cart to bring him here?"

"Who is this man?"

"A gentleman who needs our help," she said impatiently. She heard her own words, and in a flash of memory saw the dangerous mud-smeared face, with the thin line of a saber cut running down one cheek. *A gentleman?*

"Please go at once, Hébert. I have asked Bruno to harness the cart for you, but you can't take him. I want to send Bruno for the doctor."

"Where is Papa?"

"He has ridden out to inspect the cane fields." The arable land along the river had been planted with cane to take advantage of the high profit in sugar during the blockade. "We cannot wait for his return. The man is too seriously hurt. Go, please, and I will get Mattie and prepare a room for him."

Hébert stood up, his serviette in one hand. "Estelle, please ask my man to bring my coat."

"Oui, michie."

Marie-Thérèse did not wait. She hurried down the hall and out onto the rear veranda. *"Ti'frère!"* she called to a small black boy who was playing with a baby raccoon.

"Run and tell Mattie to bring her potions and come to the big house."

"*Oui, ma'mselle,*" the boy said, tucking his pet under one arm.

She went down the steps and across the yard to the stable, where she told Bruno to take one of the horses and ride for the doctor as soon as he had the cart ready for Hébert. Then she turned back to the house to instruct her *femme de chambre* to make up a bed in the guest chamber with fresh linens and to find clean rags for Mattie.

All the while she was conscious in some part of her mind of the wounded man's blood seeping into her makeshift bandage. Would he still be breathing when they reached him, or would they be too late? When all was in readiness, Estelle fixed her a lemonade, and she sat down on the front *galerie* to quiet her racing pulse while she waited for Mattie and watched for the cart.

Papa rode in from the fields before Hébert arrived. Their quarrel over the matter of her marriage was not mentioned as Marie-Thérèse told him of the man she had found on the bank. She had scarcely finished her account of how Beauté had pulled him out of the river when the cart appeared, turning in at their drive from the levee road.

Monsieur Dufret walked down the steps to inspect the victim, and Marie-Thérèse followed him. The man was unconscious, but it was soon evident that he was alive, for he moaned when the two grooms lifted him from the cart, one grasping him under the arms and the other carrying his legs, staggering a bit under his weight.

His appearance was even more dismaying in the well-appointed rooms of Petit Bois than it had been on the bank. His clothes were caked with river mud, and his face was streaked with it, mixed with his blood. Marie-Thérèse flew ahead of the little group up the stairs and led the way to the guest chamber prepared for him.

Behind her she heard the man mutter hoarsely, in French, "Easy, lads, it's a rough sea tonight." Had he been a passenger in a boat, then?

"Do you know him, Papa?"

"Never saw him before. Leave us now, Marie-Thérèse. He must be stripped of those wet clothes, and bathed. Mattie!"

The plantation's healing woman had come up the back stairs, carrying her satchel of herbs and potions. Monsieur Dufret motioned her into the chamber with him and shut the door on Marie-Thérèse.

She lingered in the hall, listening to Mattie's resonant voice exclaiming over the man's wound and to her father's low instructions. She was feeling an anxiety that struck her as odd. After all, the man was a complete stranger.

Presently one of the men who had carried him in came out of his chamber with an armful of soiled clothing. She stopped him and inspected the articles. In spite of the river mud and its sodden condition, the cloth of his frock coat had originally been as fine as anything in her father's armoire. It had been made by a good tailor, the line of its tails curving away fashionably from the horizontal waist.

"Take them to the washhouse," she ordered the groom, "and tell Sophie to soak them overnight to get that bloodstain out."

Their guest was an intriguing mystery. What was his name? Where was he from, and what adventure had landed him in the river and nearly cost him his life?

The sun was climbing higher, and as mistress of the plantation Marie-Thérèse had many things to do. She went about her daily duties, planning the preparation of the day's meals with the kitchen help and seeing that the house servants, who were greatly diverted by their unusual guest, completed their work.

After that, she made her visits to the cabins of a slave who was being treated by Mattie for the ague and to another who had been delivered of a fine baby boy. But, although she tried, she could not keep her mind from dwelling on the mysterious stranger. It was difficult not to think about him, when her shoulder still ached and her buttocks were sore with bruises from the fall he had caused when he grabbed her ankle.

In the afternoon Bruno returned with the news that the doctor could not come before morning; he was busy with a patient, the wife of a prominent planter, whose difficult delivery could take all night.

"He say Mattie knows to clean the wound, and tell her to keep the man flat on he back if she have to put him to sleep to do it. He send you some laudanum."

Marie-Thérèse went to the guest chamber and knocked softly on the door, and when Mattie opened it, she told her what the doctor had said.

"You will have to spend the night with your patient, Mattie," she told the old woman. "Go and take a rest, now. I'll stay with him."

"Yes'm," Mattie said, eyeing the brown bottle she carried. "What's that?"

"Laudanum."

"That keep him quiet."

"How is he?"

"He hurt bad in the head, *ma'mselle.* An' some bruises. Mostly, he wore down fighting the river, I think. He be in the water long time."

Marie-Thérèse closed the door behind Mattie. The room had been darkened, and it felt warm and stuffy. She walked across to the floor-length window, which opened on the

galerie and cracked the shutters to let in more air. Light fell
across the shadowed bed, and when she turned to look at
it, she drew in her breath with a sharp gasp.

The patient had thrown off the light cover and lay
sprawled on the sheet as naked as *le bon dieu* made him.
Mattie had sponged the mud and dried blood from his face
and tied a neat white bandage around his forehead and his
dark locks. Her cleansing had exposed the surprisingly
handsome looks of a man who was younger than Marie-
Thérèse had thought.

But it was not his face that held her transfixed.

Her father's slaves wore little clothing in the heat of
summer, and she had gone with Mattie as part of her duties as mistress to treat both male and female workers who
were ill, but she had never seen a grown man totally bare
before. His skin looked the color of old gold against the
white sheet, and he was astonishingly beautiful. Marie-
Thérèse had never felt this strange warm sensation looking
at a patient.

With stunned pleasure, she gazed at the glistening sym-
metry of his body, with its smooth ripple of muscles. An
elongated wedge of silky black hair extended to his flat
stomach, then disappeared to reappear on his shapely legs.
Even his feet pleased her.

The soft bulk of flesh between his thighs caught her attention, and although she felt an uncomfortable flush
flooding her body, she felt compelled to look at it. She had
grown up seeing the naked male children of the slaves
playing around their cabins, but this was different. She was
invading his privacy, and she felt a warm and tingling
shame.

Then, to her horror, she realized that his eyes had opened
and were regarding her with an unmistakable masculine
interest.

"Sorry, sweet," he said quite clearly in French, "but I don't think I'm up to it."

Her face burned with mortification at having been caught looking at him. She felt such searing embarrassment that she took refuge in anger. How arrogant he was! Even half-conscious, he assumed that she was some serving girl offering herself to him!

Almost at once she realized he was probably delirious, but whether or not he was fully awake, he looked amused, and that fueled her ire. *Just wait!* she thought, and vowed she would make him pay for the bruises he had inflicted on her by frightening Beauté.

But when his eyes dulled and closed again, it occurred to her that in his delirium he might not have seen her at all, but rather someone else. He would probably not even remember the incident.

She pulled the sheet up over his nakedness and sat down beside him, feeling both curiously excited and repelled. She studied his arresting face, with the saber scar running down his angular cheek. His eyebrows were dark and bristling, but the lashes fanning his cheek were long and silky. Now that she was becoming used to the sinister scar, she could see a vulnerability in the firm curve of his mouth, and she wondered what manner of man he was.

When Mattie came back, refreshed, to relieve Marie-Thérèse before the evening meal, she brought one of Monsieur Dufret's old nightshirts. She turned back the sheet and lifted one limp arm and inserted it in a sleeve, then lifted the bandaged head and pulled the shirt over it. The sleeping man did not waken. Mattie lifted the other arm and deftly pushed it into its sleeve. The shirt was rolled up around his neck, and she looked down at the wide, bare shoulders.

"If Estelle could lift him . . ." the older woman began.

Marie-Thérèse came back to the bed and slid her arms under his shoulders.

"*Ma'mselle!*" Mattie scolded. "What your papa say?" But she was already smoothing the nightshirt down over his body with Marie-Thérèse's help.

It was like holding him in her arms. For a moment, Marie-Thérèse was close enough to smell the clean but mysteriously masculine scent of his skin. The experience was disquieting.

"Now he be warm tonight," Mattie said. "But don't tell *michie* I let you help me!" She looked down at the exhausted man. "He bad hurt, *ma'mselle.*"

Marie-Thérèse felt a sharp anxiety. It would be too sad if he did not survive, after he had fought so hard to escape certain death in the river.

That night she had difficulty sleeping. Her bruises ached, and she could not find a comfortable position. When she closed her eyes, she saw the stranger the way she had first spied him, a sodden lump lying half in and half out of the river, as if already dead. She relived the terrible shock of that moment when the hand of what she thought might be a corpse had curled its fingers around her ankle, toppling her on her back. When at last she slept, she dreamed about him.

She was standing in the chamber next to her own, looking down at his unclothed body as she had that afternoon, her heart beating with shameless admiration of his strength and beauty. In her dream she laid her fingers on his chest and felt the strong beat of his heart beneath his skin and thought, "He lives!"

His eyes were closed, and she bent over him, whispering urgently, "What color are they?"

His thick, dark lashes swept up, and she saw that his eyes were a golden color, only a little darker than his skin. A feeling of being utterly liquid traveled through her body...

A loud crash wakened her. It sounded as if something had hit the wall behind the rosewood headboard of her tester bed. She heard Mattie's voice, then the deep rumble of the stranger's angry cursing, and some heavy thumps, as if a lumbering animal were thrashing about. She jumped out of bed and snatched up her cotton robe, then hurried into the hall and burst into the sickroom.

"Mattie? Are you all right?"

"Yes'm," Mattie said. Marie-Thérèse rushed to help her support the big man, who was skating precariously across the floor, lurching from side to side, obviously determined to stand and just as obviously too weak to be on his feet.

He looked as if he were still asleep, but he was mumbling orders. "Have my horse saddled. I must go now. Did you hear me? My horse! It's urgent, dammit!"

"He weak as a kitten," Mattie panted, "but he strong enough to throw the potion *michie le docteur* send clean across the room!"

Marie-Thérèse followed her gesture and saw the dark stain on the wall opposite his bed and the broken brown glass of the laudanum bottle on the floor.

She put her arm around the big man, lifting his arm over her shoulder, as Mattie was doing on his other side. Abruptly he collapsed on them, nearly bringing them both down. He was cursing fervently now, and Marie-Thérèse had a flash of insight, instinctively understanding the rage of a strong man who discovers he is too weak to stand alone.

"I'm surprised Papa hasn't heard," she whispered. Hébert, on the other hand, wouldn't wake if his bed shook.

"Your papa gone to visit his lady friend," Mattie whispered back. "We won't tell him you wake up. That's it, *ma'mselle,* jus' guide him," she said, puffing. "If you can help me get him back in bed without he fall, we won't wake nobody else."

They got him to the bed, and he fell back on it heavily. Mattie slid her arms under his hips and Marie-Thérèse picked up his feet, and they laid him straight on the bed and covered him. She wished he would open his eyes. Were they really golden? She had been so startled to see him observing her yesterday afternoon that she could not remember their color.

But he was sinking into exhaustion again. The laudanum would not be needed, after all. She went back to her own room, but not to sleep. Who was he and where was he headed with such urgency that it brought him up out of bed half-conscious? Did such a man have a woman? What would she be like?

In the morning the doctor came in response to Papa's summons. Dr. Boudreau was employed by several of the plantation owners with sugar mills on the stretch of the river known as Pointe St. Antoine who maintained hospitals for their workers. He had driven down this morning from New Orleans, where he had his residence, a rotund little man with a pointed beard and kind, sad eyes.

Monsieur Dufret took him into the sickroom. Marie-Thérèse and Hébert joined them in the hall after the doctor's examination.

"I fear your friend has cracked his skull," the doctor said. "Who is he?"

They stood just outside the open door. The long windows to the side *galerie* were also open, and a cool breeze blew in from the river.

"He is not a friend," Monsieur Dufret said. "I have a wide acquaintance, as you know, *monsieur,* yet I have never seen him before. From his delirious babblings, I assume he is a seafaring man."

"Hmm," said the little doctor. "He looks too much the gentleman to be one of the notorious Lafitte's band of cutthroats."

Hébert laughed. "I'm told the notorious Lafitte is often mistaken for a wealthy merchant when he walks the streets of the city."

"Fie, Hébert!" Marie-Thérèse exclaimed, fighting the sick feeling any mention of pirates gave her. "Wealthy, yes, but a merchant? A merchant of smuggled Africans and booty stolen by murdering innocent victims!"

"Exactly," said the good doctor, who knew how bitterly Marie-Thérèse hated the men who were responsible for the loss of her beloved mother and sister. For a moment, they were all silent. A survivor of the tragedy had said the brigands who had attacked the American coastal vessel had robbed the passengers, then cast them adrift in small boats. Few of them were ever seen again.

Privately, Marie-Thérèse was tortured by nightmares in which she saw the women ravished before they were tossed into the sea. In spite of the delicacy of her friends and family, such stories had reached her ears. Hanging was too good for the beastly men responsible for the deaths of her mother and Adorée!

The doctor cleared his throat. "I would say this man is more likely himself a victim of pirates," he said, and Marie-Thérèse felt a great surge of sympathy for the unfortunate stranger.

"Then how did he come to be in the river a dozen miles below the city?" asked Hébert.

"There are brigands right in our port," said his father.

"Most assuredly," said Dr. Boudreau. "But there is another possibility." He cleared his throat. "He could be a British officer, reconnoitering the river. Indeed, it is more than likely. Word is circulating in the city that the British fleet has sailed from the West Indies and is now in the Gulf of Mexico, approaching us."

"Is this true?" Monsieur Dufret exclaimed.

"It would seem so, *monsieur.*"

"Then we can expect to see their ships in the river," Monsieur Dufret said heavily.

"You know that a detachment of the militia is stationed just sixty miles down river at English Turn?"

"Yes. It is becoming our war, no?"

"Citizens are arming themselves," the doctor said unhappily.

"But our guest is French, not British," Marie-Thérèse protested. Her thoughts had remained on her mysterious patient.

"At least he speaks French," Monsieur Dufret said.

"How was he traveling?" the doctor asked.

"We don't know. I've had the area searched. If our guest was on horseback, the animal was drowned. Perhaps he fell or was thrown from a boat."

"But he could not have traveled upstream in a small boat. The current is too strong," Hébert pointed out, "and no large boat has gone up the river recently."

"True," said his father. "So he has not come from the British fleet, no?"

"But he could be traveling downriver to meet the British fleet at Belize," the doctor persisted.

"Well, whatever his errand, he has been unfortunately delayed and can certainly do no harm to anyone at present. Will he regain consciousness soon, *monsieur le docteur?*"

"I can't say how soon, *monsieur,* but he will recover if his wound doesn't become infected. He must be carefully watched for signs of fever. In the meantime, he must be kept absolutely quiet. Do not allow him to get out of bed. I am going down to Jumonville, where I have some patients in the hospital. I'll stop in on my return to the city tomorrow evening to check on his progress."

The doctor looked through the open door at Mattie, who was beside the bed. "Continue what you're doing for him, Mattie," he said, smiling. "It can't harm him, and it may help."

Mattie rolled her eyes, but she said only, *"Oui, michie."*

Looking past the rotund little doctor, Marie-Thérèse studied the strong profile of the man in the bed. He looked paler than he had when Hébert brought him home. Was he truly going to recover? She wished he would open his eyes again. Her head ached from her nearly sleepless night, but she had no memory of her dreams, only that he had worried her thoughts.

Papa invited the doctor to stay for their midday meal. It was while they lingered in the dining room that the messenger arrived with a letter for Monsieur Dufret from Governor Claiborne. He read it and said grimly, "Your rumors are confirmed, Monsieur Boudreau. We must all return to the city. I have been ordered to report to the governor and assume command of my old regiment. He is asking for volunteers, Hébert."

"Then I'm his man!" Hébert declared, his eyes flashing.

"He says it is no longer an American war, as we Creoles have been telling each other. Now it has become a matter of protecting our homes and property and our loved ones from the British invasion. He reminds us that the generals believed to command the forces of invasion are the same who defeated Napoléon's great army, and that they intend to burn New Orleans as they burned Washington!''

"They'll never burn us out! I'll enlist tomorrow in the militia's Louisiana brigade," Hébert announced. "I'll look fine in that blue-and-gold uniform, eh, Estelle?"

The housekeeper laughed, but Marie-Thérèse said tartly, "I think that the brigade will require more of you than wearing their uniform!"

Until now the war had been something happening between two nations she felt no love for, England and the rebel United States—in spite of the fact that Louisiana was now one of those states. Until Britain had sailed up the Potomac and burned the capital, they had fought mostly in naval engagements at sea or on the northern lakes, far from Louisiana. It was a war she had never expected to come to their own little bit of France here in the new nation.

The men were laughing at Hébert's youthful enthusiasm. Marie-Thérèse asked, "What of our guest, Papa? The doctor says he must remain flat."

"It would be dangerous to try to move him now. He must remain quiet for a few days, at least," the doctor said.

"Then we must leave him at Petit Bois in Mattie's care until he can be moved," Marie-Thérèse's father told her. "You will have to stay behind, *chérie,* to see that he is cared for properly. Mattie can stay with him nights, and you can choose someone for his day care under your supervision. We will take only our valets, so all the servants will remain with you. Keep one of them always with you," he cautioned. "We can be accommodated at the barracks or visit friends until you come up and bring the servants to open our *pied-à-terre* in the city. I can trust my overseer to look after the cane fields."

"You should be safe enough," the doctor told her. "The invasion is not yet imminent. If the British fleet attempts to come up the river, it will be stopped at English Turn, which is over sixty miles from here. General Jackson has strengthened the defense forces at the forts there."

"Yes, you are safe here," her father said. "If you were not, I would not leave you."

"I will return tomorrow, and again later if it is necessary," the doctor said, "and let you know immediately when your guest can be moved."

"Thank you, *monsieur*," her father said, and turned back to Marie-Thérèse. "You will be one of many Creole women who will have to carry on while their men are away fighting for New Orleans. You have always acted with great good sense, *chérie*, and that is what I expect of you now. Your mother trained you well to take your place as mistress of a large plantation, although none of us expected you to become mistress of Petit Bois." His voice caught for a moment, and he coughed to cover his emotion. "You can manage, with the help of Estelle and Mattie, and Boddy, I'm sure."

"Yes, Papa." The prospect of staying behind to supervise the care of the mysterious stranger did not dismay her. He was a guest, after all, and as mistress of the finest plantation on the river, she had much experience in dispensing her father's hospitality to his friends. She would be well protected by her staff of servants, and the invading British were still far out in the Gulf.

Between them, she and Mattie would bring the injured man to himself, and she would hear his story. She looked forward to that with anticipation. Her friends would envy her this adventure!

It was after they had waved the doctor off in his one-horse carriage and Marie-Thérèse had gone upstairs to her chamber to rest for an hour that Sophie, the laundress, came to her. "*Ma'mselle,*" she said, hesitantly, holding out a soaked roll of oiled cloth, "I find this in *m'sieu*'s clothes. It is money, no?"

"No," Marie-Thérèse said, unrolling it. "It is not money. It looks like a letter. You did well to bring it to me, Sophie. Perhaps it will tell us who the gentleman is."

In spite of the care with which it had been placed in a protective packet, water had seeped in, and the ink in which the missive had been written was badly smeared and largely illegible. What was left was only a scrap of a letter, and that so wet as to be falling apart. It was addressed only "Dear Friend."

Puzzling over it, Marie-Thérèse read:

I have met again with C regarding the British offer which he remarked is incredibly generous, but that there is some suspicion among his advisers that the letters are forged. He will consult with . . .

From there the words were unreadable. The bottom of the page was torn and soggy, the signature missing.

Regarding the British offer. The phrase smacked of treason.

A victim of brigands, indeed! Of course he had been traveling downstream. If the British fleet was in the Gulf, he was planning to rendezvous with it when it reached the mouth of the river.

Feeling a little sick, Marie-Thérèse was reluctant to believe the truth, but she found it inescapable. She must show Papa what Sophie had found. The stranger she had rescued was either carrying letters for a traitor or was himself a British spy!

Chapter Three

With great care, Marie-Thérèse loosely rolled up the square of oiled muslin to which the letter clung and left her chamber. As she went toward the front stair, she passed Hébert's open door and heard him say to his valet, "Surely I've enough clothes at the town house to last me until my new uniforms are ready. Pack only my morning coat, Apollo."

"Oui, michie."

She paused. In the guest room across the hall, her *femme de chambre,* Mattie's daughter, was sitting beside the bed. "He hasn't stirred, *ma'mselle.*" Doula said when Marie-Thérèse looked in. "But he very hot. Maybe he has fever."

If he had fever, that meant his wound was infected, and that meant he could die.

Marie-Thérèse observed the sleeping man with confused emotions. He was the enemy! He was carrying a message of betrayal to the British. *"It's urgent, dammit!"*

She remembered the desperation she had sensed in his outstretched hand, and thought of the tremendous strength it had taken to battle the Mississippi's current. She had felt that strength in him even when he would have fallen if she and Mattie had not held him up when he tried to get out of bed in the night. And she had felt the urgency that made him rage against his weakness.

"They intend to burn New Orleans as they burned Washington."

He was dangerous—a spy! Why, then, did she still feel this treacherous sympathy for him?

Moving quickly across the hall to her brother's room, she asked, "Hébert, where is Papa, do you know?"

"Probably in the office. He said he wanted to talk to old Boddy before we leave."

Marie-Thérèse considered. Boddy, who was Mattie's husband and Doula's father, was a refugee from Saint-Domingue, one of the light-skinned Negroes who had sided with the whites in the revolution there. Papa had hired him, one of the *gens de couleure libre*—free people of color—as overseer because he had learned about sugar culture on a plantation in the West Indies. Papa would want Boddy to know about this, too, because she would have to depend on the overseer while he was away.

"Come with me. I have something to show you both."

"What is it?" Hébert demanded.

He was seventeen, and she knew he often chafed under the authority their father had conferred on her as mistress of the plantation. Now the prospect of enrolling in the prestigious Louisiana Brigade was making him feel very mature. Officiously so.

She glanced at Apollo, who was folding Hébert's damask morning coat, and her brother caught her meaning and joined her in the hall.

She lowered her voice. "Sophie found a letter our guest was carrying in his clothing."

"Let me see." Hébert held out his hand for the letter.

"Not here. It's in very bad condition. I must take it to Papa before it falls apart."

Hébert scowled but followed her down the back stair and across the rear *galerie*. The passage between the house and the buildings that housed the plantation office on the left and the kitchen and storeroom on the right, was roofed to shield it from the rains that sometimes fell suddenly, in torrents. She knocked once and entered the office with an apology. "Forgive me, *cher* Papa, but if this means what I think it does, it is something you must see."

She laid the oiled cloth on his desk and carefully unrolled it.

Her father's annoyance at her interruption faded as he looked at the mutilated letter and took in its meaning. "*Mon Dieu!* Where did you get this?"

"Sophie found it in his clothes."

"Is he awake?"

"No, Papa. Doula thinks he is feverish."

Monsieur Dufret tapped his desk with nervous fingers while he considered the document. "I'll take this with me to New Orleans and give it to the proper authorities." He rolled it back up and tucked in into an etui containing his papers. "They will want to interrogate him as soon as he begins to recover. Hébert, you will have to stay here at Petit Bois with your sister while he is recovering and see that the traitor does not escape."

"Papa!" Hébert protested, flushing with disappointment. "Surely I am needed more urgently in the city!"

"You flatter yourself, *mon fils.*" Monsieur Dufret said, and Hébert colored with humiliation. "At present you are needed here. This may be important. I want you to keep an armed guard on our prisoner day and night."

Hébert squared his shoulders. "Your pardon, Papa, but if the British are going to attack, my place is with the militia."

Monsieur Dufret's eyebrows almost met as he glared at his son, but Hébert persisted, "I would regret losing this opportunity to join the Louisiana Brigade. We can put the prisoner in a cart and take him with us. That's surely good enough for a British spy!"

"Enough, Hébert! You will do as I say."

"I am no longer a lad, Papa!" Hébert shouted. He turned angrily on Marie-Thérèse. "You should have let the bastard drown!"

"Au contraire, monsieur," Monsieur Dufret said, with a formality that Marie-Thérèse knew struck her brother with a chill. She felt a pang of sympathy for her rash young brother.

"Your sister has given us the opportunity to discover who among us is treating with the enemy," her father said. "He must be fully recovered from his wound, and I want him kept confined for his inquisitors."

He turned to Marie-Thérèse. "You, *ma fille,* will see to his recovery. And you, *mon fils,* will be responsible not only for his confinement, but for his safety until the authorities send for him. Do you understand me?"

Hébert's jaw clamped in defeat. *"Oui,* Papa."

Monsieur Dufret turned to his overseer. "Boddy, pick with care two men my son can trust with arms. Keep in mind that the British have threatened to incite the slaves to rise against us, as they have tried with the Indians."

Boddy nodded.

"Apollo can handle a gun. Give him a trustworthy companion and let them guard the prisoner at night."

"Papa," Hébert protested stiffly, "I have need of Apollo—"

He might not have spoken, so completely was he ignored. "You, Hébert, will guard the prisoner by day. See to it, Boddy."

"Oui, michie."

Monsieur Dufret grunted his satisfaction. "I will take one of the grooms with me to care for our mounts," he told Marie-Thérèse in a gentler tone. "He can carry messages for us. I will keep you informed of what is transpiring in the city, and you will send a letter back with him advising me of your welfare and your concerns. I expect the army will send for the spy as soon as he can be moved. The doctor can advise you about that. But if the British fleet is sighted on the river, you must leave for the city immediately, whether or not he is recovered."

His stern gaze demanded and received a promise.

"Oui, Papa."

"Now leave us, if you please. Boddy and I have more work to do before I go."

Jacques opened his eyes and quickly closed them again as the unfamiliar room began spinning around him. When he felt more securely anchored in his bed, he looked again at the young black girl sitting on a chair beside him.

"Where am I?" he asked her.

"This plantation is Petit Bois, *michie,*" she said, softly. "I am Doula."

"How did I get here?"

"Ma'mselle herself drag you from the river."

"Mademoiselle?"

"My mistress, Ma'mselle Dufret."

Petit Bois. Dufret. The names meant nothing to him. What was he doing here? Where was his horse? *Jean!* He had important information for Jean!

The room was whirling again, and the walls became muddy water that broke over his head, filling his mouth and nose. He thrashed about with his arms, his head rolling from side to side, reliving his involuntary journey down the river.

Doula filled a large spoon with the potion her mother had left and poured it into the man's gasping mouth. He choked and spit. "For shame, *michie!*" she reproached him. "Now I have to give you a clean sheet."

But the patient had exhausted himself and slipped back into sleep.

When he opened his eyes again, Jacques blinked confusedly at the large black woman beside him. Surely she had been much younger the last time he saw her? Or had she been white? Had he been hallucinating about a raven-haired beauty hovering temptingly over him?

He murmured, *"Mademoiselle?"* but his lips were so dry the word was scarcely recognizable to his own ears.

A rosy-cheeked young cock dressed to the teeth and carrying a musket loomed above him. "Awake, are you, *m'sieu?*" he drawled with theatrical menace.

"Water?" Jacques croaked.

The black woman slipped a supportive hand under his head and held a cup to his lips. Jacques tried to gather his wits while he swallowed. The sight of the gun had triggered an alarm in his befuddled brain.

"Where am I?" Had he asked that before? He was not sure. Anyway, he didn't remember the answer, and he needed more time to ponder his strange circumstances.

"You are at present a guest at Petit Bois," said the young man with the musket.

"At gunpoint?"

"For the nonce."

"How did I come here?"

"My sister dragged you from the river. What are you called, *m'sieu,* and what was your business on the river?"

Jacques was silent. So the raven-haired beauty was not an illusion. What else was real in those visions he had seen? What secrets had he told?

He mumbled, "How long—?"

"You have been here two nights. The doctor has visited you twice, and dressed your wound."

Two nights! *What would Jean do if he failed to return in time?* The worry brought a sharp pain in his head.

"Well, *m'sieu?*" The musket was held negligently, but it was pointed down toward the bed, and the lad did not look friendly.

"I'm afraid I—I don't remember."

"You surely know your name, *m'sieu!*"

Jacques closed his eyes and exhaled despondently. *"Non."* He could not tell this unfriendly jailer he was a lieutenant of the notorious Lafitte—who was still in hiding from the United States Army charged with murder.

"Enough, *Michie* Hébert," he heard the dark woman's rich voice say. *Hébert,* he thought, struggling to retain the name as he sank back into sleep.

Marie-Thérèse nodded to Apollo, who sat holding a musket in the hall outside the guest room door. "How is he, Mattie?" she asked upon entering the room.

"He be resting easier." Mattie looked tired. She was starting her night care of the patient, and she had spent a good part of the day with him, also.

A second armed guard was stationed beyond the window on the side *galerie*.

Hébert had sat glumly in their prisoner's room all day with his weapon across his knees. It seemed unnecessary, Marie-Thérèse thought, when the man was so weak.

"Has he talked?"

Mattie shrugged. "Just nonsense, but French. He speak French like the planters in Haiti."

"Really, Mattie?" She thought, *The British fleet has been in the West Indies.* "Hébert said he doesn't remember his name."

"That happen when a man's hurt in the head."

"Take a rest, Mattie. I'll stay with him for a while."

After the herb woman left, Marie-Thérèse did not immediately take her chair, but stood looking down at her prisoner's striking face. It was quite brown against the white pillow and spoke of days spent under the sun. The scar that ran down his cheek held a dread fascination for her. It looked like the dueling scar that marked a notorious gentleman acquaintance of her father's.

The man lying immobile under the sheet looked as if, in good health, he would be a dangerous man to cross. There was a threat in that scar. She forced her gaze away from it, observing instead the way his hair sprang up from his forehead and spiraled in loose curls in front of his shapely ear. The hair of his head looked so springy that she had to repress an urge to touch it. And his extraordinary lashes, surprisingly long and black, curled upward from his cheek like a woman's.

Suddenly they swept up, revealing his eyes. She studied them curiously. They were not golden as they had been in her dreams, but a dark brown, with gold sparkles around the pupil. She felt a little shock at encountering his gaze. It was as if an inanimate object had come to life. His gaze was unreadable, yet once again she sensed the strength of will that had enabled him to save himself.

"You must stop this," he said, enunciating very clearly.

"What?" Marie-Thérèse asked, startled.

"Popping in and out of my dreams. You're not real, are you?"

"Quite real," she assured him, trying to conceal her strange reaction to his words. She was not sure whether he was delirious or in possession of his senses. "I am Mademoiselle Marie-Thérèse Dufret, mistress of Petit Bois since my mother was—taken from us. And you are, *Monsieur—?*"

After a lengthy pause, in which she found it impossible to look away from his hypnotic gaze, he muttered, "If you are real, you may call me Jacques."

"Mais non!" she protested, "It would not be proper to call you by your Christian name, *monsieur*." She waited, but he did not reply, and she said impatiently, "You have a surname, surely?"

His eyes flickered. "I said you may *call* me Jacques." He paused, then muttered, "The truth is . . . I don't know who I am."

His voice was clear and sounded sincere, but she regarded him skeptically.

"I've been told that you pulled me from the river . . . and I'm grateful. Regrettably . . . I've no memory of that, either."

That much might be true, considering the condition in which she had found him. "And how did you get into the river? Do you have no recollection of that?"

"None, *mademoiselle.*"

"You were apparently riding a horse. At least you asked in your delirium to have him saddled. And you were carrying a message."

His lashes drooped, concealing eyes that she thought, with deep suspicion, were suddenly wary. Or was that her imagination?

"A message?" he croaked, his eyes still closed.

"It was found in your clothing. Do you recall that message?" Marie-Thérèse persisted.

"Non, mademoiselle."

"It indicated that you are carrying certain information to the British, *monsieur!*"

His eyes flew open. "Impossible!"

She thought she saw genuine surprise in his eyes.

"That is why I am being treated as a prisoner?" he asked. "Why my jailers carry muskets?"

"You deny that you are spying for the British?"

"*Spying* for them!" He scowled, looking infinitely more dangerous. "I have no love for the British, *mademoiselle!*"

"And how do you know this, if you have lost the memory even of your name?"

The indignation gradually faded from his eyes. After a moment he said wearily, "I don't know, but it is true." His eyes closed, and after sitting quietly for a few minutes she saw that he was sinking into the sleep of exhaustion.

A fine beading of sweat covered his forehead. Her feeling of being threatened by his fierceness faded, overcome by a healer's anxiety for her patient. He was still very weak, she realized, and she wondered how much of what he had said she could believe.

Chapter Four

The house seemed unusually quiet when Marie-Thérèse wakened the next morning.

Papa had gone to the city, and Hébert was still sleeping. So, apparently, was their prisoner—and perhaps his guards were, too. She heard not the slightest sound through the thick cypress wall behind the headboard of her bed that separated their rooms.

She arose and pulled her white cotton robe around her. Unlocking her door, she went out into the hall. Apollo stumbled sleepily up from the chair facing the guest room, grasping his musket, when she said good morning. He was a handsome mulatto who was quite aware of his good looks and whose job was to care for Hébert's wardrobe.

She entered the sickroom, and Mattie, who sat dozing beside the bed, came awake with a jerk. *"Ma'mselle!"*

"How is he, Mattie?"

The big woman's capable hands went out in a gesture that was pure Creole. "He got to eat something. He's taken nothin' much but water for three days. I'll send Doula up with some broth from the kitchen."

"Get some rest, Mattie. I'm here now."

"Mos'ly he want to sleep. But somebody have to bathe him. An' he need a shave."

Somebody have to bathe him. A picture of the sleeping man's uncovered body, as she had seen it that first day, with its powerful bronze muscles, sprang to her mind, and a rush of warmth flooded her body as she quickly banished the thought of caressing him with a soapy washcloth. Why had that image come to her? She examined the shadow of a beard darkening his face. It increased that tinge of the sinister in his handsome features because it made the pale line of his scar more noticeable.

She imagined herself taking his chin in her left hand while holding a razor in her right, the way Papa's valet did when she had been allowed to watch as a fascinated child. It was a wickedly exciting fantasy. Would he allow it? He didn't have much choice, did he?

But what if he grabbed the razor?

She shivered.

"There's some things it not fittin' a young girl do," Mattie pronounced, lumbering to her feet. Marie-Thérèse was startled by the woman's seeming perceptiveness, until she realized that Mattie must be thinking of her daughter, Doula, who would soon come in for the day shift.

"Apollo can bathe and shave him, I think," Marie-Thérèse said quickly. And Hébert would stand guard with his musket.

"Oui, ma'mselle."

Mattie left, and Marie-Thérèse sat down beside the bed and observed her patient critically. After the loss of her mother, she'd had to deal with many minor health problems on the plantation, often working with Mattie and her herb remedies. She watched the slight movement of the sheet as the man breathed in and out. Alert for signs of fever, she placed her palm on his forehead. The damp heat of his skin penetrated her fingers. Not hot enough for fever, she decided.

But wasn't his breathing shallow and too rapid? Was his heartbeat weak, then? Should she send for Dr. Boudreau again? She leaned over him to place her ear near his chest, so close that the wiry hairs on his chest tickled her cheek and she breathed in the male scent of his perspiration. Now she could hear his heart beating. It was regular, and sounded strong enough. Perhaps a little fast.

The shadow along his jaw and the thought of him shaving his face daily the way Papa did changed her perception of him in a curious way. Tentatively she touched his beard.

Prickly, but softer than she had imagined. In fact, the short, dark stubble was surprisingly soft.

With sudden swiftness, his hand came up and captured hers in a firm grasp. His fingers had an exciting texture that was neither rough nor as smooth as the hands of her father or Hébert.

His eyes were still closed. Was he awake or wasn't he? She tried to free her hand, but, astonishingly, he carried it to his mouth and planted a kiss in the middle of her palm! The soft movement of his warm lips against her skin brought a quivering sensation that traveled up her arm and spread to her other limbs.

He was awake, all right! *"Monsieur!"* she gasped.

Many a man had bowed over her hand, bringing its back almost to his lips. It was not *comme il faut* to actually touch it with the lips, although inevitably someone's beard or mustache brushed it. But she had never been kissed in the palm! And never with such a disquieting effect. It was so... intimate!

He opened his eyes. They glittered with gold lights. "Yes, *mademoiselle?*"

She glared at him. "You are holding my hand!"

"Yes," he murmured and released it.

Marie-Thérèse fled.

* * *

Jacques felt a welcome stirring of desire that brought a surge of confidence. He was recovering if he could feel even so small a positive response to the presence of a *jolie fille*. And Mademoiselle Dufret was *jolie* indeed. Her hair glistened with health, her eyes were vivacious and full of the joy of life, her bosom was divine, and that creamy Creole skin had flushed a becoming rose when he had kissed her hand.

He felt his bristly jaw, which she had touched so delicately, and assessed his situation. From the condition of his beard, he judged it must be true that he had been in this accursed bed at least three days. He did not feel in any condition to travel, yet he must. Jean must know the result of his not entirely successful mission. Unsuccessful, yet not without hope. He had missed his rendezvous with the boat that would take him to Jean, who was still in hiding after the plundering of his warehouses on Grande-Terre.

His captors apparently thought he was a British spy. That was ironic because that was what he might well become if they did not let him go to Jean.

Jean had been half-crazy with worry over his brother, Pierre, who was lying ill in that foul Creole jail. When the governor and his advisers had spurned his first overtures, he had masterminded a jailbreak. His friends had gotten Pierre safely away to a friend on Bayou LaFourche, but the American government had sent an army unit to destroy Jean's headquarters, capturing eighty men, including Dominique You. Jean had escaped into the bayous, and had sent Jacques to offer the Americans help against the British in return for dropping the piracy charges against his band of privateers.

Jean must be anxiously awaiting his return. And now *he* was imprisoned here by his illness. If he did not reappear,

Jean would assume he had failed to negotiate with the government and throw in with the British. The Lafittes' well-armed, well-trained band could make a difference in the coming battle. Possibly the fate of New Orleans itself was at stake.

Jacques's own future hung in the balance, as well. If Jean sold his loyalty to the British, Jacques could find himself sailing his brigantine under a British flag. Somehow he must escape to carry back Livingston's message.

What he needed was a good horse! The plantation's stable must include at least one swift stallion. If he could find some way to overpower or eliminate his night guards, he might have a chance to steal a horse and get away without being shot. It would be sheer folly to attempt escape in the daylight, when there would be many people about.

He had no money with which to bribe his guards. Everything he carried with him, including his money, had been in his saddlebags, now lost forever. The guards were obviously Dufret's slaves. Could he bribe them with promises of freedom after the battle was won?

Not as long as the big black woman sat all night beside his bed. He lay quietly, concocting various schemes, until he broke out in a sweat and realized that he was still too weak to carry out any of them. He needed an ally, and he knew instinctively that the old nurse was incorruptible. She would not help him escape.

If he could not bribe one or both of the night guards, that left only the young black nurse and Mademoiselle Dufret herself, who had blushed so entertainingly when he planted a kiss in her palm.

Could he persuade her to help him? She was not invulnerable, he told himself hopefully. What woman was, to a man with purposeful charm?

His strategy for the present, then, must be to not let his captors know he was regaining his strength. When the young Creole, looking as if he would gladly use his musket on him, came into the chamber followed by one of his night guards carrying shaving equipment, Jacques pretended to be asleep.

I am going to be so weak you will have to hold my head up while your servant shaves me, you arrogant young turkey cock! he told young Dufret silently. *And if I find no one else who will help me escape, I am going to seduce your sister.*

At nine-thirty Marie-Thérèse ordered her mare saddled and rode the levee upstream to visit her friend, Annalise Bourget, on the next plantation. The Bourget house was built in the old-fashioned West Indian style, raised on brick pillars, with the ground floor serving as storage area. Galleries all around the house added to the living space. An outside stair at one side rose to the *galerie*. The house, a pioneer's home, was older than Petit Bois, comfortable but much less formal.

When Marie-Thérèse cantered up the drive to the foot of the stair, Annalise came out on the *galerie* to call down a delighted greeting. She was a short, bouncy girl, full of good humor, a year younger than Marie-Thérèse and half a head shorter. She had been unofficially betrothed since her fourteenth year to a young man still at college in Paris, who was unwilling to travel because of the blockade. But that did not keep her from enjoying the many balls her parents attended.

"We're all in an uproar, packing to return to the city," she called. "Come up, Marie-Thérèse."

Turning her mare over to the small groom who ran up to take the reins, Marie-Thérèse climbed the steps. Annalise came to meet her, carrying a Parisienne fashion doll.

"See what Papa bought for me at the Temple? It's the latest fashion, smuggled in from Paris. I'm going to have it copied exactly. There are bound to be military balls, with all the men in uniform!"

Marie-Thérèse shuddered and turned pale. "How can you handle anything plundered from some ship by those dreadful pirates? Do you never wonder what happened to the poor woman whose trunk was ravaged to get that doll?"

Annalise sobered instantly. "Please forgive me, Marie-Thérèse! I didn't mean to be insensitive. I myself believe that the goods Papa buys down at the Temple were taken from enemy ships by gentlemen privateers. But I understand your feelings, *chérie*."

"No, Annalise, you can't possibly understand. No one can."

"Oh, *chérie,* I'm so sorry." She threw the doll down on a chair and flung herself into another. "I've ordered our *cafés au lait* served here." She said no more about fashion, but began repeating the gossip her father had brought back from the city.

Gradually color returned to Marie-Thérèse's face as she conquered the nausea that any mention of the pirates or the fate of her mother and sister brought her.

"Papa says we are needed in the city to help defend our homes from the British attack," Annalise said. "He says the women are mobilizing, too. Madame Claiborne has invited me to the governor's house to help cut and roll bandages."

"Papa has already returned to the city," Marie-Thérèse confided, sinking into a chair.

"And left you here?" Annalise exclaimed.

"Hébert and I will follow him when our prisoner can travel."

"Prisoner!"

Marie-Thérèse was glad to have some news with which to divert her friend. She gave Annalise an account of her rescue of the mysterious spy.

Annalise squealed, "You caught a *spy?* The most exciting things happen to you, Marie-Thérèse," she said enviously.

Lowering her voice Marie-Thérèse said, "He is very handsome, Annalise, and very strong, even in his present weakened condition. It took both Mattie and me to keep him from falling one night when he got out of his bed in a delirium, calling for his horse."

"You went into his chamber in the night?" Annalise said, scandalized.

"Mattie is nursing him," Marie-Thérèse told her firmly, "but she couldn't handle him, and the terrible racket they made wakened me. Of course, Hébert slept through it all! It would take a cannon to wake my brother." She said nothing about her father's visit to his mistress. Surely it was not a lie to let Annalise assume that Papa had been home when this happened.

"Papa has charged me with supervising his recovery. He wants the man returned to health, so he can be tried for treason—or spying. Oh, Annalise, you should have seen him raging against his weakness like some caged animal! He is such a man as you have never seen!'

"You are blushing, Marie-Thérèse!" And it was true, for a vision of the beautiful muscles of his bronze legs below Papa's nightshirt had flashed into her mind.

"Do you have a *tendresse* for this spy?" Annalise cried, obviously both scandalized and excited.

"Certainly not!" Marie-Thérèse snapped, feeling a tell-tale warmth rising in her cheeks. Annalise's suggestion was ridiculous! It was only sympathy she felt, although that in itself was puzzling. Why should she feel anything for a traitor? "That would be quite a folly, wouldn't it?" she said coldly.

"It would be insane," Annalise agreed.

A young black maid wearing a clean white apron came up the stair bearing a large silver tray. She set it on the small table before Annalise. It held a pot of hot black coffee and a plate of still-warm sugared *beignets*.

Annalise dismissed her and poured their coffee into small, fragile cups.

Marie-Thérèse took the cup her friend offered, but only pretended to drink from hers. Her stomach was churning unpleasantly. "Papa is insisting that I choose a husband," she confided, biting her lip.

"Has he picked a husband for you at last? I thought he was never going to let you go, Marie-Thérèse. He has depended on you to manage his houses and do all his entertaining ever since the tragedy. Entirely selfishly, I am convinced."

"Rubbish, Annalise! You know I love being Papa's hostess."

"But to be hostess in your own house—wouldn't that be more exciting? Well, tell me! Who is the man he has picked?"

"I am to pick. But Papa advises me to accept Gabriel Duvallier."

"*Non!* Not our Gabriel!" Annalise exclaimed. "Won't he bore you to death with his tedious poems?"

"Papa doesn't know about his verses." Marie-Thérèse laughed. "Perhaps if I tell him it will change his opinion of Gabriel. Annalise, do you imagine Gabriel will keep writing verse to me if I marry him? Papa says I must have the protection of Gabriel's family if both he and Hébert are lost in the battle against the British.''

"Sweet Mary, mother of Jesus, forbid!" Annalise said, making a quick sign of the cross. "But what a prosaic reason for marriage! Still, if your Papa arranges it, you have no choice."

Marie-Thérèse said glumly, "Only if Gabriel does not survive the coming battle, and I could not wish for that. His poems are well-intentioned. At least they all praise my looks and my womanly charms, including 'a heaving bosom that points at the moon.'"

Annalise cried, "Oh, Marie-Thérèse, you are shameless! Did he really say that?"

"I swear it! Papa did give me an alternative—our dear Etienne."

"Etienne Picou? Oh, *chérie,* don't choose *him* for a husband! Marry Gabriel and take Etienne for your lover."

"And you say *I* am shameless!"

Between peals of laughter Annalise said, "Do come to town very soon, Marie-Thérèse. I shall miss you."

Hébert sat on the *galerie* outside their guest's room with the floor-length windows open so that his gaze could sweep the entire sickroom, brooding over one of his father's fat cigars, his loaded musket lying across his knees. He was thinking that he should be at his tailor's now, being measured for his uniform. And he would have been, but for the big rascal lying so still in the guest bed, pretending to sleep.

He shifted restlessly and caught the musket just as it was about to fall off his knees. Why in the name of God had Marie-Thérèse gone down the levee to examine a *corpse?* That rogue in there would be one now, if she had minded her own business! And he would be in the city, being sworn in to the brigade. *Mon Dieu!* By the time he arrived, his tailor would be inundated with orders for new uniforms. A pox on his sister!

He heard the dainty trot of hooves on the drive at that moment and got up to walk to the front *galerie* to watch Marie-Thérèse come up the drive. She was an accomplished rider, and she made a handsome sight on her little mare. Pride in her vanquished his irritation over her rescue of the damned spy, but it was mixed with a hurt because Papa had given her authority over him, as well as the plantation, during his absence.

His father didn't realize he was a man now, that was the trouble. But by God, he'd find a way to show him! He strode back to his chair just outside the guest room and swept his gaze around its interior. Nothing in the room had changed.

Marie-Thérèse came toward him from the front *galerie*.

"He's only pretending to sleep," Hébert said, under his breath but with heavy scorn. "I think he's faking a loss of memory, too."

"Probably," Marie-Thérèse agreed. It was a challenge that excited her. She was eager to match wits with this man who thought he was deceiving them. The social experience she had gained as hostess for her father left her confident that she could hold her own with any man. As long as she stayed out of his reach, she amended, remembering the outrageous liberty he had taken with her hand.

But he was still weak, so weak that she could knock him over with a gentle push, she reminded herself, conveniently forgetting her own curious weakness at his touch.

"The Bourgets are returning to the city early tomorrow," she told Hébert, pulling off the riding hat that bound her hair.

"Then we will be almost alone on this bank of the river," he said gloomily.

Chapter Five

The next day, Marie-Thérèse was going through her clothes, deciding which Doula should pack to take with them when they returned to the city, when Estelle came up to find her.

"Boddy say he have to speak to you."

Marie-Thérèse went down the back stair and joined her father's overseer, who stood on the rear *galerie*, holding his woven straw hat in his hands. Behind him, mist was rising from the swamp in the cold air, obscuring the cypress trees.

"What is it, M'sieu Boddy?"

His face was full of concern. "That prisoner, *ma'mselle*. He's offering gold to the men I sent to guard him if they help him escape."

"Gold!" Marie-Thérèse exclaimed. "He has nothing but his ruined clothes."

"He promised them gold and their freedom if they steal a carriage and a pair of fast horses and take him away from Petit Bois."

"Indeed!" Marie-Thérèse flushed with a swift rush of anger that was strangely painful. "And what did they say to that?"

"They laughed. They know they couldn't leave here in a carriage without waking everybody."

Marie-Thérèse bit down on her lower lip. "Can I trust them?"

"It's my opinion that they are loyal, *oui.*"

"Where did he want to be taken?"

"He said he would direct them once they got away from the plantation. I quizzed them about that, but I believe they're telling the truth. He is unable to travel, *non?*"

"When he tried to get out of bed in the night, he couldn't stay on his feet. He is stronger now, but—no, he cannot travel."

"I told them it's the fantasy of a sick man, *ma'mselle.* I told them he is a British spy, and that the British would sooner flog them than feed them. I say they have a master who employs freedmen and has been known to free slaves. They would do well to remain where they are."

"Thank you, M'sieu Boddy. Will you change the guard?" she asked.

"*Non, ma'mselle.* I chose the most trustworthy man I have to sit with Apollo. I don't believe your workers have been tainted by British offers for their loyalty, as some planters fear. But there are few I would send to the big house, and none other I would trust with arms. *Ma'mselle?*"

"Yes, M'sieu Boddy?"

"Your patient . . . he is ill, *oui,* but Apollo does not believe he has lost his memory."

"I've suspected as much," Marie-Thérèse said. "Thank you, M'sieu Boddy."

She went upstairs to the sickroom, her anger mounting with each step. No memory, indeed! So he would play them all for fools, would he? But her anger was directed mostly at herself. The sympathy she had entertained for this man who had fought the mighty Mississippi's current and won was misplaced, she told herself ruefully, but it was absurd to feel as if she had been betrayed. Why wouldn't he try to escape Petit Bois, after all?

Entering the sickroom, she put her hand on her brother's shoulder. She knew how bored and frustrated he was by his inaction when all his friends were probably marching and practicing maneuvers with the famed Louisiana Brigade. "Where's Doula?"

"Gone to get some soup for our patient."

"Go and have your dinner, Hébert."

Hébert got up and stretched, still holding his musket, then stood the gun against the wall. Marie-Thérèse saw the flicker of a thought in the eyes of the man watching from the bed, and her anger hardened. Was he wondering if he could get to the musket before she could?

"Take your weapon with you, Hébert. I want it out of M'sieu Jacques's reach."

Hébert looked surprised, then grinned at her. "Getting some sense, are you?"

Their prisoner gave her a look so wounded by her distrust that she knew it was feigned. Nevertheless, it had the effect of softening her rage like butter left in the sun. What a rogue he was!

"I'll stay with him," she told Hébert.

"Good." He straightened and put his musket over his shoulder.

After her brother left, Marie-Thérèse put her arms akimbo and glared at her patient. "So you have regained your memory!"

The prisoner said, softly, "Only a fragment, *mademoiselle*." His face, dark against the pillow, looked thinner, with sharply angular planes. It made him appear even more handsome, and slightly more vulnerable. Marie-Thérèse hardened her heart against the evidence of his suffering.

"You have remembered that you have gold! And apparently you have also remembered where this gold is hidden. You are too weak to get out of bed, yet you offer to pay well anyone who will carry you away from Petit Bois. Are you so dissatisfied with the way we have cared for you here, *monsieur?*"

He looked up at her with a bemused expression that did nothing to gentle the aura of danger she had sensed emanating from him, an aura that even his weakness could not destroy.

"You are remarkably comely, *mademoiselle*," he murmured.

It was in the dark eyes that danger lurked, she thought. The slanting look he gave her—wary and self-contained, but intensely confident—held a threat that made her heart flutter. It came from beneath black brows that began in an elegant line on each side of his nose and thickened to a black smudge below Mattie's white bandage. The challenge in that look was infinitely exciting.

"Almost comely enough," he said, "to make me forgive you for detaining me at gunpoint in order that I may experience your tender care."

She flushed at his sarcasm. "Have you remembered who gave you the message you were carrying?" she demanded. "And to whom you were taking it? What is your name, M'sieu Jacques?"

He said nothing, regarding her with that look that made her insides churn.

"And where would you have my guards take you if they should accept your bribe?"

He flashed a smile that made her draw in her breath sharply. A man so dangerous should not be so handsome!

"To New Orleans, of course, *mademoiselle*."

"You will be taken to New Orleans, *monsieur,* but in chains. In the meantime, I assure you that nobody on Petit Bois is going to accept an offer of unseen gold, to be paid sometime in the unknowable future, for betraying me."

He looked at her with a glint in his eyes. "Someday soon, *mademoiselle,* I am going to stop that sweet, tart mouth of yours with kisses."

A bolt of pure outrage shot through her. "How dare you!" No man had ever ventured to speak like this to her. The sheer audacity of it took her breath away. But the confidence with which he spoke shook her. She felt a thrill of peril that made her lips tremble.

He was smiling at her as if he were promising her some unimaginable pleasure. "Then," he said in his soft West Indian voice, "I am going to open that pretty bodice and fondle those twin mounds of passion you keep lowering over my head until you beg me for more."

She drew in her breath sharply. The gleam in his eyes was unmistakably desire. She was schooled in coquetry, and in her own set she would have found it a deliciously amusing challenge to respond to a flirtation. But no man she knew would dare to use such explicit language. It was insulting! And an unmistakable threat.

"You will, you know," he murmured, his eyes daring her, "beg me for more."

In a confusion of feelings, both shock and a fearful fascination with this man, Marie-Thérèse took refuge in laughter. After all, he was still so weak that she could push him over with one hand. "Talk is cheap, *monsieur,* when you are bedridden."

The gleam in his dark eyes brightened. "Laugh, *mademoiselle!* But do not think me impotent because I am in bed. Admit you are panting for me!"

She knew her face was scarlet. "You are quite mad, *monsieur!*"

"Someday you'll admit it. There will come a day when you'll beg me to take you into my bed."

Her laughter pealed like cold bells. "When hell freezes over, M'sieu Jacques!"

"Shall I tell you what I will do to you when that day comes?" His voice was thrillingly low and intimate. "Do you want to hear what skills in making love I have for your pleasure? Shall I tell you of all the places where I shall torture you with my kisses?"

Mon Dieu, and she had thought Gabriel's insipid poetry naughty! Her Creole suitors were too mannerly to say such things. She could not listen to his audacious talk—no gentlewoman should!—but since she knew she was perfectly safe with him, she had to admit she was finding it highly diverting. In fact, she was trembling inside with a curious excitement—but she would never admit it!

"You are foolish if you have persuaded yourself that you can seduce me with words, *monsieur.*"

"It usually works," he said plaintively, and she could not help laughing again.

"What a rogue you are, M'sieu Jacques!"

Doula came in with his tray, setting it down on the bedside table. When Marie-Thérèse bent over him to plump up his pillows, he looked pointedly at her bosom, and she fought an impulse to cross her hands over her breasts. She knew her cheeks flamed again when she and Doula put their hands under his arms to help raise him against the pillows. Touching the muscles of his back was like putting her fingers on a hot flatiron. Pressing her lips together, she went to sit in Hébert's chair and watched Mattie's daughter help him eat.

His outrageously free talk would have enraged both Hébert and her father, had they heard him. But in spite of his bravado, she could see that he was tiring. She felt a reluctant admiration for his audacity. She recognized in it the quality that had brought him success in fighting the mighty river current. That, and his resolve.

Whatever piece of treachery he was involved in must be terribly important to him.

Downstairs, Hébert finished his solitary meal and walked out of the house to get a little air before returning to guard duty. Sitting in the sickroom holding a gun for twelve hours out of twenty-four was incredibly boring. It was hard to stay awake.

The man in their care was recovering. Why did they have to wait for the army to come for him? Why couldn't they bundle the spy into the carriage and take him with them to New Orleans? Dammit, he should be with the brigade!

He had all afternoon ahead of him, at least another four or five hours of killing inaction, and he wondered how he could bear it. After several hours sitting in that room, he wanted to stand up and shoot off his musket just to hear its boom.

He rejected the idea that his duties in the brigade, as they waited for the British to attack, could be equally boring. Just wearing the handsome blue uniform would make all the difference, he thought. Women loved that uniform!

Walking toward the office, he met the overseer. "Afternoon, Boddy."

"Good afternoon, *m'sieu.*" The free quadroon stopped and removed his hat. "Did *mademoiselle* tell you the prisoner tried to bribe Apollo and my night guard?"

"*Non!*" Hébert exclaimed.

"I think he's shamming a memory loss. He claims to have gold to pay anyone who'll help him escape from here. He's probably too clever to try to work you, *m'sieu*," the overseer said diplomatically.

"Damn right!" Hébert said. He was furious with both Apollo and with Marie-Thérèse for saying nothing to him about an attempt at bribery. It was unfortunate that Papa had left Marie-Thérèse in charge of the household. Although she was two years older than he, his sister was gullible.

She thought she was so mature, entertaining all Papa's friends as his hostess with her natural coquetry, but she was still an innocent, and too softhearted. It was foolish of her to waste her compassion on a scoundrel like that traitor. He would have to protect her from her own generous impulses.

And Apollo! He would give him a piece of his mind!

"Damn right," he said again, forcibly. "The traitor knows I'd as soon shoot him as not." A disquieting thought followed that one. "I suppose word's spread through the cabins about the British offer to the slaves of gold and freedom if they will rise up against their masters? Some of ours are bound to take the bait, eh, Boddy?" he asked uneasily.

"I'm watching it, M'sieu Hébert. I've got my spies, you know. Don't worry. I'll hear about it if an uprising is planned."

Needing the exercise, and wanting to reassure himself, Hébert walked briskly down the road between the two rows of cabins, alert for any sign of revolt. The men and some of the women were out in the fields weeding in the newly planted cane field. A few children were playing in the scythed grass around the cabins, and they called, "*Michie* Hébert! *Michie* Hébert!"

He stopped to tease some of them. He had always had a good rapport with the children of the plantation, having grown up with some of their fathers. It was unthinkable, after all, that his old playmates could come after him with their machetes, wasn't it? He felt better after his stroll but his concern about his sister remained.

Jacques was miserably hot, and his head ached. He lay still because thrashing about trying to find a cooler, more comfortable spot took too much energy. The exchange of words with Mademoiselle Dufret spun itself out in his throbbing head, and he distracted himself from his discomfort by thinking of her, and how she had reacted to his teasing.

She was a pretty baggage. Hair black as midnight, with an exquisite shine. Eyes that mirrored her every thought, changing instantly from laughter to a tender concern for his pain to a blazing anger when she discovered his deceptions. A woman of passion, he thought, rueful at his incapacity to take advantage of it.

Skin like a magnolia blossom. A full underlip of the most delicate rose, made for kissing. He meant to taste those lips before he left! And she had the carriage of a queen. Full of herself, she was, *mais oui!* And what a tongue!

There was a layer of maturity and sophistication over the convent-trained child, but she was a virgin. He was sure of it. An experienced woman would not have reacted as she had to his threat of seduction. He could have laughed at the shock in those midnight-blue eyes when he began telling her what he would do to her. Yet, jolted as she was, she had listened—and been affected by it, he'd swear.

If he seduced her, would she help him escape? He would not ordinarily consider seducing a virgin—he prided himself on having more responsibility than that. But his case was desperate.

No, on second thought, he had no time for seduction. He needed a horse, now, tonight!

Nevertheless, the fantasy of making love to Mademoiselle Dufret was pleasant to contemplate. Filled with dreamy thoughts of how he would arouse her passion and leisurely enjoy her, he fell asleep.

When he awoke, Doula was gone and Hébert, his jailer, was back on the chair with his musket. Feeling stronger, Jacques immediately put his mind to work on thoughts of escape. Once he would not have hesitated to take on two armed men. Furious at the weakness that made overcoming his two night guards impossible, he set himself to devising some trickery.

He vaguely remembered being given laudanum when he first awoke in this room. If only he could drug his guards! But how could he induce them to take it without food to put it in? He had never seen the guards take anything to eat or drink while on duty. Besides, the laudanum had been taken away with his trays. Or had he thrown it across the room? A vague memory of the sort troubled him. If he'd done that, he'd been foolish.

How could he trick his guards into leaving their posts? He had nothing with which to work. And no clothes! He could do nothing but wait for an opportunity, and pray that, if one came, he would be strong enough to seize it, because he would probably have only one chance.

Marie-Thérèse was dressing for the evening meal when she heard a male shriek of anger and fear from the *galerie*. She opened her shutters and looked out in time to see the guard hurl something over the rail and fire his musket at it.

Drawing her robe around her, she rushed out through her window. Apollo had joined Rami, the guard, at the railing.

"What was it?" she cried. "Rami, why did you shoot?"

She heard Hébert come running up the stairs, shouting, "What the hell's going on?" He crossed through the sickroom to join Marie-Thérèse and the others.

Apollo muttered, "Gris-gris."

Marie-Thérèse stood beside her brother and stared down at the tiny bundle of feathers and bones barely visible on the grass below.

"It was on his chair," Apollo said.

Marie-Thérèse glanced back at her patient. He had raised himself in bed and propped his head on his hand, trying to see what was happening.

"Who put it there?" Hébert asked. Apollo shrugged, and Rami just stood there with his smoking musket, trembling.

"Who could have brought it into the house?" Hébert asked Marie-Thérèse.

She shook her head. "These things just appear, you know that. No one is ever seen. That's why it seems like magic. And it's no use trying to tell Rami it's harmless, Hébert. Look at him!"

Rami was shivering.

"Do you know who your enemy is?" Hébert asked him.

Rami shook his head numbly.

"Reload your musket," Hébert told him, "and don't waste any more shot."

Rami nodded. He sat down on his chair and took out his powder. The others walked through the sickroom and out into the hall. Hébert asked Apollo, "Do you know who is playing these voodoo tricks?"

Apollo looked uncomfortable. *"Non, m'sieu."*

"I'll speak to Boddy. He'll know."

From the bed, Jacques saw how the burly Rami's hands shook as he poured powder and shot into his musket. The big man was as superstitiously frightened by a voodoo charm as any black slave on Haiti would be.

At this moment, there was only one loaded musket, Apollo's, and his attention was diverted by the two Dufrets standing with him in the hall. Once Jacques would have seized the moment to rush out of the room and jump from the *galerie,* counting on surprise. But Rami's shot had alerted everyone on the plantation. And he was still too weak—and he was wearing nothing but a nightshirt, dammit.

Marie-Thérèse found it difficult to get to sleep that night. The wind had shifted from the north, and now was bringing in warm, moisture-laden air from the Gulf. The fog cleared from the swamp behind the plantation, and she heard the incessant croaking of the frogs celebrating the return of warmth. The change of wind direction also brought to her ears the occasional bark of an alligator and the *whoo-whoo* of an owl and other, more mysterious night cries from the swamp.

She tossed and turned beneath her mosquito net thinking about the man in the next room, who had lied to her, deceived her, and tried to bribe her father's slaves to turn against her. And then promised to seduce her! She could not forget the scandalous things he had said to her, and the strange excitement he had aroused in her would not let her sleep.

After she had finally managed to doze off, she was wakened by the sound of voices. She was groggy with sleeplessness, and it took a moment for her to realize that what she was hearing was the murmuring of the two guards, one outside the door of the sickroom, the other on the *galerie.*

They had evidently opened both door and window and were talking across the prisoner's room to each other. The voice of Rami on the *galerie* had risen, and it came distinctly through the wooden louvres of the shutter covering her open window.

Her first impulse was to get up and silence them. Then she became aware of what they were saying. They were discussing the voodoo charm. Apollo said, "Rami, you smart enough to know a bundle of sticks and feathers can't kill you!"

"Maybe," Rami said. "But it say something to me. It say there be somebody out there who want me dead. An' that's something that hang over my head."

"Who wants you dead?"

"Somebody," Rami said morosely.

Hébert was sleeping through the conversation—she could hear his gentle snoring from across the hall. Probably the prisoner was sleeping, too. It was only because she was so wakeful that she had heard the soft voices. Relaxing, she drifted into sleep again.

Sometime later she was awakened by a furtive sound outside her window. It was not a loud sound, but it puzzled her, even in her sleep, with its difference.

Then she heard the warning chirp of an awakened bird. There was one frightened bark from a dog, then silence.

Marie-Thérèse got out of bed and drew on her robe. Unlocking her door, she looked out into the hall. There was no one sitting on Apollo's chair. She stepped to the open door of the sickroom and looked straight through it at Rami's empty chair on the *galerie*. Then she looked at the bed.

It was empty!

Now she knew what she had heard. Her patient had been moving down the veranda, step by careful step, leaning against the wall of the house for support.

"Hébert!" she shouted, as loud as she could. Then, without waiting for an answer, she ran down the back stair and outside.

There was no one visible in the yard, but she heard a nervous nickering from the stables. Something—or someone—was disturbing the horses. She ran across the grass and burst into the tack room.

At first she could see nothing. The dim light of the partially obscured moon flowed in behind her, and as her eyes adjusted to the darkness, she made out the figure of a man lying on the floor. It was the second groom, spread-eagled and trouserless, his face upturned, his eyes closed, a trickle of blood running from his nose.

She stopped, momentarily frozen with shock. One of the horses neighed and began kicking in his stall. Marie-Thérèse glimpsed a figure in the stables beyond the tack room, a tall man bare to the waist, with a pale face and burning dark eyes. She gasped when she realized she was looking at M'sieu Jacques. He had discarded both his bandage and Papa's white nightshirt, which would have made him too visible, and was wearing the groom's too-tight trousers.

He had a saddle in his arms, but he was too weak to throw it on the horse. He staggered under its weight until he fell back against the stable wall, cursing under his breath.

Marie-Thérèse ran to him, crying, "*Monsieur!* What do you think you're doing?"

She pulled the saddle out of his hands, dropping it on the floor.

He put his arms around her waist, pulling her so close that her breasts were crushed against his bare chest. When she drew in her breath to shout for help, his hands moved swiftly up to hold her head, and he placed his mouth squarely over hers, stifling her scream with a kiss. He was so weak that he was leaning on her, yet she could not break his fierce embrace.

His mouth was hot but strangely sweet, as was the touch of his hands on her bare neck. His hot tongue invaded her mouth so unexpectedly that she stopped struggling in surprise. Thrilling tremors ran through her body, setting off sensations she had never before experienced.

Pressed against his nearly nude body, with only a sheer night shift and her cotton robe between her soft breasts and his hard chest, she was having difficulty breathing. His tongue, exploring the softness of her mouth, was turning her to jelly.

She was stunned by the intensity of her reaction. She had no strength to struggle. Indeed, she felt the most astounding inclination to put her arms around his neck and press herself even closer to him. He staggered from one foot to the other in an attempt to keep his balance, and she herself felt so deliciously weak that she feared they both would fall.

"Ma'mselle!" It was Apollo, running to her aid. He grabbed M'sieu Jacques by his hair and pulled his head back. Marie-Thérèse heard the crack of his fist against the jaw so near her own. The arms holding her dropped limply, freeing her. Just as M'sieu Jacques staggered backward, Hébert came running in from the tack room in a rage and struck him a blow over the head with his musket. Jacques crumpled, sliding to the floor with his head against the wall. His wound had opened, and his head was bleeding again.

"Hébert!" Marie-Thérèse shrieked, her head spinning and her heart pounding. "Now see what you've done!" She burst into sobs.

Her brother took her in his arms, cradling her trembling body. "There, Marie-Thérèse, you're all right now, *chérie.*

Don't cry." Over her shoulder, he shouted at Apollo, "What in hell made you leave your post?"

"I had to relieve myself, *michie*," said Apollo reasonably.

"So where is Rami?"

"I left him on the *galerie*. When I get back, he out cold."

"*Mon Dieu!* Marie-Thérèse, please stop crying!" Hébert begged. With his arm around her, he led her out of the stables.

In the tack room, the head groom was bending over his young helper. Marie-Thérèse could not stop weeping. "You shouldn't have struck him with your musket, Hébert!"

"He struck Rami, didn't he? And the groom? Look, that spy isn't worth your tears."

"I don't care what he did!" she sobbed. "Papa charged us with his welfare. Is this the way you're keeping him safe? You've probably killed him!"

"If I haven't, the army will," he said bluntly. "We're at war, and he is a spy, or worse, a traitor. Can't you get that through your head?"

Marie-Thérèse shook off his arm and ordered the groom to get Mattie up and bring her herbs. "Tell her she must look after the groom, and Rami, too." Then she went to the kitchen to waken the cook's helpers and order water heated for Mattie.

The moon had gone behind the clouds scudding up from the Gulf, and the night was black as pitch. Dawn was still several hours away. Mattie joined them, and Marie-Thérèse took her upstairs.

Rami was sitting up on the *galerie* floor, groggy, asking what had happened. Marie-Thérèse sent Mattie to look after him while she remade the guest bed. Then they waited until Apollo and the head groom carried up the man who called himself Jacques, unconscious and bleeding.

There was no need for armed guards for the rest of the night. Hébert stayed for a few minutes, watching as Mattie and Marie-Thérèse busied themselves dressing his reopened wound. While Mattie prepared another bandage, Marie-Thérèse washed away the fresh blood with shaking hands.

Her mouth and lips still tingled strangely, but she would not let herself think about what had happened to her in those few moments before she was torn from Jacques's arms. The strange sensations the spy had aroused in her did not bear thinking about.

Chapter Six

"The wound will heal again," Dr. Boudreau assured Marie-Thérèse, "but he is feverish. And no wonder, if he went out in his weakened condition wearing nothing but his nightshirt. It has given him the ague. But his wound is not infected, and that is good. You know, *mademoiselle*, how to prepare a poultice for the congestion I can hear in his chest."

"*Oui, monsieur.*"

Marie-Thérèse had had little sleep, because she had spent most of the night with Mattie, hovering over the patient. Watching the doctor sponge the trickles of blood from the reopened wound before he deftly applied a fresh bandage, she did not know which was more painful, her aching head or the ache in her breast as she looked at the bruises discoloring M'sieu Jacques's handsome features. There were blue half-moons under his eyes, and one whole side of his face was purplish. But her gaze was drawn to the crisp and beautiful shape of those lips that had touched her own with tingling fire. Marie-Thérèse's heart felt squeezed between anger and pity, but mostly anger.

"Can we not take him to the city?" Hébert asked impatiently. Marie-Thérèse glared at him.

"*Oui,* when his fever breaks," the doctor said. "But when you do, he will be thrown in the New Orleans jail and forgotten while the city engages in chaotic preparations for a siege. They will have no time for him in these hectic days of trying to assemble a volunteer army. It would probably mean his death."

Marie-Thérèse stared at him in horror, and Hébert was silenced.

"If the authorities want to keep him alive for questioning, they should leave him in your care, *mademoiselle,* especially since a fever is threatening his recovery. Right now, you can give the patient better care here than he would find in the city."

"But we should be there!" Hébert exclaimed. "How long must we remain behind, coddling this traitor?"

"You are quite safe here at the moment, *monsieur.* The forts below you are fully manned, and there has been no movement of the enemy up the river."

"How can anyone be sure? The fog gets thick enough before morning to hide an army."

"We know because the British fleet has been sighted entering Lake Borgne."

"Lake Borgne!" Hébert exclaimed. "But that is just beyond the swamp at our backs!"

"The swamp is your protection," Dr. Boudreau said patiently. "And American gunboats are preparing to engage the fleet on the lake. The British must deal with them before they can advance to Lake Pontchartrain and disembark for an attack on the city."

The good doctor took his leave, and Marie-Thérèse found a square of muslin and ordered Doula to spread it with liberal amounts of lard and mustard for a poultice for her patient's chest. Then she tore up an old undershirt of her father's for a piece of red flannel to place under the hot poultice to protect his skin. She was glad that Hébert did not think it necessary to sit by the door with his musket to keep a barely conscious man in bed. She still felt very provoked with her brother. But she was even more provoked with Monsieur Jacques.

As she tenderly sponged his bruised face with the cloth wrung out of cool water that Doula brought her, she began softly scolding the unconscious man. "What in *le bon dieu*'s beautiful world were you thinking of, M'sieu Jacques to wander outside in nothing but your nightshirt? Have you no sense at all?"

No sense at all…no sense at all…at all… The voice was feminine, low and musical, but the words ricocheted in Jacques's aching head like billiards. He opened an eye, squinting against the light from the window behind the head of the woman whose hands were so gentle on his sore face. Ah, Mademoiselle Dufret herself! His disastrous attempt to escape came back to him.

Last night he had silenced her with kisses. Would that he could do the same this morning, for every low word she spoke reverberated in his head with pounding pain.

"How far did you think you could ride when you are not strong enough to throw a saddle over the horse you would steal?" she reproached him, all the while softly stroking his forehead. "Tell me *that!* And now you've got a fever that will have to break before you can travel."

Behind her Doula came into the room, carefully carrying a large square of fabric that she had liberally smeared with lard and mustard, as she had been instructed. Marie-Thérèse took it and told the drugged Jacques, "This will burn like fury, and it serves you right!" But her warm voice caressed him even as she scolded him. "Did you think a man could go through your ordeal in the river and ride a strange horse away three days later? Is your treachery so urgent that you must throw away your life? How exasperating you are, Monsieur Jacques! If that is your name.''

''Other lives are at stake,'' he wanted to say, but his tongue was still thickened by laudanum. What a shrew she was! And how lovely . . .

Her hands were busy with something he could not see, and as she worked she continued to whip him with her soft words. Although her ministrations aggravated his headache and irritated the hell out of him, they also made him feel abundantly cared for.

''And without so much as a *'merci, mademoiselle'* for saving you from the hungry river that was about to suck you to your death! How just plain *stupid* can a man be?''

Jacques had closed his eyes against the onslaught of her low voice, but he opened them wide when she pulled back the sheet and reached for the tail of his nightshirt. Her thumb brushed his inner thigh, and in spite of the laudanum his body reacted instantly. Had she noticed his involuntary reaction?

She had. Her eyes were squeezed shut against the sight of him. The expression on her face tickled his belly with amusement, but he restrained the laugh, because the vibrations it set off were so painful.

Marie-Thérèse flipped the front of Papa's nightshirt up over her patient's bruised face and opened her eyes. Of its own volition, her gaze moved over his shapely brown torso and her breasts tingled with a memory of how it had felt to be pulled strongly against his bare chest. Her fingers trembled as she placed the square of red flannel on the tight black coils of hair, smoothed the poultice over his chest, then bound it all in place with a long strip of muslin that, with Doula's help, she passed under him.

When she pulled his nightshirt down to cover the poultice, his eyes were open and focused on her with a glazed but quizzical gleam. He mumbled something that sounded like, "Taking your clothes off, too, *chérie?*"

"*What?*" she cried. Oh, he was impossible! Marie-Thérèse pulled his nightshirt lower with a jerk and covered him to his chin with the sheet.

His laugh erupted and changed into a moan. He turned his head away from her and soon lapsed into a drugged sleep again.

Marie-Thérèse stood looking down at his sleeping face with confused feelings. He was a spy and a rogue, and his nefarious activities had got him into the state he was in. So why should she feel as if it would be an unbearable loss if they could not save him? She tried to tell herself it was because then Hébert would be responsible for his death, but she knew she was thinking more of M'sieu Jacques than of Hébert. She couldn't let him die!

Later that morning, Estelle came to her with the news that she had a visitor.

"Who is it?" She had been so intent on her task of bathing her patient's fevered face with cool water that she had not heard the arrival of a horse or a carriage.

"*Michie* Duvallier. He say to tell you he have a letter for you from *michie.*"

"A letter from Papa!" Marie-Thérèse exclaimed. "Please find Hébert and ask him to come to the salon to greet Monsieur Duvallier."

The housekeeper hurried away.

Marie-Thérèse left Doula with the basin of cool water and bade her bathe the patient's face every few minutes. She went to her chamber to straighten her dress and her hair before going below, but she gave herself only a cursory glance in the mirror. The pale yellow of her morning dress did nothing to offset her pallor or minimize the dark shadows that lack of sleep had left under her eyes, but there was no time to try to make herself pretty for Gabriel.

She found him standing in the salon, looking resplendent but quite ill at ease in light-colored breeches, a dark blue frock coat over an embroidered waistcoat of lighter blue and a white stock. After her recent days and nights in the sickroom, his attire struck her as excessively formal.

"Bonjour, Gabriel," she said, extending her hand in welcome. "It is good of you to come. I have sent for Hébert and ordered refreshments. You have brought us word from *cher* Papa?"

"*Oui, chère* Marie-Thérèse." He brought her hand to his lips, a dark curl falling over his forehead becomingly as he bent his head. His eyes had a soulful look that was somehow annoying to her on this distressing morning. He gave her a folded and sealed paper, and she opened it at once, saying, "Please excuse me, Gabriel, but I must see what he says!"

Gabriel coughed delicately. She looked down at the paper in her hand and blinked. What she saw was: "Your eyes aglow with love are the window to my heaven..." *Mon Dieu!*

"What is this, Gabriel?"

He said eagerly, "It is a new poem dedicated to you. It is meant for your eyes only."

"But Papa's letter!" she cried, wanting to weep, because she could guess what was coming. Papa had sent Gabriel—they must have discussed her, reached a bargain. What was she going to say? What *could* she say, but yes? Dr. Boudreau's voice echoed in her head, saying, "He will be thrown in the New Orleans jail... It would probably mean his death..."

"Ah, yes, Monsieur Dufret's letter," Gabriel stammered, patting his pocket flap with an awkwardness that was totally unlike him.

"I'm sorry, Gabriel," she said quickly, apologetically "but we are so anxious here. Did Papa not tell you?"

Gabriel looked stricken. "*Mais oui,* the British spy! I'm afraid I had forgotten."

"He tried to escape last night, and Hébert all but killed him. I've not slept—"

"You must forgive me if I seem to have lost my senses, Marie-Thérèse. I am distraught with happiness because your father has given me permission to speak—"

He faltered as Hébert burst into the salon and wrung Gabriel's hand in greeting. "How good to see someone from the city, Monsieur Duvallier! How does it go? Are you one of the brigade?"

"Yes, indeed. And we shall see action soon, perhaps. There is already word that American gunboats have been ordered to engage the British fleet."

"I am eager to join, myself," Hébert said.

Duvallier shrugged. "It could be over before you arrive in town, Dufret. It's rumored from Jamaica that the British are bringing twelve thousand men, seasoned by fighting Napoléon. The governor will be lucky to raise twelve hundred."

"You're saying we will lose New Orleans?" Hébert cried, obviously shocked.

"There are some prominent citizens who advise negotiating to save our property."

"Traitors!" Hébert exclaimed.

Gabriel smiled slightly. "We have been governed by Spain and then by America, and we have remained French. We will still be Frenchmen under British rule, *n'est-ce pas?*

Some say that would be preferable to rule by the American 'barbarians.'"

"Fie, Duvallier!" Hébert cried. "Creoles will never accept British rule! They are royalists, aren't they? And they have bragged that they will burn us out as they burned Washington!"

"Gabriel brings us a letter from Papa," Marie-Thérèse said, trying to hide her impatience.

Gabriel began patting his pockets again. "I have also a letter from your friend, Mademoiselle Annalise, who sends affectionate greetings. You know that the Bourget family has returned to the city?"

"*Mais oui. Chère* Annalise!"

Gabriel handed the letters to Marie-Thérèse who slipped Gabriel's poem and Annalise's fat letter into her pocket and opened the sheet from their father, excusing herself to read it.

Papa's letter was concise and to the point:

There is frenzied activity here to meet the British threat to the city...

Then all the city did not share Gabriel's resignation to defeat!

The governor is closeted day and night with the American general Jackson, who is now in command. The general has inspected all the approaches to the city and strengthened their defenses. The citizens admire his energy, and he has gained their confidence. The army is swamped with volunteers who must be trained in only days to meet the British. The only good news I have to report is that the government has wiped out the nest of vipers on Grande-Terre, capturing eighty pirates, including the notorious Dominique You. The others, including Jean Lafitte, escaped into the bayous. The contents of the pirate warehouses were confiscated, and I have been asked to examine some jewelry to see if I can identify any pieces, a dolorous task...

Marie-Thérèse gasped. *Mama's jewelry, after all these years? Oh, no, please God! She could not bear it.* The familiar pain, so strong it brought a feeling of nausea, sliced through her.

I have delivered the scrap of message the spy was carrying, but no one has time to act on it now. Since the message was intercepted, and he is confined to his bed, the authorities prefer to wait to interrogate the man until he is recovered enough to be brought to them.

Gabriel Duvallier has kindly offered to carry this letter. He has my permission to speak to you privately, Marie-Thérèse. Please give him a letter for me telling me how it goes at Petit Bois and how soon you will arrive.

Your loving papa

Without a word, Marie-Thérèse passed the letter to her brother.

Estelle arrived with a tray holding coffee and cakes, looking startled when Hébert exclaimed, "Damn, damn, damn!"

"*Merci,* Estelle," Marie-Thérèse said, as calmly as she could. "Coffee, Gabriel? Or would you prefer something stronger?"

"*I* would!" Hébert declared, striding to the table that held Papa's decanters and some glasses.

"I will join you in a brandy, Hébert," Gabriel said. "Is it bad news, then?"

"Papa confirms what Dr. Boudreau advised us—that we are still stuck here in the country. It's damned tedious!" Hébert complained. "I don't see why we have to wait for the army to send for the spy. Marie-Thérèse, let's return to the city with Gabriel and take the spy with us. If he gives us any trouble, I'll simply shoot him."

"*Hébert!*" Marie-Thérèse screamed at him.

"We're at war, aren't we?"

"The army wants him alive!" Marie-Thérèse said. "Gabriel, he is only a boy showing off! Pay no attention to him."

"Someday soon, when I am in uniform, you will pay attention to me, *ma chère soeur*. Eh, Gabriel?"

"A uniform helps," Gabriel admitted modestly.

His nervousness about speaking to her no longer aroused Marie-Thérèse's sympathy. On the contrary, she was beginning to feel quite irritated with him. She was eager to have all this over and to get back upstairs to her patient.

"Can you dine with us, Duvallier?" Hébert asked, handing Gabriel his brandy.

"I regret that I cannot. I was given only enough leave by my officer to deliver your father's letter and to await your reply." He swallowed and said, "Perhaps if you were to pen your answer, Hébert, I could have the privacy your father granted me to speak with your sister?"

"Oh, of course," Hébert said, trying to sound very adult and succeeding only in provoking Marie-Thérèse even further. "Is that all right with you, Marie-Thérèse?"

"Perfectly. But tell Papa what you did to the poor man upstairs," she said, "or I shall have to add a postscript."

"She has a tart tongue," Hébert warned Gabriel, tossing off a third of his drink. "All right, Marie-Thérèse, I'll be in Papa's library."

Gabriel lifted his own glass and took a gulp from it. His courage thus fortified, he asked coyly, "Will you read my poem, *mademoiselle?*"

She restrained herself from tapping her toe in impatience. "Oh, Gabriel, of course I will! But this is not a good time. I am needed upstairs in the sickroom. Mattie is sleeping—we were both up all night—and her young daughter is with the patient...."

"*Chère* Marie-Thérèse, did your father not tell you that he has given me his permission to offer for your hand?"

"Of course he did, Gabriel, but I cannot discuss marriage when things are this chaotic. We don't know from one day to the next whether we will be driven from our homes."

Gabriel protested, "But that is why your father sent me now. He wants you to place yourself under my protection."

Until that moment, Marie-Thérèse had thought she might say yes when Gabriel asked for her hand, and that that would be all there was to it. She considered herself a dutiful daughter, although a much-indulged one, and she really wanted to do as her beloved Papa wished—eventually. But Gabriel here, alone with her in her father's salon, was not the same Gabriel she had enjoyed flirting with at the opera or at a ball, or on an extended plantation visit when they were surrounded by their teasing intimates. She knew Gabriel was essentially eligible as a husband, but marriage to him was still in the realm of fantasy.

On the other hand, life was shatteringly real in that room upstairs where she had spent the past days and most of the nights. If Gabriel persisted with his bad poetry and the romantic ritual of bending one knee to her now, she knew she was going to say no. She had no time for such trivialities.

"Gabriel, I do respect my father's wishes," she said hastily. "But you must not ask me now. I have been up all night with my patient, and I have not the time to listen to you this morning."

Gabriel looked pained, and she realized belatedly how cold and unfeeling she must have sounded.

She pulled his poem from her pocket and said, "Thank you for this, *cher* Gabriel. I will read it after I have had a good night's sleep, and can enjoy it."

"But I may not be able to return," he said, going pale.

She felt a pang of contrition, and wanted to comfort him. "I will be in the city soon."

"I shall be with the brigade," he said stiffly, "and who knows where we will be dispatched to meet the enemy?"

It occurred to her that he was thinking that he might be killed in battle, and she felt a chill. But with an attack on their city approaching, that was true of every Louisiana male, including Papa and Hébert. She said, gently, "I'm sorry. You honor me, Gabriel, but I must return to my duties, and you to yours. Someday this war will be over, and then we will talk. *Au revoir, cher* Gabriel."

He bowed formally, his voice cool. *"Au revoir, mademoiselle."*

Hébert came back with the letter he had scratched out and handed it to Marie-Thérèse to read. As she had guessed he would, he made himself out as a hero in striking down their prisoner, who he said had tried to steal his father's best trotter in order to make his escape.

He ended the letter, "Dr. Boudreau said that the prisoner is still unable to travel and that he may die. If he is going to die, I pray it may be soon, so that we can join you."

Marie-Thérèse handed it back with compressed lips but without comment, and Hébert said, "I'll just seal this, Duvallier."

As soon as he left the room, Gabriel put his hands on her shoulders and pulled her close. "Do not make me wait for an answer, *chérie*," he said in a low voice, and he pressed his lips to hers in a long, bruising kiss that ended only when Hébert's step sounded in the hall.

Marie-Thérèse stood very still when Gabriel released her and stepped back. He had caught her by surprise, and surprise was all she felt. He had held her in almost the same way Jacques had held her in that incredible moment in the stables, but that had been a kiss full of fire and fury, a kiss that had left her whole body tingling. She realized now that Gabriel must think her as stiff and unyielding as a palmetto branch.

She regretted that. But it was done. And she knew now that she could never bring herself to marry him.

Gabriel accepted the letter from Hébert and took his leave with a defiant hurt, promising to see them in the city.

Marie-Thérèse forgot him almost immediately, running quickly upstairs to see if Jacques was still burning with fever.

She found her patient very hot, but sleeping so quietly that she had not the heart to wake him with a fresh poultice. She sent Doula back to the kitchen with it. "Tell them to keep it warm for you, and bring me back more cool water."

She sat down beside his bed. Was not sleep healing? On the other hand, should his sleep be so heavy? Should she be doing something more? To distract herself from her worry, she pulled the letter from Annalise out of her pocket and opened it.

Chère Marie-Thérèse,
I think of you often down there at Petit Bois, and all that you are missing by not being in the city. The American general Jackson has taken command of the city's defenses, and the most delicious stories are circulating about him.

Marie-Thérèse was beginning to feel a headache. But she read on.

Apparently he arrived after an all-night ride, and one of our hostesses—I shall not name her—opened her house to give the famous general his breakfast. Imagine her shock when a tall, lanky, dust-grimed man, dressed more like the "Kaintuck" frontiersmen who come down the river on flatboats and walk our streets, than a general of the United States Army, sat at her table, set with her finest china and crystal and a rich variety of foods, and refused everything but a few hominy grits!

The words seemed to come to Marie-Thérèse from another world, making little sense. And yet they described a world that had been hers as little as a fortnight ago.

Madame S. had begged for the privilege of honoring the general at dinner that evening, and she was warned and immediately warned her other guests what they could expect of *l'américain* who had come to save the city. And imagine their surprise when General Jackson turned up in a resplendent uniform and proved to be a perfectly charming guest!
Papa heard later that the unfortunate general has been suffering from dysentery while fighting the In-

dian uprising in Alabama and then riding posthaste to our rescue, but that after a half hour's rest he immediately took charge of planning the city's defense. His name is on everyone's lips!

How she and Annalise would have laughed together only a few days ago. Now she looked anxiously at her patient's feverish color.

We are expecting momentarily to hear that hostilities have begun. It is frightening, and we are all fearful for our loved ones, but there is also a wild excitement and a recklessness infecting the entire city, which is unlike anything I have ever experienced.

All our beaux are called up or are volunteering. Gabriel is fortunate to be able to visit you and has offered to take this letter for me. You must tell me *everything* that takes place when you two meet. Promise! And you must come soon, *chère,* or you will miss everything.

Your affectionate friend,
Annalise

Marie-Thérèse folded the letter and put it back in her pocket. Dear, pleasure-loving Annalise! The war was an adventure to her. She felt a thousand miles removed from her old friend, and many years older. And yet, until the man lying in the bed before her had been washed up out of the river into her life, she knew she had been almost as giddy as Annalise.

Her patient stirred and began muttering unintelligibly. She looked at the rosy spots on his cheekbones, and her heart cramped with a powerful emotion. Suddenly he flung out a hand and caught at her arm. His eyes opened wide and he said, clearly, "Quick, we must hide! See the torches? See their machetes?" His eyes were not seeing her, but rather something in a dream, or a delirium.

She gently removed his hand from her arm so that she could take the wet cloth Doula handed her. When she touched it to his hot forehead, he raised his head from his pillow and screamed, "*Mon Dieu!* It's burning!"

Startled, she dropped the cloth on his face. He flung it away as if it were a burning brand, and she knew he did not know where he was or what he did. The fever had him out of his head! It must be broken, and soon.

She said quietly, "Doula, give me the basin and go and bring back the fresh poultice, please."

There would be another sleepless night. Mattie was perfectly capable of caring for him, but Marie-Thérèse knew she would be at his bedside, too, because she could not stay away.

He could not die!

Chapter Seven

Jacques awoke from a long sleep feeling weak but rested and miraculously free of the congestion in his chest. *Mon dieu,* but it should be gone! The determined *mademoiselle* had nearly burned the hair off his chest with her poultices. There was no burning poultice now, but he was still warmly wrapped round with cotton under his nightshirt.

Neither *mademoiselle* nor the big dark-skinned nurse she called Mattie was in his room now, but young Dufret was back in his chair. And without his musket! Jacques looked around as far as he could see without moving his head, but he could find no gun.

Damnation! The fever had really drained his strength. This was another opportunity, and he was too weak to take it. He had overestimated his stamina once, and been soundly beaten for it. But how much time had he wasted here? How many days were left in which to negotiate the truce his friend wanted with Governor Claiborne? The man had been Jean's sworn enemy for a decade, vowing to drive him and his band of pirates out of Louisiana.

But if the governor did not agree to drop all charges and release Jean's men from prison in return for the support of his five hundred fighting men, Jean would be forced to deal with the British. If that happened, Jacques believed, the city was doomed.

He watched his jailer through slitted eyelids. Hébert had fished a letter out of his pocket and was reading it, muttering, "Damn, damn!"

Abruptly young Dufret rose. He stuffed his letter carelessly back in his pocket, and when he swiveled to leave the room, the folded paper dropped to the floor.

Jacques lay absolutely still, expecting him to return, his awareness of the dropped letter heightening with each passing minute. A certainty grew in him that the missive concerned his imprisonment here. He had long sensed that young Dufret was dissatisfied with his present situation as a jailer, and his curiosity about the message swelled.

He listened acutely. Low feminine voices conversed somewhere on the upper floor, but there was no sound of movement in the hall. He tested his strength by pushing himself up against his pillows, and a wave of pain in his head made him stop all movement.

He rested a moment. The upper hall was still silent, so he threw his legs over the side of the mattress and sat up. Dizziness swept over him, and he had to wait until it passed before he could push himself to stand and move gingerly from the bed.

Marie-Thérèse had stumbled to her chamber toward morning after she and Mattie had finally succeeded in breaking their patient's fever. After getting Hébert's reluctant promise to see that M'sieu Jacques's needs were met, she had slept heavily until midday, when Doula had had water brought up for her bath.

While she bathed, she thought of her patient, and how her impression of him had changed over the days of caring for his needs. Although he still kept his secrets, his aura of danger had shifted perceptibly. The danger he posed now lay in the strength with which she was drawn to him and in her feeling that, in spite of the mystery surrounding him, she understood him intimately.

His delirium in the night had revealed a vulnerability that touched her deeply. It had been so like the nightmares she had suffered these past four years that she had experienced his terror even as she tried to quiet his fears.

Doula helped her into a simple day dress of sapphire blue trimmed with narrow bands of white lace. After drinking her café au lait and eating a buttered piece of a fresh-baked *baguette,* Marie-Thérèse went to the sickroom. No guards were on duty; they had not been necessary while she and Mattie were battling their patient's fever.

The sight that met her eyes gave Marie-Thérèse an angry shock. M'sieu Jacques was standing in the center of the room, his shapely legs revealed beneath one of Papa's nightshirts. He should not be on his feet—and especially his bare feet! And the doctor had said he must be kept quiet for at least a week to let his body recover from the new concussion Hébert had given him.

But it was neither that alone, nor the embarrassing intimacy of his attire, that upset her. It was what he held in his hand. She recognized it immediately. Somehow he had gotten hold of Papa's letter, and was reading it!

"M'sieu Jacques! What *are* you doing?" she exclaimed, rushing forward to snatch the letter from him.

He staggered back, still clutching the letter. She tried to grab it. His knees were damnably shaky, and he reached for her shoulders. He seemed always to be grabbing at her to keep from falling, and it infuriated him. This must stop. He had to get away from this woman and this place!

"Get back in bed at once!" she ordered, propelling him toward it.

Mon dieu, but she behaved as if she were in command of his brigantine and he were a lowly seaman! She needed a lesson. But where had his strength gone? He struggled to be free of her, and at the same time to hang on to the letter, which interested him greatly. In it Dufret revealed that he had talked to Governor Claiborne, who had conferred with the American general. General Jackson had not only vowed he would not deal with those raffish, thieving Lafittes, but had agreed to send an army unit to drive them off Grande-Terre! Dominique was in jail, and Pierre and Jean were in hiding. And what in hell had become of his brigantine? He wanted desperately to finish reading the letter.

But he was lurching as if he were blind drunk, and instead of fighting Mademoiselle Dufret off, he was forced to cling to her. He backed into the bed and fell over on it. Because he did not let her go, *mademoiselle* fell with him.

He was on his back, and she was lying on top of him. He could feel the nipples on her soft breasts rise at the close contact, and it excited him. Her thigh lay against his groin, and incredibly, his fever-weakened body was responding to her close, intimate weight. She lifted her head in sudden awareness and turned her startled gaze up to him. Her lips were very near his, full and rosy.

He did what any real man would do in such a position, feverish or not. He kissed her. This was not a kiss of aggression, to silence her, but a kiss of pure enjoyment. He relaxed on the bed, holding her, enjoying her nearness and the fragrance of her hair. He nibbled. He ran his tongue over her lips, measuring their fullness and their shape while tasting them.

She shuddered, and then her lips parted, and he felt a wave of triumph as he sensed her rising innocent passion. His own desire flamed in instant response. This was the answer to his problem. This little darling was his way out.

She was struggling now, belatedly making noises of outrage and fury. He let her go, still caressing her with his eyes.

She rolled away from him and to her feet in one graceful movement. Her cheeks were flushed and her eyes flashing, her lips so scarlet they looked bitten and seemed to throb from the kisses he had given her. Never had a woman looked so thoroughly, so temptingly, aroused, he thought, enraptured.

She demanded in a low voice, "Do you want to give my brother the excuse he is looking for to kill you, *monsieur?*"

She was probably right about that. "*Non, mademoiselle,*" he said ruefully, "but what man could have resisted stealing a kiss when you flung yourself down on me like that?"

"I did not!"

"No one with red blood in his veins," he went on, "even at the risk of his life!"

"You mock me, *monsieur,*" she said with an emotional throb in her voice. Startled, he saw that her eyes were suspiciously moist, and he realized for the first time how vulnerable she was under her tart exterior. He felt a pang of contrition for planning to deliberately exploit her inexperienced but passionate nature to enlist her help.

He caught her hand. "No, I do not mock you," he said seriously, and discovered that he meant it. "You, *mademoiselle,* are a prize worth any risk."

She looked at him with brimming eyes, and a surprising tenderness swelled in his breast. He pulled gently at her hand until she sat down on the edge of his bed. She was biting her lower lip, trying to get control of herself again. Jacques seemed to know what she was feeling, and, what was more surprising, he seemed to care.

"I would gladly risk my life to hold you in my arms again," he heard himself say, and to his dismay, he sounded sincere. Risk his life for a woman? *Jacques Bonnard, when have you needed to lie to win a woman's favor?*

Her eyes grew mysteriously darker. Suddenly she bent over him and gave him her lips with a sweet surrender and an inexperienced passion that shook him to his depths. What a desirable woman she was! He could lose himself and all that he was trying to do in her kisses! Obeying an irresistible impulse, he reached up and cupped her breasts in his two hands, and she made a soft, inarticulate sound of surprised pleasure.

The intimate knowledge that she was not bound by stays or corsets intoxicated him. He pulled her closer, drowning in the sweetness of her kiss and her surging response to his desire. He knew in that moment that it was only a matter of time before he could take her, but the strangest thing was happening. He was seized by a desire to be completely honest with her.

With his hands on her cheeks, he drew her away from him so that he could look into her eyes. They were dazed with an emotion that he knew by instinct was new to her. He saw that he had shaken her world, and the knowledge shook him. He was suddenly drunk with his power over her, but he was equally determined to tell her the truth.

"Let me love you," he said passionately. "But do not fall in love with me, *chérie.*"

Still dazed she said, "Why?"

Marie-Thérèse vibrated with the passion his kisses had aroused in her. So this was what it was like to want a man, this ache to be touched in the most secret places of her body, this urge to give herself to him, to pleasure him and let him pleasure her. It occurred to her that in her ignorance she had often played with fire. But until now she had not known that the divine fire this man's caresses ignited in her body even existed.

And she had passively accepted the idea of marrying Gabriel Duvallier! Why was it that this man could inflame her, when Gabriel's kisses left her stiff and unmoved?"

"Why?" she said again.

"Because in the life I lead there is no place for a woman as magnificent as you. I can only hurt you."

Her eyes widened, and that drugged look of passion faded from their dark depths.

"So you do remember the kind of life you lead!" she said sharply, standing up and lifting her hands to straighten her bodice and smooth her hair. His warning had brought her to her senses just in time! Her cheeks flamed with shame. What devil had prompted her to kiss this traitor with such abandon that *anything* could have happened? Her breasts burned with the imprint of his hands through her gown. "And what is this life, pray?"

"I didn't say I remembered it. But I know it's not like your life here at Petit Bois, *chère mademoiselle*. It could not be to your liking."

Oh, but he had a smooth tongue! All along he had been making fools of them with his lies. He remembered everything and told them nothing. "I'm sure it would not," she said haughtily, "since you will be in prison."

"But you can keep me out of prison," he said softly.

These words were the last straw. He was using her. "And why should I do that?"

"Because of what I feel for you, and what you—"

"And what do you feel? You have deceived me, lied to me, tried to incite my father's slaves against me—"

"No!" he exclaimed. "Never that!" He caught her hand and brought it to his lips. "You will help me, *chérie*, because of what you feel for me."

She tossed her head. "You flatter yourself, *monsieur*. There is no place in my life for a man. I have told my friends that only a grand passion could tempt me away from the pleasant life I enjoy as mistress of Petit Bois. You, *monsieur,* are quite safe!" She turned on her heel to leave.

She was taking the damned letter with her, and Jacques watched the graceful sway of her hips with helpless anger as she went out of his room. Damn! He owed her his life, but the stakes were too high to worry about honesty and the hurt he would inflict. Regardless of the consequences, he had to hunt Jean down in his maze of bayous and deliver Livingston's message.

Time was short. He had no choice but to seduce Mademoiselle Dufret so thoroughly that she herself would arrange his escape. And remembering the feel of her soft, unstayed body in his arms, he knew he was going to enjoy every moment of it.

In her retiring room, Marie-Thérèse scrubbed at her lips with a cloth lathered with French soap. She could not forget who she was—the daughter of Monsieur Paul Dufret and hostess of his famous sugar plantation, Petit Bois. To fall in love with a British spy who admitted he would love her and leave her was madness! She must be bewitched!

Hébert was right. The sooner they put M'sieu Jacques in the carriage and left for New Orleans, the better! But there was a new, raw hurt in her breast. She did not want to care what happened to the patient she had nursed with a devotion that she could not justify, but she did care—passionately.

That night, when Hébert took a stroll after their evening meal, Boddy, the overseer, approached him. "*Bonsoir,* M'sieu Hébert!" He lowered his voice and said, "I have learned who Rami's enemy is, *m'sieu.*"

"Yes, Boddy?"

"He's a big fellow named Gama. One of the cane-cutters. Do you know which one I mean?'

"Yes, I know him. He's been somewhat of a malcontent?"

"That's the one, *oui*, a man full of hate. He quarreled with Rami out in the field last cutting season, and things have worsened between them since then."

"Did Gama sneak that gris-gris into the house?" Hébert asked sharply.

Boddy said, "He wouldn't risk it. He probably sent someone."

"I've questioned the maids. I trust them."

"Maybe a child, one of the little boys? Gama is a man who carries a grudge. And maybe he's jealous of Rami, coming to the big house and allowed to tote a gun."

"What did they quarrel about? A woman?"

"I don't think so."

"I don't want Gama anywhere near the big house!" Hébert exclaimed. "See to that, Boddy. Is he trying to incite the slaves to a rebellion, do you think?"

Boddy scratched his head. "He's the kind the British could maybe get to, *non?*"

"Yes."

"I'll have him watched, *m'sieu.*"

"And try to convince Rami the damn gris-gris can't do him any harm, unless it scares him to death! Does he really believe that a charm made of a bone and a few feathers can hurt him?"

"It's not the gris-gris, *m'sieu.* It's knowing Gama wants him to die."

Hébert felt a chill. That was what voodoo was all about, it was said—the belief that an enemy could wish one to death.

"I heard a rumor Gama stealing your chickens," said Boddy. "Maybe that's how he pays the voodoo woman for her charms." He chuckled. "I think I discuss that with him."

"Good idea, Boddy."

He told Marie-Thérèse about their conversation later that evening. "Do you remember Gama?" he asked her.

"The big one who always cuts the most cane? Of course I do! He must be six-foot-three!"

"At least."

"He was never friendly when we played among the cabins with the children. I was always afraid of him."

"You were right to be afraid. Boddy says he's a man full of hate."

Marie-Thérèse shivered. "What's going to happen, Hébert?"

"Boddy's keeping an eye on him."

Jacques awakened in darkness. He had heard a step on the *galerie*. His guards had not been restored after his fever, and a sharp feeling of alarm brought him fully out of his sleep. What *mademoiselle* had said about giving her brother an excuse to kill him had lodged in his mind, telling him to be wary of young Dufret. He slipped silently out of bed and stood for a moment, fighting a wave of dizziness, then crossed the floor to peer through his window shutters.

Moonlight illuminated the *galerie* and revealed a dark figure moving as stealthily as Jacques himself. All of Jacques's nerves tightened. As his eyes adjusted to the darkness, he saw that an enormous black man was approaching from the rear of the house. He was no one Jacques had seen before, but with horror he recognized the gleaming object in the man's hand as the blade of a cane-cutter's machete.

It was like the nightmare that he could never wholly escape, the nightmare that was his earliest memory of Haiti: a horde of hate-filled faces, murderous machetes gleaming in the light of torches...

Was he about to experience another slave uprising?

The dark figure had paused. Again the moonlight flashed on his murderous weapon. Jacques realized the man had stopped at the window next to his own—the room he had deduced was *mademoiselle*'s—with his machete poised to chop through the bar that secured the wooden shutters.

There were no guards! No doubt another assassin was outside Hébert's door. But there was no time to sound an alarm, if he was to save Marie-Thérèse Dufret from imminent death.

Chapter Eight

Jacques ripped the bandage from around his head, producing a strip of muslin a yard long. He doubled it, holding the ends in his two hands, and slipped through his window just as the machete came down with a crashing blow on the shutters of the next room. The big slave entered *mademoiselle*'s room, and Jacques ran in his bare feet after him.

Inside her mosquito *barre* Marie-Thérèse, wakened by the sound of shattered wood, sat up and screamed. The opened windows threw a square of pale moonlight into the room. Silhouetted in it was the figure of the slave who had always inspired unease in her. She could not see his face, but his height and bulk identified him. Another figure, mysteriously white, was behind him. Marie-Thérèse did not pause to try to identify it. Behind the gauze, she leapt out of the other side of the bed, shrieking, "Hébert! Hébert!"

Her scream galvanized Jacques. The husky slave stood just outside the gauze *barre*, his machete raised again, when Jacques threw the muslin bandage over his head and pulled it tight around his throat.

Gama's head jerked back, but his machete was already on its way down. It slashed through the mosquito netting but tore out of it as Jacques pulled him back.

Jacques tightened the pressure on the slave's throat, praying that the muslin would not tear, and that the surge of strength *mademoiselle*'s scream had triggered would last long enough for him to subdue the rebel. Her terror had reached that hidden cancer in his mind where nightmares were spawned, giving him the power to hold on while the big man thrashed about, trying to use his weapon with one hand and clutching at the strangling cloth at his throat with the other. He was trying to shout, but could make only choking sounds.

Jacques was dragged about the room with him, putting all his fear-induced strength into tightening the noose.

Marie-Thérèse ran to her door and unlocked it, and Hébert burst in with his musket. He raised it and fired at the two men struggling in the moonlight. The burst of powder filled the room briefly with a flash of orange light, illuminating both men as they fell. Marie-Thérèse screamed again when she saw that it was Jacques lying under Gama. The machete skittered across the floor.

For an instant, Gama lay looking up at the smoking gun. Even in the dim light, his face expressed pure hatred.

"Kill!" he shouted. *"Kill the white devils!"* He rolled off of Jacques, coming to his hands and knees, and crawled on all fours, but with incredible swiftness, out of the window. Outside, he straightened and ran, his bare feet thudding unevenly down the *galerie*.

Marie-Thérèse stared at the trail of blood Gama had left on the cypress floor. She did not have the courage to look at Jacques. Her heart was pounding.

Hébert stood over their prisoner with his now-empty gun. He was looking at the blood and listening to the sounds of Gama's escape, apparently indecisive.

From the floor, Jacques said calmly. "It's not a slave uprising, or we'd all be dead."

Hébert lowered his gun, but he was still listening alertly. "No. Gama is not well liked enough to command a mob. But he must have an accomplice. He wouldn't dare break in here unless someone was outside my room planning to kill me."

Marie-Thérèse gasped. Abruptly Hébert ran out into the hall, and she cried after him, "For the love of God, be careful, Hébert!" His steps drummed down the back stair.

Now that the threat of immediate death had been removed, Marie-Thérèse was shaking like a leaf in a breeze, her legs trembling so violently that they could not support her. She sank to her knees and leaned over Jacques, who was still on the floor. He was pale with exhaustion, but to her great relief she saw no bleeding.

The big plantation bell began tolling, making a deafening sound that would waken and warn every soul within hearing of danger, including those on the nearer plantations—if there were any but slaves left who had not already gone to New Orleans to defend the city!

"Are you hurt, *m'sieu?*"

"No, *chère.*"

The casual endearment started her shaking again. "You saved my life, M'sieu Jacques." She could still see the towering figure and the gleam of his machete just outside her *barre* when she'd wakened. Nothing would ever erase that image from her memory.

Groaning, Jacques pushed himself up to a sitting position. "Then we start even," he said.

She laughed nervously, releasing some of her tension. Still in her night robe, with him barely covered by Papa's nightshirt, she helped Jacques back to his room. It did not even seem strange to have his arm lying across her shoulders. There was comfort in being close to him, and a feeling of being protected.

His room was shadowy, but she knew it well, and her eyes had adjusted to the darkness. She did not try to light a candle, but guided him to his bed and pulled the sheet and the light coverlet up over him. He relaxed with a great sigh of exhaustion.

"Rest," she said, touching his cheek. It was cool, and yet she felt a heat from the contact. But it was not the heat of fever, she noted thankfully.

He caught her hand and brought it to his lips. "I was frightened for you," he murmured.

Marie-Thérèse wondered that she had ever thought him dangerous. A tremendous glow of tenderness suffused her. She thought of that terrifying moment after Hébert's gun had exploded, when she had seen him lying under Gama's bulk. "And I for you," she said.

When she went back to her room, she found Estelle, who had been wakened by the shot, already mending her mosquito netting by the light of a candle. Hébert came running back upstairs, calling "Marie-Thérèse, are you all right?"

"I'm here, Hébert."

"I should have followed him," he said, chagrined, "but by the time I reloaded, he would have gotten away." The truth was that he had been afraid to return to his room for ammunition, because he feared a murderer was awaiting him there, but he would have died before admitting it.

He walked across the room and picked up Gama's machete. "Gama slid down a pillar and escaped. Boddy thinks he was acting alone. The others say he was crazed with hate. Boddy's taking a few trusted men out to search the plantation for him, and I've sent a messenger to the sheriff, offering a reward and warning that the runaway is armed and dangerous."

"Armed?" Marie-Thérèse asked.

"Boddy says he may have stolen another machete. He won't get far," Hébert said grimly. "He signed his death warrant when he broke into your chamber. If I'd had a loaded gun, I'd have followed and killed him on the spot. But he won't get away! At least I wounded him and he's leaving a trail."

When he left her, Marie-Thérèse went back to bed, but not to sleep. She felt as if she were in the center of a hurricane. Everything was changing. The ground seemed to be shifting under her feet. She no longer knew Petit Bois, or herself. A man she had never seen before he washed up on their bank, dark and intriguing and obviously on a dangerous mission, had somehow become the center of her existence, the core around which her thoughts and emotions revolved.

It wasn't love. It couldn't be love. Where was it all leading? What would Mama have said? Tears came to her eyes, and she cried, again, for Mama and Adorée and their terrible fate.

At breakfast the next morning, Boddy brought word that Gama was not on the plantation, but had left a trail of blood going into the swamp.

"Then he'll come back soon, or not at all," Hébert predicted. "He can't survive long in the swamp."

"What did he and Rami quarrel about?" Marie-Thérèse asked.

"Rami didn't want to say," the overseer told them. "He said, 'I get in Gama's way.'"

"I think he's still frightened," Hébert said. "And Apollo claims ignorance about the whole thing. Now that your patient is improved enough to have tackled Gama, I'm putting them back on guard duty."

"He saved my life!" Marie-Thérèse protested.

"Just the same," Hébert said.

Later Marie-Thérèse got the story from Mattie, who knew everything that went on in the cabins. She was horrified at the attack on her mistress, but she knew what fueled Gama's hatred. "Gama been telling everybody 'bout the British. He say the British don' own slaves, and don' carry black men from Africa on they ships anymore. Be that true, *ma'mselle?*"

"I've heard so," Marie-Thérèse admitted.

It was the nightmare of every plantation owner that the British were trying to subvert both the Indians and the slaves to their side in the coming conflict. Leaflets had even appeared in New Orleans urging the Creoles themselves to join in their "liberation" from the Americans.

She wondered who had posted those leaflets in their very midst. Some spy, of course. Was that what Jacques had been doing? It seemed doubtful, since he was the one who had saved her.

Marie-Thérèse wrestled with her wayward emotions. How could she have arrived at this state of confusion? She was all but promised to Gabriel Duvallier, and yet the prospect of marrying him affected her about as emotionally as an appointment with her *modiste.* Her feelings were totally involved with her exasperating patient, to whom she now owed her life.

The audacious things he had said to her were burned indelibly into her memory. She could not exorcise them. His dark gaze often rested on her bosom, and she knew—she *knew*—what he was thinking, and was appalled that she could feel an ache there for his lips.

Her own words often came back to her. She had spoken them to Papa and more than once when her friends had quizzed her about her romantic feelings, "I have everything I want at Petit Bois. Why should I marry, except for a grand passion?"

Now she was mortally afraid that she had met her grand passion, and that it was one that had no chance of leading to happiness.

That day Papa's groom arrived with another letter for them. *"Mon cher fils et ma chère fille,"* it began, in an excess of paternal affection that was unusual and somewhat alarming. Then it went on:

We are told that the British fleet has entered Lake Borgne, avoiding the pass at the mouth of the river, where General Jackson has been expecting them. A small American flotilla of gunboats lies between them and the entrance to Lake Pontchartrain, but they face at least fifty British vessels. This is most serious, because there are several routes open to the city from the lake.

Hébert, I do not say that you were not justified in your attack on the prisoner, but it has obviously delayed your return. The authorities now wish to question him, and we have not much more time.

Christmas week is almost upon us, and I would like us to be together, even if it will be a somber holiday. You may be as safe or safer at Petit Bois than you would be here, but if we are facing defeat I would prefer to have you with me.

Your loving papa

Marie-Thérèse penned their answer, telling her father the prisoner was so far recovered as to have saved her life from Gama, who had tried and failed to incite an uprising, and that they would probably arrive in two days. Then she went to her prie-dieu and prayed that Jacques would not die in the New Orleans jail.

That afternoon they heard distant cannon fire from beyond the swamp. The threatened British attack had begun—not from the river, but on Lake Borgne, between the American gunboats and the British fleet.

The cannonade kept up all the next day. Marie-Thérèse gave Apollo the laundered breeches and shirt Jacques had been wearing when she found him, and a frock coat of her father's to replace the one that had been ruined in the river. When he was properly clad, Apollo took him out on the *galerie* and offered him support while he walked, trying out his unsteady legs.

"You were steady enough to bring Gama down," Apollo said slyly. "Where be all that strength today, *michie?*"

"Fear is a great stimulant," Jacques admitted.

Apollo laughed. "You feared for *ma'mselle,*" he said admiringly. "And you were smart to be a-feared. That Gama crazy as a loon."

When they had walked all the way around the house, Estelle brought up a tray of coffee and cakes, and Apollo helped Jacques into a chair. Hébert joined them, his musket loaded and within easy reach.

"Coffee at gunpoint?" Jacques asked with an ironic lift of one eyebrow.

"You are at liberty to refuse it," Marie-Thérèse said coolly. But she could not take her eyes off him, dressed as he was in Papa's ill-fitting but finely made coat and his own shrunken breeches, which he was thin enough to wear. Even so, they were tight-fitting enough to reveal the shape of his body, narrow-hipped and beautiful. He looked every inch the gentleman.

"Tomorrow, we all go to the city, where you will be turned over to the army," Hébert explained with satisfaction. "Until then, we must rely on my trusty musket to keep you with us, *monsieur.*"

Marie-Thérèse saw the glance Jacques gave Hébert's weapon and read it clearly. He was thinking that he could perhaps seize the musket before Hébert could use it. Their gazes met, and she saw by his amused expression that he had also read her mind.

He said, "I look forward to returning to New Orleans."

Both of the young Dufrets looked skeptical. But in New Orleans, even in the city's accursed jail, he would find some way of getting word to Livingston that he had been prevented from reaching Jean. It was imperative to persuade the governor that Jean's offer was sincere, and that his letters detailing the British offer were authentic.

The naval battles now being fought within their hearing proved that time was running out. Perhaps Mademoiselle Dufret herself could be persuaded to take a message to Livingston for him?

He smiled at her, and was gratified when she colored faintly. The cough and echo of the cannons rolled across the wooded swamp that separated them from Lake Borgne. There was no way of knowing which fleet was scoring a hit. Their view of the river and the opposite shore was calm and peaceful, and the laughter of children playing came from the rear of the house, the same direction as the leisurely cannonade.

The contrast between the peaceful scene and the sound of distant cannons made Marie-Thérèse feel disoriented, as if she were experiencing a disquieting dream. Now that they were actually going to New Orleans on the following day, she was eager to leave Petit Bois. Tomorrow would be the last time she would see Jacques. Maybe then she could forget his mocking, yet tender gaze, and the way her lips had tingled long after he had kissed her. In the city, the military balls and the other war-related activities Annalise had described would help her forget him.

But could she truly forget him when he was in the city jail only blocks from her father's town house? She should feel happy to be relieved of her duties as nurse and healer, but she felt strangely sad, as she feared Jacques would not be well cared for.

Jacques watched the play of moods on Marie-Thérèse's face, thinking of taking her in his arms and burying his face in her bosom. The very thought of it made him ache with desire. But how was he going to manage to be alone with her now that his two sentinels were back?

He had no money with which to bribe the prison guards, so he must persuade her to bring Livingston to the jail. But how? There would be few opportunities for a private word with her. He couldn't very well manage it while they were riding in the carriage, with Hébert listening!

The thought that after tomorrow they might never meet again was unacceptable. He promised himself that, whatever happened, he would see her again. And take her in his arms. Sometime. Somewhere.

On this side of the house, facing north, they could see the levee and the river to their left, and the dark foliage of the cypress swamp behind the plantation to their right. A drainage canal that served to carry off the excess water after a torrential rain extended from near the levee through the cane fields and into the swamp. It lay beyond the garden. Several black children were fishing from its bank with bamboo poles.

As the group on the *galerie* sipped their coffee, an astonishing thing happened. A handful of red-coated soldiers appeared on the levee road, coming toward the house. At the same time, out of the dark foliage behind the plantation buildings that marked the swamp, several long, shallow boats appeared on the canal. More red-jacketed men jumped ashore and began unloading cannons. Other soldiers came running through the fields bordering the canal, making them blossom with scarlet.

Hébert leaped to his feet. "*Mon dieu!* The British have bypassed the forts!" he cried. "I thought only an Acadian could navigate that damned swamp!"

The redcoats were running toward the house, and behind them more men came pouring out of more boats with muskets in their hands. Marie-Thérèse was on her feet, too, and she was dimly aware that Jacques had also pushed himself up from his chair to look.

"I must get word to Papa," Hébert said, and before Marie-Thérèse realized what he meant to do, her brother had grabbed a pillar and slid down from the *galerie*. He fell but rolled over and was on his feet again in seconds, streaking across the lawn between the levee road and the pool where the canal began.

Marie-Thérèse cried out as several British muskets fired at her brother. "Oh! No! Hébert!"

But he had disappeared into the copse that separated Petit Bois from the Bourget plantation. Marie-Thérèse covered her mouth with her hands. Her heart was in her throat. What a rash but heroic thing to do! And how dangerous! But how like Hébert, young and impulsive as he was, to realize immediately that Papa and the generals must be warned that the attack had begun and in this unlikely place!

He disappeared among the large oaks and several of the red-coated soldiers ran into the woods after him. The fear that they already had wounded him fatally pierced her breast. She was alone now, and solely in charge.

Things were happening too fast. The British were rounding up the slaves and forcing them into the grinding shed. Several of the red-coated officers had already reached the house. Marie-Thérèse picked up Hébert's musket and ran through her brother's chamber to the central hall of the upper floor.

She was at the head of the stairs when two officers burst into the foyer below with pistols in their hands. Several soldiers with muskets crowded in behind them, their muddy boots soiling the polished floor.

"Stop there, or I'll shoot!" she shouted, raising Hébert's loaded gun.

Jacques followed her into the hall. *"Mon dieu!"* he said under his breath. He put his arms tightly around her from behind, catching her arms in his embrace and forcing the barrel of the gun upward. He said sharply in her ear, "Do you want to get us both killed, *mademoiselle?*"

The gun wavered as she struggled against him. His heart swelled at her foolhardy courage, but he muttered, "Don't be an idiot! You are one against a regiment."

"Put the gun down very carefully, *monsieur,*" the British officer called, in passable French. "If it goes off, you will both die instantly."

His tone was utterly convincing. Marie-Thérèse's burst of courage collapsed in a wave of sheer panic as she looked into the muzzles of the guns aimed at her and Jacques. For a moment she could not speak. The men below cocked their pistols.

Jacques took the musket out of her nerveless hands. He laid it carefully on the landing and held out his empty arms.

An older officer whose red coat was covered with medals and gold braid entered the house, and the soldiers parted to let him through. He strode forward with the arrogance of a man whose slightest wish was always obeyed, looking critically into the rooms on the left and the right of the hall as he came: the salon, where Mama's beautiful portrait hung, the music room, which doubled as a small ball-room, the formal dining room and Papa's library. His sharp blue eyes directed their gaze from the Turkey rug on the floor to the gilt wall sconces and the crystal-hung cande-labra.

Then his gaze followed the handsome staircase up to the landing and rested on Marie-Thérèse and Jacques.

"A well-appointed house. It will do nicely for my head-quarters," he said to his aide. "We will occupy it immedi-ately." He was speaking French, which told the stunned Marie-Thérèse that he wanted her to understand him. "I want nothing removed except the painting in the salon. Have my lady's portrait brought from the ship to hang in its place. Move my things into the master's chamber."

Marie-Thérèse's terror was forgotten in her blossoming rage. He was moving into Petit Bois as if it were his own, as if he planned to stay! Her fury was stronger than any she had ever known. It boiled up, fueled by the thought of these enemy hands desecrating her mother's portrait, and over-rode her fear.

She threw back her shoulders and lifted her chin. Her movements thrust her breasts forward, and a collective sigh was released by the soldiers below her.

Jacques felt her cold rage like a blast of winter, and his own anger flared surprisingly at the reaction of the red-coats to her beauty. But he put a restraining hand on her arm. She wrenched away from it and took two quick steps down the staircase.

"Your filthy hands will not touch my mother's portrait!" she shouted. "Nor will you move into my father's cham-bers! I will not allow it! *Monsieur,* you are not welcome in this house. You will leave immediately, and take your in-solent sold—"

The officer's aide was running up the stair toward them, his pistol drawn.

Jacques leapt down the two steps and put his hands over Marie-Thérèse's mouth and nose so tightly she could not breathe, choking off her voice.

Of course, Marie-Thérèse thought, feeling a terrible pain, a pain so strong she was near fainting. After all, wasn't Jacques the *enemy*?

Chapter Nine

Marie-Thérèse was very uncomfortable. She had been confined to her chamber for several hours, sitting in a straight wooden chair with her hands pulled through the slots in its back and tied together. Her arms and shoulders ached from the unnatural position, and her mouth was dry and her jaws hurt from the gag stuffed into her mouth.

Her pride had been trampled, but her heart was even more sore.

Rage at the invasion of Petit Bois had long since burned itself to ashes, leaving only pain and anxiety. She had accused Jacques of spying and treachery, but until now the reality of a British attack had not been imaginable. Like a child, she had believed that her comfortable life would continue, no matter what happened.

Now she wondered if this British plot to seize Petit Bois and mount their attack on New Orleans from here was what Jacques had been hiding while he was stealing her heart.

He was worse than a rogue. He was not only treacherous, but callous!

She tried to tell herself Hébert had escaped the British and was even now in New Orleans, and Papa would come with his regiment and drive these invaders off his plantation. But another vision came and went behind her smarting eyelids—that of her beloved younger brother lying wounded in the woods, felled by a British musket, perhaps dying.

The tears she had been fighting flooded her eyes and rolled slowly down her cheeks. She could not even lift a hand to brush them away.

The door from the hall opened, and Doula entered with a tray. "Estelle send you some soup, *ma'mselle,* and the soldier say untie you." A warm tantalizing odor rose from the tray, and a sharp pang of hunger reminded Marie-Thérèse that she had not entirely lost her appetite.

For a moment after Doula removed the gag, her mouth was so dry that she could not speak. Her tongue felt swollen. Doula offered her a cup of water, but her arms were so numb as to be useless. Doula held the cup to her lips, and then Marie-Thérèse managed to say, "Help me to my retiring room."

A few moments later, relieved and her hunger appeased, with the blood returning to her limbs, she plied Mattie's daughter with anxious questions.

"Soldiers made everybody gather in the grinding shed except us in the big house. They tell us do our work, tell cook make dinner for them, tell Estelle make beds—"

"Monsieur Hébert? Did he get away?"

"Nobody know if he get through. The soldiers let nobody go into the woods."

Who would have thought the British could transport an army across territory that was so strange to them, territory considered hostile even by her Creole friends? Coming out of the swamp in that stunning surprise had given the enemy a terrific advantage. They had surrounded Petit Bois before anyone could react. Except Hébert. And where was *he* now? Marie-Thérèse felt horribly alone.

"And what of our patient?" she asked painfully. "Has he put on his red coat?"

"He tied up like you, *ma'mselle,* in he room. Apollo take he tray now."

Jacques tied up, too? Why was that, if he had been spying for the British? Could she and Papa have been mistaken about him?

And Hébert, beating an injured man and reopening his wound! Oh, no! she thought. She remembered again the giddy intoxication of that moment when she had been pulled down on top of him, and in that embarrassingly compromising position had flung off all the restraints her mother and the nuns at the convent had placed on her and responded shamelessly to his kiss. Had her heart been right to trust him, even when her head did not?

A tiny hope blossomed in her breast. She said indignantly, "Can't they see he is a man who has been very ill? And is not yet recovered?"

Doula nodded. "They see. He still wear the bandage of my mother 'round he head."

"Mattie! Is she in the grinding shed with the others?"

"*Oui, ma'mselle.* Like animals in a pen!"

If she was not to be allowed to look after Jacques herself, Mattie must come to the house. "Quick, Doula! Bring me a silk gown—that rose-colored one will do! And help me into it. Where are the British now?"

"They all over the plantation!"

"Their officers," Marie-Thérèse clarified.

"In the dining room, eating cook's food."

Doula had just finished brushing her hair when the British soldier who had been posted at her door entered and gestured toward her chair. Obviously he meant to tie her up again. Marie-Thérèse remained standing, her slender body defiantly erect, her head high. Her mother's necklace of rubies was fastened around her long white neck.

Seeing the jewels and holding them in her hand had brought back the familiar pain, a pain that had not lessened in the four years since her mother and her sister were captured by pirates. This was not as horrible as what they must have suffered, she told herself, building her courage. She and Hébert were all Papa had left, and Hébert might be gone. She could do what had to be done.

Marie-Thérèse made no move to sit again. The soldier's eyes took in her proud carriage and her jewels, and he hesitated for a fraction of a second. She seized the moment.

"Inform *monsieur le général* that Mademoiselle Dufret wishes to speak to him when he has finished his repast."

"You wish to speak," the British soldier said incredulously, in bad French, "to my general?" His mouth widened, as if he were about to guffaw.

Marie-Thérèse quelled him with a look. "Are you hard-of-hearing?" she snapped.

His grin vanished. "No, milady."

"Then go. Inform the general that I await his pleasure here. Doula, you stay with me," she added with casual arrogance.

"Oui, ma'mselle," Doula said meekly, but a tiny smile hovered on her lips as the British soldier's confused expression changed to a sullen respect and his officiousness wilted under Marie-Thérèse's aristocratic hauteur.

"Yes, milady," he said, and left them.

She paced the floor of her chamber, her indignation growing as she pictured Jacques, still weak from fever, bound to an uncomfortable chair in the next room. Yesterday he had been her prisoner, and today she was a prisoner herself. But he was still her patient.

"Will he come?" Doula ventured.

"We'll soon know."

A half hour later, there was a knock at her chamber door. Marie-Thérèse nodded to Doula, and the maid opened the door. The red-coated officer who stood there was the gold-spangled and bemedaled one who had inspected her father's house with critical appreciation and announced that it would do nicely for him. The general himself had indeed come.

He was tall and commanding, with gray hair that was still peppered with black. His keen, cold eyes appraised her change of costume and her jewelry instantly, but his tone betrayed no reaction. "Mademoiselle Dufret."

"Monsieur le général," she said with icy courtesy. "Come in, if you please."

"Well, *mademoiselle?*" His French was almost perfect. His slightly ironic inflection told her he was a man who said little—and that little directly.

Marie-Thérèse chose her words carefully. "I am in your power, *monsieur,* but since you are obviously a gentleman, I hope you will honor my two requests."

"Which are?"

"First, I fear my young brother may be lying in the woods, wounded by your soldiers, who fired at him."

The general's heavy eyebrows shot up. "Indeed? And where was he going? Straight to Jackson?"

She felt a thrill of fear. Had he not been aware of Hébert's attempt to flee before she spoke? But she had to tell him. What if Hébert was lying unconscious, his blood seeping into the grass under the oaks? "To the next plantation, I presume."

"I will have the woods searched, *mademoiselle,*" he said grimly. "Your other request?"

"The man who was with me when you invaded my home is recovering from an injury and a fever. If I am not to be allowed to attend him, I would like to have my herb woman released from the grinding shed and brought to the house with her potions to see to his needs. Her name is Mattie. She is a West Indian healer, and a free woman of color."

"With her potions, eh?" There was suspicion in his tone now. "Who is this man, and how was he injured?"

Her heart leapt with the hope that Jacques was not a spy, after all. "That I do not know. He was washed up on the bank of the river, apparently thrown by his horse. He claims to have lost his memory."

The suspicion deepened in the cold eyes. "Why do you feel a responsibility for this nameless man?"

"We Creoles are a hospitable people, *monsieur,* and he is my guest," she said haughtily. "He has been very ill, and he is still my patient."

The general eyed her silently, his expression becoming quizzical. "You are very young, *mademoiselle,*" he said at last, "to be mistress of so fine a mansion."

"I have managed my father's household for four years, *monsieur.*"

"Indeed! Where is your mother?"

Her hand crept up to touch the rubies at her throat. In a voice that sounded as if it were not her own, but rather came from far away, she said, "She was captured by pirates, *monsieur,* as she was returning from a visit to France."

The English general's naturally stern face grew sterner. "No doubt by the same dastards who have seized so many of our vessels! I am sorry, *mademoiselle.*"

She inclined her head in thanks, and waited.

"Mademoiselle Dufret," he said finally, "I will make a bargain with you. I will grant your requests in return for some of your Creole hospitality. Unfortunately, you must remain here until the battle for New Orleans is successfully concluded. But I confess, *mademoiselle,* that I do not relish keeping a young woman of your obvious talents bound and gagged. So I would appreciate it if you would manage this house and your servants, to make it a comfortable headquarters for myself and my aides, in the same manner as you managed it for your father.''

Marie-Thérèse stiffened with outrage. "*Monsieur,* do you ask me to treat you as guests in the home you have invaded and appropriated for your own use?''

"Would you rather spend the weeks or months of our siege tied to your chair?''

She was silenced.

"It is your choice, *mademoiselle.* You must know there is no possibility of escape from my troops now that we are here. You can treat us as your guests and be honored as our hostess, or you can remain my prisoner. If you accept my terms, I will see that my men conduct themselves as they should before the lady you obviously are. I will ask only one thing of you—that you sit at the table with us and take the first taste of any food your cook serves us.''

Marie-Thérèse stared at him, appalled. This was as insulting as being gagged and bound to a chair! What would Papa say?

He was watching her closely, and with an infuriating hint of a cold smile.

"If you do as I ask, I will send a party out to search the woods and, if they find your brother, bring him back. My own physician will attend him.''

Did she really have a choice? If it saved Hébert's life . . .

"As to your mysterious guest, he may have the services of your healing woman. I will release him to return to his bed if it is necessary and place him under guard.''

It would ease her mind about Jacques. If she remained free, she could visit him and ask him why the British treated him, too, as a prisoner of war. *Who was he?*

"Is it a bargain, Mademoiselle Dufret?"

"I should prefer to take my breakfast on a tray in my chamber. That is my custom."

"I think that is a lady's privilege," he said, "but I shall hold you responsible for the food we are served. Fair enough?"

"Oui, mon général."

"Good. You will be under house arrest," the British general told her. "You will have the freedom of the house and the kitchens, and you may consult with your servants as necessary. I trust you will not be foolish enough to try to escape from the plantation, as the size of my force surrounding it is formidable.

"The men quartered here will be limited to myself and my aides, but I will expect you to feed close to twenty officers, some of whom will have sleeping quarters in other buildings. My aide-de-camp will inform you how many to expect. You may notify him when you are in need of supplies."

Marie-Thérèse nodded. She was feeling a painful release of tension now that she had achieved her goal, and she was holding herself erect only with effort.

The general started toward the door, then turned back. "I shall want a cup of tea, very hot, brought to my desk every morning promptly at eleven."

"Oui, m'sieu," Marie-Thérèse said. "I hope I shall not be expected to taste that!"

The general paused as if startled, then laughed in genuine amusement. "You like your coffee, eh, *mademoiselle?* Never fear, I shall make other arrangements to protect myself from your tea." He inclined his head and left the room.

Marie-Thérèse collapsed in her chair and motioned to Doula.

"You were wonderful, *ma'mselle!*" Doula murmured, coming close.

"Get word to Mattie that I need her. And ask all the servants—cook and her helpers, too—to come to the rear *galerie*. I will talk to them there."

"*Oui, ma'mselle.*"

While Doula was assembling them for her, Marie-Thérèse walked out into the hall and met Apollo coming out of Jacques's chamber with his tray. She looked at it critically. Jacques had eaten everything. That was a good sign.

"He is not to be tied again," she said to the armed red-coat standing outside the door.

"I received the general's order, milady," the soldier said. "Released, but confined to his chamber."

Marie-Thérèse walked past him into Jacques's room. He still sat in the chair to which he had been bound. His face was pale, and the scar running down his cheek was livid. He looked as dangerous as a trapped animal. He said, glowering at her, "So you have dealt with them."

She felt his words like knives in her heart. "I— Perhaps we misjudged you, M'sieu Jacques," she said in a low voice.

"Indeed?" he said sarcastically. "Why do you say that?"

She glanced at the door, aware they could be heard by his guard. "I didn't expect you to be tied up by our captors."

"I told you I was not their spy. Did your brother escape their guns?"

Her voice caught in her throat. "They...they will search the woods, and bring him back if he is wounded. The general's physician will treat him. And the general will allow Mattie to come with her herbs to dress your wound."

Jacques was silent, which led her to say defiantly, "I am to manage the household as usual, to serve the general and his aides. That is all."

He shot her a dark, questioning look. "And will he share your bed?"

She paled at the insult. "You wrong me, *m'sieu!*" *Mon dieu!* Was this what she had done by responding with abandon to his kisses? Had she given him the impression that she was immoral?

She reminded herself that he must be hurting from being so uncomfortably bound. "Come, now," she coaxed, "let me help you to your bed so you can rest."

He got to his feet and, shrugging off her help, threw himself full-length on his bed. "Do not think me ungrateful, *mademoiselle.* I owe you much. But I am no longer your untrustworthy patient."

Then who are you? she wanted to cry, but she restrained herself because of the soldier just outside his door. She did not know why, but she explained further, "The British general has promised me the...the respect of his officers."

"Don't trust them. Don't even trust me," he said harshly from his bed.

Doula came to the open door. "*Ma'mselle,* cook and the others are on the rear *galerie* below."

"*Merci.*" Marie-Thérèse turned away from Jacques, confused again. Was he friend or foe? And why did he have such power to hurt her?

They gathered around her with anxious faces, wanting to hear what the future held: Désirée, who had many times been called from the kitchen by Papa's friends and toasted as the best cook in all New Orleans; Estelle, who was housekeeper and supervisor of the housemaids, all of whom were present; Apollo, Hébert's handsome and sassy valet; and Désirée's helpers in the kitchen, as well as the gardeners, the woodcutters who kept the stoves and fireplaces supplied, and the handymen who kept the house in good repair—all individuals necessary to the smooth running of a large plantation house. And, of course, Mattie and her daughter, Doula, who was not only her mother's understudy, but had also recently been made Marie-Thérèse's *femme de chambre*.

"We are prisoners of the British army, which has come to attack New Orleans," Marie-Thérèse told them. "I hope Monsieur Hébert was able to get to the Bourget plantation and get a horse. If he did, he will take the news that Petit Bois has been taken to my father, and—" Her voice broke. She cleared her throat and said, "And Papa will return with his regiment to rescue us. Until that happens, we are forced to accept these men—these British officers—as our guests at Petit Bois."

A murmur of indignant protest rippled among the servants.

"I have agreed that we will continue in our daily tasks, just as we would if I had invited them into our home. If we do that, they will treat us with...with courtesy. Since we are their prisoners, they could be much less kind. But they, they seem to be gentlemen, and, and I am forced to rely on their promise. They will search the woods for M'sieu Hébert, and if he is wounded, they will bring him back to us."

There was a pregnant silence.

"Are you all right, *ma'mselle?*" Désirée asked softly.

"I was kept bound and gagged in a chair from the time they came until now. No one harmed or molested me, but I was released only because I accepted their terms. Will you help me?"

"*Oui.*" The murmurs were soft, and giving. "*Oui.*"

"*Oui, ma'mselle.*"

Marie-Thérèse laughed through tears. "And, Désirée, you must not put any poisonous mushrooms in their food, because I will be asked to taste everything before the general is served. *And* he drinks tea!"

"Mother of God!" Désirée muttered.

Chapter Ten

When Marie-Thérèse descended to the salon that evening, she found the familiar room filled with young men in red uniforms. They stood in groups, conversing animatedly in English, glasses of spirits in their hands, or they lounged on the damask chairs, waving their drinks and laughing. It was overwhelming, and she paused in the doorway to brace herself for the ordeal of being pleasant to the enemy invaders of her home and her privacy.

A young officer leaning against the mantel under her mother's portrait caught her attention, because he had hair as gold as a Spanish doubloon and eyes of an intense blue seldom seen in Louisiana. He turned his head suddenly and met her gaze.

"Egad!" he exclaimed, staring.

His exclamation attracted the interest of others, and suddenly all eyes were upon her. She heard the buzz of comments that rose, but understood only the tone of admiring appraisal.

As if I were a prime piece of horseflesh! she thought in anger.

The general reached her side in several long strides.

"*Mademoiselle,*" he said. He bowed and kissed her hand in the French manner, and continued in her language,

"May I present my staff? This is my aide, Major Ashley, who will relay any message to me." The young man at his side, dark-haired, with topaz-colored eyes, bowed over her hand.

"Forgive me," the general said, "if I do not tire you before our repast with a long list of English names. You will meet them individually later." He turned to face the room.

"Gentlemen! May I present Mademoiselle Marie-Thérèse Dufret, who is our lovely hostess? She has agreed to keep us comfortable, and I have in turn assured her that she can expect your utmost consideration in return for her hospitality here at Petit Bois." He spoke in French, and his officers apparently understood him.

The room echoed with male voices saying, *"Mademoiselle"* and some exclaiming, *"Enchanté."* Across the room, the officer with the golden hair kissed his fingers and flung them toward her with a dazzling smile in what he apparently thought was a proper French gesture but she thought would have been more appropriate as a tribute to Papa's wine.

They were very confident of victory, these young men. She trembled inwardly for the fate of New Orleans.

The general offered her his arm, saying, "Apollo has brought word that we can be served." Together they crossed the hall toward the dining room, where the table had been set as she had ordered with Petit Bois's finest china and silver. Not all of these eighteen men present were quartered in the big house, but most would take their meals with her, the lone woman at her table.

When her father invited only male guests, she usually took a tray in her chamber. Now she was forced to sit with these enemies who brazenly occupied her father's home, to endure their bold stares and pretend to enjoy their company without understanding their barbaric language. She found it comforting that Estelle stood just inside the door, with a maid beside her at the serving table. The housekeeper's warm dark gaze said, "Courage!"

Marie-Thérèse took the chair the general held for her and sat waiting while Apollo seated the general and the others took their chairs. Apollo then ostentatiously opened two bottles from Papa's stock of smuggled French wines and filled the wineglasses.

The crystal caught the gleam of the candles on the table as the British general lifted his glass. "To our charming hostess, Mademoiselle Dufret!" he said, and a chorus of male voices echoed, *"Mademoiselle!"*

Marie-Thérèse forced herself to smile in acknowledgment in spite of the anger and loathing in her heart. With no appetite whatever, she picked up her fork to ceremoniously taste the food placed before her.

Upstairs in his room, Jacques sat at a small table, looking at the tray that Apollo had brought him, and brooding. Why had it bothered him that Mademoiselle Dufret had made a bargain with the British general? What else could a woman do in her circumstances?

He wished he had not asked if she would share the general's bed. The question had just been a visceral reaction, one he was not willing to call jealousy. No, it couldn't be jealousy! It was his situation, captured by a British general—normally his prey!—who was covered with gold braid and as arrogant as any man he'd ever encountered. And he was powerless! He had no weapon, no fast little brigantine under his command, no men willing to risk their lives to carry out his orders. And the slow recovery of his strength was infuriating.

He had churlishly insulted Mademoiselle Dufret, to whom he owed his life. Deep down, he didn't believe she would trade her body for her freedom. The point was, why should he care if she had?

These past days had been the most frustrating Jacques could remember. His failure to reach his friend was all the more maddening because he owed Jean and his family so much. What would he have become if Jean had not taken him home with him on that night straight out of hell, when the slave uprising had erupted like a volcano on his father's plantation?

To fail Jean now was unacceptable, especially since his friend was at a turning point in his life. Some of Jean's men, including one of his family, Dominique You, had not been very selective in the merchant vessels they attacked. Jean himself had not been averse to attacking the vessels of Britain's ally, Spain, which were loaded with gold from their colonies. His family, Jean said, had been poorly used in Spain, and after three generations he still held a grudge against all Spaniards.

But one of his lieutenants, a rough, brutal man, had ill-advisedly captured an American merchant schooner. It was a clear case of piracy and had made the United States government determined to wipe out the Baratarian community of privateers and smugglers which Jean commanded.

Jean wanted to rectify that mistake by defending New Orleans, his adopted city, against the British. In spite of the persecution of Louisiana's American governor, who deplored the way the city patronized the smugglers, Jean's loyalty was to America. And he would have the opportunity to prove it, if Jacques could give it to him.

He must forget the woman, Jacques told himself. Forget how magnificently foolhardy Marie-Thérèse had been in her angry defiance of the men appropriating her home, forget her tenderly fierce battle with his fever, forget how soft and yielding her body had been in his arms. Thanks to her care, his health was nearly restored. But he must put her out of his calculations now, and plot his next move without her.

He had missed his rendezvous with the boat that was to take him to Jean's hiding place in the bayous. Now he must find another way to pass on the information he had. Or, perhaps, get back to New Orleans, and try to get the answer Jean really wanted.

Marie-Thérèse excused herself immediately after a bottle of Papa's best port was brought to the table. She was nearly out of the door when a voice behind her called urgently, "Mademoiselle Dufret!" She paused, and turned. The golden-haired officer was walking down beside the table toward her.

She regarded him coolly. *"Oui, monsieur?"*

"Lieutenant Roland Bacon," he said. "May I have the pleasure of your company, and a little conversation? Perhaps a stroll on the *galerie?*"

His French was passable, but his accent was atrocious. "I beg you to excuse me, *monsieur,*" Marie-Thérèse said. "I am quite fatigued."

He bowed in acquiescence, but his blue eyes were so bold as their gaze roamed over her that she shrank as from an unexpected touch. "Another evening, then?" he suggested confidently.

"Excuse me, if you please, *monsieur.*" She made a quick curtsy and escaped.

Upstairs she walked through her bedroom and out on the upper *galerie*. The floor-length windows to Monsieur Jacques's room were shuttered, and a British soldier stood guard before them. It didn't matter. She never wanted to face him again, or hear the voice that had asked sarcastically, *And will he share your bed?*

She walked to the rail and stood beside a pillar, heavy-hearted, scarcely able to believe what she was seeing. The plantation was dotted with small bonfires. They glowed in the canefields, they desecrated her garden.

It was a typically French garden, divided into sections by hedges of shrubbery. Within these areas, figures moved in the light of the fires, soldiers cooking their evening meal and trampling down the flowers and shrubs in her garden, just as they were doing to the young cane shoots in the fields.

She gulped down a sob and rushed back into her room. Doula was waiting to help her out of her clothing and brush her hair. Before she undid a single button, the maid barred the repaired shutters and locked the door to the hall.

"Stay with me, Doula," Marie-Thérèse said. "I don't want to be alone."

"Oui, mademoiselle," Doula said. "My *maman* told me to bring my bed." She unrolled a pallet on the floor beside the tester that was Marie-Thérèse's bed.

It brought Marie-Thérèse comfort, but a part of her mind acknowledged that if any of the general's officers wanted to assault her, Doula could not prevent it. She had to trust the general's word that she would be safe.

For hours they heard conversation, laughter and the tread of boots in the rooms below them. The conversation was loud enough to keep them awake, but it was in English, which they did not understand. From the garden, they heard shouts and laughter and some singing, drowning out the familiar night noises of tree frogs, cicadas, and the occasional cry of a night bird.

When at last Marie-Thérèse sank into an exhausted sleep, the nightmare began. The ship was pitching in a heavy sea, but that didn't stop the big, bearded men with long hair tied back with bandannas and gold rings hanging from their ears from boarding and brandishing their wicked knives. Adorée screamed, "Save me!" as a black-bearded ruffian grabbed her around her slender waist, swinging her off her feet. Marie-Thérèse rushed at him, but *Maman* was there first, only to be impaled on his sword.

"Murderer!" Marie-Thérèse shrieked as her mother's blood flowed and the pirate carried off Adorée.

Her sister's screams wakened her. She became aware of Doula, bending over her, saying softly, "*Ma'mselle!* Wake up, *ma'mselle!*"

"I'm awake," she said. But why were the sounds of guns popping off and men shouting curses still assaulting her ears?

She heard drums and a bugle horn sounding an alarm. She sat up. The awful images of blood and fury she had pictured aboard the ship slowly faded from her vision, but her heart was still pounding and the noises of battle still continued.

A terrible shock rocked the house and rattled all the windows, followed a few seconds later by a loud explosion. Bewildered, Marie-Thérèse wondered what was happening. When the shock and the sound were repeated, she realized it must be cannons she was hearing. The explosions had sounded terrifyingly close.

"Doula?"

"I'm here, *ma'mselle,*" Doula whispered. She had dropped to a crouch on her pallet in terrified confusion.

The bugle horn was still sounding. Above the slow and ominous warning of the drums, she heard Jacques's voice outside her window.

"Are you all right, *mademoiselle?*"

In spite of the anger with which she had left him, Marie-Thérèse responded to his familiar voice with a warm rush of relief. She pulled her robe on over her night shift and unbarred her shutters. The battle cries and the tocsin of the drums became louder. The acrid odor of gunpowder sullied the night air, and she heard the utterly terrifying sound of a man screaming.

She stepped out on the *galerie*. The house rattled as another cannonball shot over it. Jacques stood before her, his strong shoulders still draped with Papa's nightshirt, which was tucked into his trousers. He was alone on the veranda. His guard had apparently responded to the bugler's summons and left his post.

"I heard you screaming." He put his arms around her. "Are you sure you're all right?"

"It was a nightmare," she said, trembling at his touch. Her anger was forgotten in the warmth and safety that his nearness brought to her treacherous body. "What's happening? Is it cannons I hear?"

"There's an American gunboat on the river bombarding the British encampment." He turned her toward the river, and she gasped when she saw the flash of powder as another cannonball was fired from the gunboat.

"Unfortunately, we are in their path. There's fighting in the trees across the canal," Jacques told her. "The Americans have apparently launched a surprise attack."

"So near? Thank God," she breathed. "Hébert must have gotten through to Papa." That meant he was safe. She had no doubt that her father had come with his regiment of the militia to drive the British off Petit Bois, as she had firmly believed he would. But she began trembling violently. Papa and Hébert could both be facing the shot from the muskets of those redcoats who had succeeded in arming themselves and were firing into the trees.

With his arm around her, Jacques guided her to the rear corner of the house. He held her close to him against a pillar on the rear *galerie* where they could look out on the encampment. It was a scene of utmost confusion. Officers were shouting orders, the buglers' urgent calls were constant, and the soldiers were scrambling to find their weapons and form ranks against the attackers. Musket balls were coming from across the canal, and the shrieks and curses of the men they hit added to the fearful din. A mixture of fog and gunsmoke obscured the action on the other side of the canal, where there appeared to be hand-to-hand combat in the trees.

Even in her fear, Marie-Thérèse was burningly aware of Jacques's hard body wherever they touched. Her hands were on his forearm, which encircled her just below her bosom, holding her in the lee of the pillar. When a volley of musket fire deafened her, she dug her fingers into his flesh.

Jacques felt a drop of moisture on his arm and realized that tears were running down her cheeks. Her grief moved him.

"I couldn't bear to hear you screaming," he said unsteadily. "If anyone has molested you, I will kill him."

He felt the shake of her head against his breast. "It was a nightmare—and I woke up to find it was real." A shudder rippled through her body. "But you know about nightmares, don't you? You know about death and destruction . . . and fire?"

He was suddenly very still. "How do you know that?"

"You told me—in your delirium."

What else had she learned, listening to him rave? Anger accelerated his pulse, but it was anger at himself. He felt again the almost irresistible urge he had once had to be completely truthful with her, not to use her, but to trust her with his secret mission and ask for her help. But it was too late for that.

"This is another nightmare," she whispered, flinching at the sound of a volley of gunshots.

They listened in silence to the sounds of the conflict beyond the garden. After a long moment, Marie-Thérèse said in a low voice. "First *Maman* and Adorée, and now Papa and Hébert... and, and look at this destruction!" she wailed. "All my mother's roses, destroyed!"

"You can think of roses at a time like this?" Jacques refrained from adding, "When the very house we're in might be hit at any time?"

"*Maman*'s roses were the most famous on Pointe St. Antoine. She spent hours with them. Her garden was her life, and I have tried to keep it as she created it."

"Flowers can be replaced, *chérie.*"

"But not by my mother." Her sorrow rose in a choking flood. "They've chopped down that lovely old magnolia that was there, shading the walk to Papa's office." She pointed at the raw stumps silvered in the moonlight. "And the oak tree that Adorée and I used to sit in for hours, when Hébert was too small to climb and was pestering us." How many years had they grown?

He stroked her hair, suffused with a dangerous tenderness. "Adorée?" he asked gently.

"My s-sister."

"Where is she now?"

She conquered her tears, and he felt the effort it cost her. "I hope and pray she and my mother are in heaven!" she said in a voice suddenly hard. "They were on a ship captured by pirates, and what they endured I can only imagine."

The tone in which she said "pirates" made him shiver with a premonition. Had the Dufret women been on board that American ship that had been attacked with such stupid greed and such fateful consequences to the Lafittes?

"What I have to endure here is nothing compared to what they must have suffered at the hands of those beasts! I have no right to feel sorry for myself."

He was hurting for her, with a pain that surprised him. "So that's the nightmare that torments you. I'm sorry, Marie-Thérèse."

She looked searchingly at him, struck by the sincerity in his voice. The scar on his handsome face no longer looked sinister to her. It was part of him, and she fought the urge to reach up with her fingers and trace its path on his cheek. He had known tragedy, too.

"Jacques?" she began tentatively, then stopped. She had never before used his name without the more formal title. "Is Jacques really your name?"

"Yes, *chérie*. I am Jacques Bonnard."

"Bonnard," she said slowly, as if tasting it. "I don't know that name. It's not a Creole name, is it?"

"Yes, but not of Louisiana. I was born in Haiti."

"And your family is still there?"

"I have no family. I was the only member who escaped the slave uprising on our plantation. Everything was torched."

It was a scene he could never erase from his memory. They had been out in the warm, sticky night chasing fireflies, when Jean cried, "Look! The cane is burning!"

Jacques saw again the reflection of the torches on the perspiring dark faces of Toussaint's rebels and on the bright blades of their machetes, heard their exultant shouts when they torched the outbuildings and swept on toward his father's plantation house. In his ears were the screams of those escaping the burning buildings only to meet the machetes. Jean had restrained him from running into the melee in the panicky belief that he could reach his mother and dragged him, numb with shock, to his own home, with the whole Bonnard plantation aflame behind them.

Marie-Thérèse sighed and murmured, "You must have been only a child when that happened."

"I was. My mother—I never saw my mother again." Jacques was in the grip of the miasma the memory of that night always brought. To this day, the sweetish smell of burning cane sickened him. That was one reason he preferred to spend most of his time at sea.

He was on the verge of a confession, and realized that he could not tell her the whole truth. Not after hearing the loathing with which she had uttered the word *pirates*.

She waited for him to continue, but he could not.

How could he tell her that the friendship of the notorious Lafitte and his family had been the most stabilizing influence in his life? The Lafittes had coaxed him out of his despair and depression. They sent him to school with Jean on Martinique, and when he was grown and came into his modest inheritance, they had helped him purchase his own brigantine.

He joined Jean and other young gentlemen privateers licensed by the United States and other nations sympathetic to their cause to run through the British blockade or capture their vessels.

At last she asked, "And what brought you to Louisiana, and to your mishap in the river?"

His arms tightened protectively around her. "Don't ask me that, *chère* Marie-Thérèse because I can't tell you. Not now." *And perhaps never.*

Her name on his lips was a pleasure that she savored. But Jacques was still keeping his secrets from her. She moved out of the circle of his embrace, putting a little distance between them, and immediately felt cold and alone.

Jacques raised his head, alert. Shallow boats had appeared on the canal. British reinforcements sprang out of them and disappeared with their muskets into the trees beyond the man-made bayou. For a time, the sounds of gunfire increased, and Marie-Thérèse sent up a fervent prayer for Papa and Hébert.

They heard three long faint notes on a bugle. "It's sounding the retreat," Jacques said. "The Americans are withdrawing."

"Oh, no!" she cried, in panic.

"It may be part of their strategy. They've probably done more damage to the British than they've received. And now General Jackson knows the size of the British force. It is said that he is a tough fighter. Trust him."

Soon the redcoats were returning in triumph, singing as they marched back on the road along the levee. "My guard will be back," Jacques said, leading her to her room. Before the long open window, he clasped her in his arms again in a reassuring hug, and she leaned into him, reluctant to part from him. She felt a spasm of pure desire, so strong that she lifted her head and turned it to find his lips.

He bent his head, a low sound in his throat, and kissed her. When her lips parted, he thrust his tongue between her teeth in a masterful way that startled her. She had never known such a kiss, nor had she ever experienced the wild emotion it aroused in her. It was a kiss that deeply satisfied the intense need it created, yet left her yearning for more.

She wanted it never to end. She wanted to satisfy the mysterious hunger the kiss aroused. But Jacques put her away from him and exclaimed, "God forgive me, I did not mean to— Forget this happened."

She stared, for a moment uncomprehending, lost in her emotions.

"I don't want you to suffer more hurt, Marie-Thérèse," he said, almost roughly. "You must not fall in love with me, *chérie.*"

A flush suffused her whole body as she understood what he was saying. He was rejecting her.

Shaken and confused, she said angrily, "What tremendous conceit! Who can think of love at a time like this?" and turned away from him, trembling with anger and humiliation.

She entered her chamber and slid the bar across the shutters, then turned to find Doula crouched, shivering, beside her bed.

"Ma'mselle?" her maid whispered.

Marie-Thérèse put aside the bitter thoughts of her own situation to reassure the frightened girl. "Doula, it's good news! Papa returned with his soldiers to attack the British! That means that Hébert reached the city safely."

"Oh, *ma'mselle!*"

"They've gone now, but they'll be back for us, never fear! Papa won't let them have Petit Bois." Inwardly, she sent up a prayer that it was true—and that Papa and Hébert were still safe.

Jacques entered his room with mixed emotions. Comforting Marie-Thérèse had been sweet, and now his arms felt curiously empty. But the kiss had been a mistake. For one thing, he had taken advantage of her emotional state. He knew that the deadly-serious fighting they had witnessed was a new and disturbing experience for her. For another, his ill-advised kiss had promised too much, and, surprisingly, it had threatened to undo him.

He felt acutely her humiliation and hurt pride at being rejected. He felt like a cad.

Damn the bastard who had been responsible for that sorry episode on the eastern coast! Before that, he and Jean and Pierre had been considered gentlemen privateers, forgiven for smuggling in the goods people needed, not pirates with the United States Army after them.

Now eighty of their men, including some of his crew, were rotting in jail, Jean and Pierre were in hiding, and he was a prisoner of the British, who were poised to attack New Orleans! He had found a woman he could cherish . . . but it was not to be.

It could never be. She was not for him, and he had no stomach for causing her more pain.

A rap on his door brought his head up sharply. "Yes?"

"Major Ashley. May I come in?"

"I am your prisoner, *m'sieu,*" Jacques said dryly.

A man of about thirty-five with dark hair and beard came into his room. "I am the general's aide. I have come to tell you that the general has ordered the guard removed from your door. Also, he has ordered that no trays be carried to your room."

"Why would he do that, *monsieur?*"

The major shrugged. "The general does not confide in me, *monsieur,* but it may well be that he does not relish your monopolizing the time of two of our men. You may not leave the house, and I advise you not to try to escape, because you will risk being shot. You are to take your meals in the common dining room from now on."

This was *her* doing, Jacques thought. Mademoiselle Dufret must have interceded with the general for him. He needed no woman to plead for him! He would tell her so.

But he would take advantage of any opportunity the new arrangement offered. The walls of his room had been closing in on him since he had regained his health. But no more. He would find a way to leave Petit Bois at last.

Chapter Eleven

In the morning, Marie-Thérèse took breakfast in her room. She had slept very little, and she wondered if she would ever sleep soundly again. Her life had changed so drastically and with such suddenness that she scarcely recognized herself when she looked in her mirror. Was it only the day before yesterday that she had been anticipating spending Christmas with her father and Hébert in the city?

In other happier years, they had enjoyed celebrating the holiday on the plantation, with piles of wrapped gifts for each other stacked around the *crèche* on the hearth. They invited guests, not only for dinner, but also houseguests for the week. There was always a feast for the slaves who worked in the cane fields and the sugarhouse.

But Christmas had not been the same since they had lost Mama and Adorée, although Marie-Thérèse had tried very hard for Papa's and Hébert's sakes to keep up the traditions of Petit Bois: decorating the house with wreaths and garlands of holly bright with red berries, making their own Louisiana orange wine and shelling pecans for the pies.

This year she had anticipated a modest observance of the holiday in the house on the rue St. Pierre. Her Christmas gifts for Papa and Hébert and Annalise and other friends were still in the trunk she had packed before the British arrived. Would they ever receive her gifts?

Where were Papa and Hébert now?

But she must not mope! The staff and the canecutters had earned their Christmas celebration. Petit Bois could observe Christ's day, British or no. She would preside over a traditional dinner in her best gown. Let them see what manner of life they wanted to destroy! And let Monsieur Jacques Bonnard see what he had rejected.

It was a matter of Dufret pride, she told herself, but it would also keep her too busy to feel sorry for herself, or to think about Jacques Bonnard and the way she had thrown herself at him.

If she had not already fallen in love with him, she had completely lost her heart the night he took his life in his hands, weakened as he was by fever, to save her from mad Gama's machete. Last night, during the long hours of the battle, she had revealed herself to him. She had told him things she could not speak of to her closest friends. And afterward she had offered herself in that kiss that she had shamelessly invited at her door. He could not think otherwise. And he had kissed her and refused her love.

You must not fall in love with me, chérie.

Pride would be her refuge. She had no other.

When she was dressed in a pale blue morning gown with flowing sleeves and an empire bodice, she sent Doula to summon Désirée and walked out on the *galerie*. The sight that met her eyes was heartbreaking.

The huge British encampment stretched to the edge of the swamp and as far as she could see into the cane fields. Everywhere she looked, she saw the blackened rings of their campfires. Down on the drainage canal some soldiers were unloading heavy cannons from shallow-draft boats, each mounted on its own cart. With no regard for her garden, they were dragging them through the orange trees and over her flower beds.

The big guns must have been brought from the British vessels on Lake Borgne. She was astonished that such heavy artillery could have been transported through the swamp, and by men unfamiliar with the maze of waterways leading from Petit Bois to the lake. The soldiers were setting up a battery near the slave cabins to fire toward the Bourget house.

Lucky Annalise, to be safe in New Orleans and to have left the plantation without seeing all this destruction!

Another battery was being positioned in the front garden, just below the levee, with its cannons trained on the American gunboats clearly visible on the river in the morning sun. She could just make out the lettering on their bows. The *Carolina* was the gunboat that had fired its cannonballs at them the night before. The smaller vessel that had joined it this morning was the *Louisiana*. She could see clearly their big guns. They seemed to be aimed straight at her.

The British soldiers had hitched the mules Boddy used to pull the cane wagons to the artillery carts and were dragging them through the garden, leveling shrubs and flowers alike in their path. Piles of cannonballs were stacked in pyramids, with no regard for the formal flower beds. Many of the plantation slaves had been impressed into labor. She saw one of the gardeners leading a mule-drawn cart through the rosebushes he had carefully pruned just days ago.

Désirée joined Marie-Thérèse at the railing. "You wanted me, *ma'mselle?*"

"Désirée, tomorrow is Christmas Day," Marie-Thérèse said desolately.

"*Oui, ma'mselle.*"

Marie-Thérèse noticed a redcoat moving between the two rows of cabins along the canal at the end of the rear garden.

"What are the British doing in the cabins?" she asked the cook.

"Some officers sleep there."

"But where do our workers and their families sleep?"

Désirée shrugged. "In the sugarhouse, or in the stable."

Marie-Thérèse's lips tightened.

"The British moved in at Jumonville, too," said the cook. "They using the hospital there. Rami help carry wounded there last night. He say many men hurt in the fighting."

Nearer the levee, where the ground was dryer, British soldiers were working with spades. "Why are they digging?"

"They bury their dead."

Marie-Thérèse shuddered. "Don't they know why we bury our dead above ground in Louisiana?"

Again Désirée shrugged.

Resolutely Marie-Thérèse said, "I want to pass out the Christmas gifts of food and sweets, as usual. Also, I want to have a Christmas feast for all hands, as we always have at Petit Bois. Can you do it, Désirée?"

The cook's dark eyes hardened. "It be no day of rest this year, *ma'mselle*. The British say, 'Fetch this, carry that.' Boats be coming all morning with more cannonballs."

"At least we can give our people food for Christmas. Surely the soldiers will allow them to eat. And here in the house I want to serve a traditional Christmas dinner of *bouillabaisse, vol-au-vent* of pigeon, and roast turkey, with the usual trimmings. Pies and a *pouding à la reine* with wine sauce for desserts."

Désirée bridled. "For the enemy, *ma'mselle?*"

"Non! For Petit Bois! Will you try?"

Désirée looked at her young mistress. She saw the misery behind her pride, and her own lined face softened. Her dark eyes gleamed. *"Oui, ma'mselle!"*

The day was a busy one, both for the British soldiers, who were digging in and setting up batteries, and for Marie-Thérèse and her household. The ingredients for the food they were preparing were all available on the plantation, which had both a sugarhouse and a mill. Slaves had already been assigned by the British to furnish fish for the encampment. There were two *pigeonniers,* housing a hundred doves, and flocks of fowl in coops. A large fenced kitchen garden was still furnishing winter vegetables, raided daily by those soldiers who camped out around the house and cooked their own food, although it was supposed to be reserved for the officers.

Marie-Thérèse had no time to think of her loved ones, of her battered heart, or even of the injured pride that had instigated all the frenzied activity in both the house and the detached kitchen. So when she went downstairs to preside at her Christmas table wearing her garnet silk dress with the bands of velvet ribbon sewn around the skirt, it was a shock to see Jacques standing among the red-coated officers with a glass of whiskey in his hand.

Seeing him chatting comfortably in English with the British officers threw her off balance. Apollo had apparently found him another suit of clothes from Papa's armoire, because he looked every inch a man of substance—a gentleman, but one with a discernible toughness.

That look of being able to take care of himself in any situation was striking now that he was recovered from his fever. It brought back the strong sense of danger she had felt when she found him on the riverbank.

What was he doing here in her salon with the British? Had they released him because it was Christmas Day? Some new and obviously important officers had arrived with the cannons from the British ships, and one of them was talking seriously to Jacques. As she watched them, all her old doubts rushed back.

The blond officer, Roland Bacon, approached her. "You do not speak English, *mademoiselle?*" he asked.

"Non, monsieur."

"Perhaps it's just as well," he said with his bold smile. "At least they can't accuse you of spying for the Americans."

She looked at him sharply. Was he making a reference to Jacques? "Are they telling secrets, then?"

"They are full of their plans for New Orleans, but I would rather talk of your charms, *mademoiselle.*"

"That subject does not interest me, *monsieur,* but what they plan for my city does."

"You wouldn't like it, I fear."

She wished she could slap his smiling face. She was grateful when the general appeared beside her and offered his arm.

"You have decorated the house charmingly, *mademoiselle,*" he said. "My compliments!"

"It's a tradition at Petit Bois, *monsieur.*" She glanced around the room and stiffened. Her mother's portrait was gone, and in its place hung a large painting of a woman dressed in white with a tiara on her hair and long white gloves that came to just above her elbows.

"My lady," the general said, following her glance with pride. "I am eager to show her Petit Bois. She will appreciate the care you have taken with it, *mademoiselle.*"

Marie-Thérèse could not prevent a small gasp escaping her lips. Did he expect to bring his wife to Petit Bois? Was that why he had ordered her portrait to be brought from his ship?

"Is your wife coming to America, then, *monsieur?*" The question burst out of her.

"She is on our flagship, awaiting the outcome of the siege with the other English ladies who accompanied their husbands."

"*Monsieur,*" she said, trying to conceal her rage, "the painting you removed is a portrait of my mother, whom we lost when the schooner she traveled on was attacked by pirates."

"I am sorry, *mademoiselle.* My condolences."

"May I ask what you have done with it?"

"Would you like it hung in your chamber?"

"I would."

"It will be done," he promised.

He took her arm, and in shock she allowed him to lead her across the hall to the dining room. The rest of the Christmas dinner Désirée and her girls had prepared was a nightmare to be endured as best she could.

She watched as Jacques filed in with the other men. What was she to think of this man who captured first her sympathy and her imagination, and then her heart? How had he so quickly come to be on such good terms with their hated captors, unless he was one of them, after all? Could she believe anything Jacques told her?

Her gaze kept returning to his arresting face as he sat between two officers down the length of the long table. She looked at the sensual curve of his lips, and her face flushed and then paled as she recalled the emotions she had experienced when that mouth had ravished her own so intimately. The memory sparked a hot glow that began at her core and spread up through her body. There was a ringing in her ears, and a fog seemed to descend between her and the conversation around her as an unwelcome longing possessed her. She became aware of a heaviness in her breasts, and her eyelids drooped.

Suddenly she felt Lieutenant Roland Bacon's gaze. He was looking at her with complete perception of what she was feeling, and his blue eyes blazed with an answering passion. She shrank from his embarrassing insight, and he smiled. It was a smile of complicity and invitation, and she shivered with revulsion.

"A delectable meal, *chère mademoiselle,*" the general said. "It's a pity we haven't the time to properly appreciate it. But I'll not forget your kindness in making our first Christmas in Louisiana a memorable one."

"*Merci,*" she murmured, but she thought, *His first Christmas, indeed!* Papa and his militia would surely make it his last. If only there were something she could do!

Perhaps there was. In a flash she saw the drawing she could make, showing the placement of the batteries around Petit Bois and the occupation of the neighboring plantations by the British. It should be valuable information for General Jackson to know how many reinforcements were pouring into the region. It was possible he and Papa would be as surprised as she had been that the British could bring such heavy armament through the swamp.

But how could she get a message to Papa? There was the rub.

The British encampment had spread to the neighboring plantations, both upriver—like Annalise's family home— and downriver. Apollo said they were forming a new encampment on the Bourget property that stretched from the river to the swamp. She could not hope to slip through the lines herself. One of the slaves would have a better chance, because they had been impressed into helping the British.

She pushed the delicious food around on her plate, her mind whirling with plans and possibilities. When Apollo began serving the port, she excused herself and left the dining room. She noted that Jacques remained behind, laughing and talking with the enemy. The hurt of his duplicity was as sharp as needles in her heart.

Later in the evening, the Negroes danced around a bonfire near the tables of food Estelle and Désirée set up on the south side of the house. Marie-Thérèse watched from the *galerie* above them, uneasy in spirit as she saw some of the British soldiers who were still bivouacked in the garden join them. Would they win the loyalty of Papa's slaves? Whom could she trust to try to get up the river to the Americans? Who would not be tempted to hand her message over to one of the British soldiers for gold?

In spite of the risk, she resolved to try. She was working on her map of the plantation and the placement of the batteries by candlelight when there was a knock at her door. She quickly dropped a shawl to cover the papers and inkpot on her dressing table, and went to unlock the door. The general stood there. Behind him was Apollo, who carried the portrait of her mother.

"I wanted to personally assure myself that the portrait was safely delivered to you, *mademoiselle*."

"*Merci, m'sieu.* Enter."

She stood back, and the two men came in. The general instructed Apollo to hang the painting for her and, to her uneasy surprise, stayed to see it done.

Marie-Thérèse watched, feeling very uncomfortable. The general must have sensed her fear. He walked over to her dressing table and casually lifted the shawl. His face hardened as he looked down at the drawing.

"Interesting," he said in a cold voice. "How were you planning to get this sketch to General Jackson?"

She said, as steadily as she could, "I have no way of doing that, *monsieur*."

"No?" he barked. "You are free by my tolerance, *mademoiselle*, and because of our bargain. You do realize that with a word I can confine you in one of the slave cabins for the duration of the war, don't you?"

She could feel the blood leaving her face, and she felt very cold. *"Oui, monsieur."*

"Then why are you doing this?"

She did not know what to say to him.

"Who are you planning to send? One of the slaves? Your overseer? Tell me!"

"No one."

"Then why are you doing this?" he demanded again, thumping the drawing.

An inspiration came to her. She looked up at him guilelessly and said, "Because, *monsieur le général,* you are making history."

She saw that he was taken aback, and that he did not know whether to believe her or not. She held her breath, praying his vanity would make him accept her explanation.

At last he growled, "Then leave it to the historians." He closed his fist over the drawing, wadding it up. "No more of this!" he said sternly and left, taking the crumpled drawing with him.

Apollo followed him, sending her a look of wry sympathy over his shoulder.

Marie-Thérèse sat on her bed and looked up at the painting on her wall. Her mother sat erect with a lacy fan in her left hand and the beginning of a smile on her lips. The grand, becoming dress she wore was one that had been made in Paris for her. Its bodice was cut from Belgian lace, lined with gold satin.

The pride and self-worth in her beautiful dark eyes seemed to be speaking directly to Marie-Thérèse, saying, "Do not despair, my darling daughter."

Tears trembled on Marie-Thérèse's lashes. Outside in the garden, the shouts and laughter had ceased. The Negroes were singing, but more quietly. Listening, Marie-Thérèse thought it was a song of acceptance and patience.

She had heard it sung before, but she had never heard its sadness so clearly.

Chapter Twelve

When Marie-Thérèse left the dining room, Jacques was deep in conversation with a British officer, but some sixth sense told him she was leaving. He didn't understand how she had gained such power over him. She was never far from his thoughts.

The Englishman was voicing his curiosity about Jacques. "You were not born in Louisiana, were you?"

"No, *monsieur.* I come from the West Indies."

"Indeed? I have recently sailed from Negril, where vessels of the British fleet had their rendezvous for this exercise. Do you know Jamaica?"

"Somewhat," Jacques admitted. "But I was born in Haiti."

"Are you familiar with Negril, sir? It is one of the most colorful ports I have seen, and I have sailed over half the globe. That is where they hanged Anne Bonney, is it not, along with her pirate friends?"

"So I've heard," Jacques said cautiously.

"I thought I was going to lose my sailors in those low haunts on the shore near the lighthouse, sir!"

"You easily could have," Jacques returned, laughing. "Living is easy in those islands."

The Briton had many questions. He was intelligent and amusing, and Jacques was enjoying the opportunity to use his English. The other's interest stimulated an uncharacteristic garrulity in him, perhaps the result of having been forced to guard his tongue for the past few weeks.

"I was sent to school in Martinique," he said, "and that is still my favorite of the islands. Do you know it?"

"I spent one night ashore there." The officer drained his glass, and Apollo discreetly approached with more port. Abruptly the Briton said, "Sir, you are obviously a seafaring man."

"Yes, sir."

"If I am not mistaken, you are now or have been one of the privateers who play cat-and-mouse with our merchant fleet in the Atlantic and the Gulf."

Jacques laughed to hide his discomfiture. He had been made careless by good food and drink and challenging conversation with a man who knew life at sea as well as he did. "You are a shrewd judge of men, sir," he said.

This must be why he had been allowed to dine with them. They had guessed what he was, and wanted information from him.

"How do you come to be here?" the Briton asked.

"That is a cat with a very long tail. To be brief, I have been recovering from a fever here at Petit Bois."

"Under the ministrations of the delightful Mademoiselle Dufret?" the officer suggested, a twinkle in his eye.

Jacques said warily, "Mademoiselle Dufret saved my life."

"Monsieur Bonnard, are you by chance acquainted with Jean Lafitte?"

The question was not unexpected, given the conversation that had preceded it. "Yes, sir."

"He entertained some of us recently at his remarkable headquarters on Grande-Terre. Lavishly, I might add. In fact, the luxury we encountered there was an eye-opener." He waited, but Jacques did not respond. He continued, "We made a rendezvous to meet later, which he failed to keep."

Jacques looked down at his glass of port and said calmly, "Then you have not heard that the United States Army raided Grande-Terre and captured eighty of Lafitte's band? I understand they are now in the New Orleans jail."

The Briton did not indicate by so much as a lifted eyebrow whether or not the news surprised him. "That must be why Lafitte didn't keep our rendezvous. Is he among those captured?"

Jacques didn't hesitate. "No, sir. He escaped, along with most of his band. He is said to be in hiding in the bayous."

"A bewildering half of the continent, more water than land, I'm told."

"Not half, no, sir, but it is a very large region of shallow lakes and interlacing waterways, in which it is all too easy to lose one's way. The Lafitte brothers know it well."

"How well do you know it, Monsieur Bonnard?"

"Very little," Jacques said cautiously, his heart quickening with excitement.

"I'll be frank with you. What I want to know is whether you can put me in touch with Jean Lafitte."

Jacques considered, forcing himself to appear indifferent. "It might be possible, if I could get to New Orleans."

"What would you do there?"

"Go to the jail. Speak with his men who are being held there."

"Would you be allowed to do that?"

"It could be arranged for me, I think. I am acquainted with Jean Lafitte's lawyer."

"Would his men tell you where Jean Lafitte is now?"

"Possibly."

The British officer studied his wineglass. "You look like the kind of man who could find out where he's hiding."

"I can find him."

"I return to my vessel at daylight. If you go with me, Bonnard, I'll see that you are put ashore near New Orleans. I will want you to bring back an answer from Lafitte. Or, better still, bring him back with you, so that we can talk."

Jacques said, "He is too canny for that, *monsieur,* but I can bring a message." His head was awhirl with possibilities. At last, fate was turning his way. By daylight he would be leaving the heavily scented air of Petit Bois behind him. He could forget it, and Mademoiselle Marie-Thérèse Dufret.

Abruptly he realized that he could not leave her behind in her ruined, occupied plantation with no one but her servants—not without telling her he was going. It was incredible, but it was true. He could not do that to her.

He was a man who had never had any strings on his freedom, or anyone he cared deeply about—except his adopted family. He told himself that there were still no strings on him—he simply owed her the courtesy of a farewell. After all, she had saved his life.

He lifted his glass and finished his port. "If we are to leave early, *monsieur,* I will say good-night," he told the Briton.

"Good. Meet me at the boat on the canal at daylight." They shook hands.

Jacques left the company to their port, cigars and talk of war strategy and went upstairs.

* * *

Marie-Thérèse had returned to the *galerie* outside her chamber and was looking down at the plantation workers, whose mood had lightened again. Boddy and his Mattie were with them, and Doula and Estelle. Doula and Sophie, the laundress, were dancing, looking unfamiliar and almost savage in their wild gyrations in the firelight. But they looked happy, Marie-Thérèse thought enviously, as if all their fears and insecurities had been put aside.

Boddy had told her Gama had not been seen again. "Swamp's got him," he had opined. "Or he's been taken aboard one of those big shallow boats going back to the British vessels. Do you suppose he's the one who guided them to our canal?"

Marie-Thérèse had shaken her head without answering. She didn't like to think about Gama. It made her wonder how far she could trust the others. In the end, she knew, she could depend on no one but herself.

She heard a step and turned to see Jacques approaching her.

Immediately she felt a quickening of the pulse at the base of her throat, and wondered if she could even trust herself. He was one of them. Why else had he been invited to share their meals?

"Lovely Marie-Thérèse," he said softly, and she shivered, hearing his voice.

She fought an irrational desire to touch him and be held by him. "Yes, *monsieur?*" she asked coldly. How could she still want him? She was out of her mind!

"I've come to say goodbye."

A knifelike pain shot through her breast. "You are leaving Petit Bois?"

"Yes, *chérie.* I have an opportunity to go, and I must take it."

Fury boiled up in her, sparked by the wholly unreasonable feeling that he was abandoning her. "You lied about having no liking for the British, didn't you? You are one of them."

"No," he said. "I am not 'one of them'! They want to use me, but I am using them." His face was unreadable in the dim light, which cast a menacing shadow over his scar.

"As you used us at Petit Bois?" she asked hotly. "As you used me? I can never believe anything you say, because you have lied about everything."

In her passionate anger, she had thrown her head back, exposing the long, beautiful line of her throat to the chill moonlight. Jacques was seized by an almost irresistible desire to kiss her there, where he could see the pulse of her rage at him. Suddenly he knew he could never leave her.

He said, "Not everything, *chérie*. But I did tell you I didn't want you to love me. That was a lie." He knew that now he was speaking the truth.

He put his arms around her, but at his touch she began beating her fists against his chest in a fury. He held her loosely, paying no attention to her blows, entirely absorbed in his discovery.

"I thought I could leave without saying goodbye, but I can't. Sweetheart—"

She was not fighting him, she was fighting her longing to embrace him, to run her fingers lightly down his cheek, to put her hands on the flat planes of his jaws and press her lips to his.

"Go!" she cried, so filled with anger and frustration that she was near tears. "If you are leaving me here, go now!"

"My brave little Creole," he said, tenderly. "I didn't want to love you." He took her wrists in his big hands and bent to kiss her.

She had hated herself for lifting her lips to him once before, inviting his kiss, yet she was doing it again. His mouth came down over hers, and she melted, weak with desire. His arms came around her to pull her close.

How could she want to give herself to a British spy? He was one of the enemy, one of those who had walked into her home and appropriated it and all that was in it and made her a servant. One of those who had taken down her mother's portrait and hung a painting of the general's wife in its place, as if to say that *she* was the real mistress of Petit Bois! How could she forgive that?

And yet she was swaying on her feet, leaning into his kiss. In a swift movement, he let go of her wrists and lifted her in his arms. She began beating on his chest again while he carried her into her chamber and laid her on her bed. He lowered himself over her and bent his head to kiss her again.

She hammered on his back, but he paid no attention, because she was kissing him as hungrily as he was kissing her. Her fingers flattened out, and her traitorous hands caressed him, feeling the tension in his muscles as he moved. Her palms crept up to tangle her fingers in the soft hair at his nape.

He was lying on the bed with her now, and they rolled from side to side, holding each other while they kissed. The scent and the warm feel of him filled her senses. There was no other world but this one in his arms. She was lost in him.

At last they tore themselves apart, gasping for air. He got up and started for the door, and she raised herself on her elbow in alarm.

"What are you doing?"

He turned the lock on her door, then closed and barred the shutters at her windows. He came back to her then, and sat on the bed beside her. "I thought I could just go and leave you," he said, "but I can't." His dark eyes glowed deeply. "God help me, but I can't do it!"

"If you love me, take me with you," she begged, utterly under his spell. "Take me away from here."

"I can't do that, my darling. But I will come back for you, I swear it. You must trust me."

Trust him? A laugh bubbled up in her throat. She could love him—oh, how she could love him!—but trust him?

Through her window came the rhythmic staccato of the slave's music, punctuated by the shrill cries of the dancers and their audience. Jacques slowly began undoing the small buttons of her bodice. He slipped one hand inside to caress the roundness of her breasts, and she shuddered with frightened pleasure.

He spread open her bodice, pushing the shift she wore under her dress off her shoulders. "I've dreamed of this," he said, his voice vibrating with emotion. "You are so lovely!"

The night air caressed her skin while he looked at her in the dim light of the winter moon that filtered through the shutters. "So lovely!" he repeated, and bent and took one hardened nipple, then the other, into his mouth, sending little shocks of pleasure through her.

She felt utterly wanton for allowing this, but she could do nothing but glory in these sensations she was experiencing for the first time. She buried her fingers in his soft, dark hair, feeling his skull through it, making her hands familiar with its shape. The urge to be close to him, all of him, was so strong it was carrying her along a dangerous current to some end she could not foresee.

"As God is my witness, I didn't intend this!" he muttered. He disposed of their clothing, and it seemed so wholly natural that Marie-Thérèse scarcely noticed until he pulled her close and she felt his naked skin all along her body. The sensations it aroused were feeding a hunger that seemed to have been growing in her forever.

"Jacques," she murmured. "Jacques."

"Love me, Marie-Thérèse," he begged. "Just this once, love me truly." He heard his own words with wonder. He had thought he would never ask that of a woman!

"I love you," she whispered, and his heart surged.

His hands explored her body, caressing every curve, touching secret places that gave her exquisite pleasure. This must be what the priest called carnal pleasure, but it didn't feel like sin. She felt she was giving her greatest gift in allowing this intimacy, and she gave it to him gladly.

He took her hand and placed it on himself. Marie-Thérèse gasped, but she accepted his invitation to explore his body as he was discovering hers. Their coming together seemed so natural that the pain of the ultimate invasion shocked her. He held her still, and they lay quietly, joined together.

She was filled with wonder. So this was how a man and a woman became lovers.

He began a slow, gentle movement, and instinctively she moved with him. And then he taught her how a man loves a woman.

The lesson went on for most of the night, and Marie-Thérèse was an apt pupil, marveling that she had lived for nineteen years, never knowing the things about her own body that Jacques was teaching her. When at last he brought her to a climax of sensation that left them both collapsed with wildly beating hearts, she felt as if Jacques had touched her soul and they had become one.

When their breath came back, they talked.

"I never believed I could love a woman as I love you," Jacques said. He brought her hand to his lips and kissed each finger. She laid her other hand on the soft hair of his chest, which had a sheen of perspiration. She felt inexpressibly close to him.

"Such capable little hands for one so lovely!" he murmured. "I marvel at what they have been able to do, how you fought my fever, how you can keep your head and manage your servants and keep this household running under such adverse circumstances. And you are so lovely! You are the woman I never expected to find, my true mate. Your gift of love means more to me than the gift of life that you forced on me."

"Yes, you did," he said, chuckling, when she protested. "You wouldn't let me die! Now my life is yours to do with as you will. I'm dedicating it to you, to keeping you safe and happy."

"Yet you are leaving me," she said reproachfully. "I'll be so alone when you go."

"I swear I'll come back, sweet Marie-Thérèse. You can't go where I'm going now, but I'll come back for you. Believe me, *chérie,* and trust me. I will come back!"

He kissed the pulse beating in her throat, and she heard the strong beat of his heart going almost as fast as her own. With her fingers she traced the pale line of the scar that both fascinated and frightened her because it spoke of dangers she could not imagine. Someday he would tell her what perilous encounter had left this reminder, but now she wanted only to kiss it, and to thank *le bon dieu* that he had lived to love her.

After midnight, the sounds of revelry below the *galerie* began dying away. Doula knocked at her mistress's barred shutters.

"*Ma'mselle? Ma'mselle?* Are you all right?" she asked anxiously when Marie-Thérèse did not answer."

"Yes," Marie-Thérèse finally said, in a drugged voice. "Go to bed, Doula."

"But my bed, *ma'mselle*—"

"Go to bed," Marie-Thérèse said again, from deep within Jacques's arms, and Doula said no more.

Sometime toward morning, a heavy downpour of rain on the roof awakened them, and they made love again. So this was not a rapture that she would know only once, Marie-Thérèse thought, transported. She would never get enough of loving him. She slept, content, in his arms.

Jacques left her before dawn. Marie-Thérèse crept out on the *galerie* in her robe, almost stumbling over Doula's sleeping form outside her window. The *galerie* was dry; there had been no wind, and the rain had poured as out of an overturned bucket. Below, in the drenched garden, Jacques and a red-coated officer were walking toward the canal, where one of the shallow boats awaited them.

Marie-Thérèse knew what that meant. He was going to the British vessels that had sent in the reinforcements. He was going to the enemy. And her heart was going with him. He had promised over and over to come back for her. Could she believe him?

She had to trust him. There was nothing left in life for her if she could not trust him.

She stood at the rail and watched as long as the boat was visible. When it vanished between the trees, she turned back to her room. Doula had not awakened. She lay on the wooden deck of the *galerie,* deep in sleep and completely relaxed. The girl had danced the night away so energetically that she had probably not even missed her pallet, but Marie-Thérèse murmured, remorsefully, "I'm sorry," to her sleeping form, and opened her chest to get a light shawl to throw over her.

What had she become? Love had completely changed her from Papa's dutiful daughter, well brought up and a member of the best Creole society, into a selfish and irrational creature who was a loving slave to a British spy! For if Jacques was not spying, what was he doing?

Having pronounced this harsh judgement on herself, she climbed into her bed and fell into an exhausted sleep.

Chapter Thirteen

The next day was drizzly. A fine gray rain fell over everything, muting the colors. The green of the oaks blended into their beards of moss, and the bright red coats of the soldiers moving through them were subdued to a warm glow.

The encampment was quiet. Marie-Thérèse heard no cannons or muskets fired, but throughout the day reinforcements continued to arrive via the canal. Occasionally a line of British soldiers could be seen marching upriver on the road beside the levee until they merged with the trees bordering it.

Marie-Thérèse went about her usual tasks in a daze: planning menus, keeping the kitchen girls busy gathering and preparing vegetables for Désirée, and seeing that the linens were changed and laundered. She was haunted by sensual memories of the hours she had spent in Jacques's arms. Sometimes she would stop and stare at what her hands were doing while she felt again the incredible sweetness of his lips at her breast, or remembered the surprising silkiness of his skin when she had touched a secret part of him. Now and then she paused in what she was saying to Estelle, hearing again the music of her name moaned in helpless passion in his deep voice.

She could scarcely believe it had really happened. She, Marie-Thérèse Dufret, had given herself—given her virginity—freely and joyously to one of the enemy! Had she not seen him leave with a British officer by the same route that had brought in British reinforcements? It was incredible. It was world-shaking.

In the chill of the morning, with Jacques gone, she could look back on what she had done and reckon the cost of her pleasure. An heiress with the highest social position, trained to manage a luxurious plantation home, she had taken for granted that she was considered a prize on the marriage market. But she was not naive enough to believe that value had not been lost along with her maidenhead.

She had even risked the unthinkable—being made pregnant out of wedlock—and by the enemy!"

I have become a woman, she thought, and there was a rueful pride in that, *but I have no husband—only a lover who probably is deceiving me and who may never return.*

She had stepped out of her safe and comfortable world into another that was still uncharted. And yet, who knew whether that safe and comfortable world would even exist after the coming confrontation with the British? And even so, how could she regret knowing the ecstasy of Jacques's love?

Her world had been turned upside down, and she knew she had been irrevocably changed. She was no longer the lighthearted girl who had chattered to Annalise about the excitement of finding a handsome and dangerous British spy on the riverbank. On this silvery-gray morning, everything looked different.

The raindrops that sparkled on the shrubs that were still standing in her garden were like diamonds, and those roses that had been spared had an aching loveliness. She saw, beyond the tiredness in Désirée's lined face, the pride in her cooking skills that fired the old woman's energy, even though she cooked for the despised enemy. And the loving concern she sometimes saw in Estelle's dark eyes moved Marie-Thérèse almost to tears.

Had they noticed the change in her? They had known her since she was a child. How could they miss it?

She would not have believed Jacques's going could make such a difference. She felt as if there were a great emptiness in her day. A dozen times she caught herself thinking she would go to his room, as she had become accustomed to doing when he was ill, to see if he needed anything.

While Doula helped her dress for dinner, she stood before her mother's portrait and wondered what that respected lady would think if she could come back to Petit Bois now. Would she call her daughter a wanton and a traitor—or a courageous survivor? She tried to compose her features into the gracious dignity the artist had caught in her mother's expression to order to mask the distaste she felt for her task as hostess—and now mistress—to the enemy.

"How can I bear it, Doula?"

"We bears what we must," her young freeborn maid said, and Marie-Thérèse sighed. "Yes," she said, thinking of Mattie, Doula's mother, and Boddy, her father, all *gens libre de couleur* but now impressed into labor by the British along with the slaves.

When she entered the salon, Lieutenant Bacon approached her with a single scarlet rosebud, still holding a drop of rain in its folds, and presented it to her.

"I cut it for you because it's absolutely perfect," he said. "Like your beauty, *mademoiselle*."

"You mustn't say such things to me, *monsieur*."

"Why not? I only speak the truth," he said in his awkward French.

She accepted the rose, hiding her dislike for him. But she could not resist saying, "Your soldiers have been hard on my roses, *monsieur.*"

"I regret that, but it was necessary. May I sit with you this evening? The general is remaining with his troops."

"Where?" she asked.

"In a bivouac we have been constructing a few miles up-river, from which we will launch the attack."

Against her family and all her friends! Her smile felt frozen.

"The general likes to bivouac with his troops. That is why he is so popular with them."

Apollo came to the door and signaled her that Estelle was ready to serve. She took the arm Lieutenant Bacon offered with a small bow. They led the way to the dining room.

He seated her and took the general's chair. There were fewer officers at her table now, since many stayed out in the field as the general was doing. Those remaining were of more serious mien after the Americans' surprise attack and the cannonade from the river gunboats on their encampment.

"This war will be over soon," Lieutenant Bacon said confidently. He looked at her. "What will you do then?"

She kept her smile intact, hiding her sudden feeling of panic. "I shall be mistress of Petit Bois, of course."

He regarded her with an expression in which she read pity, and she said, with spirit, "Do not be so sure your generals will prevail, *monsieur le lieutenant.* My father will return with his regiment to drive you out." It was the hope she clung to, her only hope.

Lieutenant Bacon smiled. "You are charming when you say that, but not very realistic," he said. His skin, like his hair, was very fair, and his teeth very white. "We are the army that defeated Napoleon, remember."

"Ah, but Napoleon was not a Creole!"

"Well said!" Lieutenant Bacon laughed indulgently. "But, *mademoiselle,* we're not here to fight the Creole French. We came to teach our rebellious colonists a lesson. And we know what *you* think of the Americans."

"We are all Americans!" Only a few months ago, she would have scorned anyone who insisted on calling her an American rather than Creole French.

"You would be wise to realize the strength of the forces we have brought from England, *mademoiselle.*"

"And you would be wise to consider the skills Americans have developed in fighting the Indians, *monsieur!*"

He laughed at her. "Those savages? They tie the legs of the trousers we give them around their waists. They still paint their faces, even if they have exchanged their feathered headdresses for hats. Would you place your safety in their hands against Britain's finest?"

"But Papa said you have been asking those very Indians to join 'Britain's finest' in your war against Americans. Why is that?"

"Touché."

"I'm sure you don't intend to keep your promise to give them back the land we have cultivated," she challenged him.

He shrugged. "All's fair in love and war."

"For shame, *monsieur!*"

Sparring with the brash officer with the hair of gold, pretending a confidence she didn't feel, helped Marie-Thérèse keep up her spirits and allowed her to forget for a few moments how much she missed Jacques. But when the lieutenant began expounding on her physical charms, she listened to his conversation without hearing everything he said, sometimes slipping away in her mind to relive those magic hours in Jacques's arms.

He must love her, to have given her his total attention for most of the night. It had been as if nothing else existed for either of them. And he had been so tender and loving, so concerned with giving her pleasure. It must be love!

It did not occur to her that she was encouraging Lieutenant Bacon, who interpreted her occasional lapses into dreaminess as a reaction to his outrageous compliments.

The next days were quiet, but they were busy ones for Marie-Thérèse and her household, and for the British soldiers. The rain hung on, and a northern chill was in the damp air. Lieutenant Bacon said that the Americans were building a rampart from the levee to the swamp near their new encampment.

"I hope it is higher and stronger than yours," Marie-Thérèse said sweetly.

He laughed. "We do not hide behind ramparts like cowards, *mademoiselle*. We meet our enemies face-to-face. They are cleverly installing it on the north bank of a dry canal so that we shall have to cross the ditch to reach them when we attack. It could be bloody, but it will be short. Our scouts tell us they have only a handful of men compared to our legions."

Marie-Thérèse listened to him and thought, *Is that what Jacques is doing? Is he a scout for the British generals?*

Why couldn't she hate him? She found it easy to detest this British officer beside her, who thought to please her with flattery yet boasted of what his army would do to New Orleans!

The next day the British bombardment of the *Carolina* and the *Louisiana* began. The American ships returned the fire. Cannonballs whizzed over Petit Bois and fell into the gardens and what remained of the British encampment. The stable was struck, and the redcoats led the frightened horses out and tied them up in the trees to the south of the mansion.

As Marie-Thérèse went about her tasks, she noticed that the British soldiers were building something curiously like an oven under the levee near the battery that was firing at the American ships. The cannonade continued until evening. From time to time Marie-Thérèse heard a bugle call. Some she could recognize now: the call to reveille, which got the soldiers up in the morning, and the call that told them they could break for food. But there were others she could not identify.

Twice during the day, she heard the drum and fife and looked out from the front *galerie* to see redcoats marching upriver in a crisp line on the road along the levee.

Lieutenant Bacon, walking back from the battery, flushed with pleasure when she spoke to him.

"Where are the soldiers going?"

"To reinforce our legions preparing for the attack."

"They are not fighting yet?"

"We've had a few skirmishes. Yesterday, I was within a hundred yards of the rampart General Jackson is building." He was eager to hold her attention. "His men fired at us, but we were able to take shelter in the plantation buildings this side of the line. With a spyglass I was able to see quite clearly what the Americans are up to."

She excused herself and went back along the covered walk to the kitchen and storeroom. Was Jacques aboard one of the British vessels now? What was he doing there? *They want to use me, but I am using them.* Damn him for being so secretive, she thought, her heart aching.

The next morning it became obvious what the odd oven under the levee was for. The British gunners were heating the cannonballs before they loaded them into the cannons. Curious, Marie-Thérèse walked out on the upper *galerie* where she could see both of the ships that were at anchor on the opposite shore.

From this distance she could see the American gunners preparing to fire their cannons at Petit Bois. The British began firing. The first cannonball fell into the river with a hiss. The British fired again and struck the *Carolina*. It shuddered in the water, and a thin trail of smoke rose in the morning air.

The fiends! Marie-Thérèse thought. They were trying to set the ships on fire!

They were feeding more red-hot cannonballs into the artillery, and their aim was getting closer. An American cannonball soared over the house, and Marie-Thérèse thought in dread, *The sugar mill!* But it fell into the cane field with a thud and an explosion of soil.

The British fired again and made a strike. Across the river, pandemonium reigned on the *Carolina*. The hot cannonballs had started a fire on deck. Marie-Thérèse could see sailors and gunners running around, their mouths open in shouts that barely carried across the water. Some were fighting the fire, but soon sailors began jumping off the ship and into the river. Smoke surged in rolls into the cool air, and then a tremendous explosion rent the morning. Flames leapt out of the ship, which was soon obscured by black smoke.

Down by the levee, the British gunners were shouting and jumping up and down in their excitement. She recognized the word *magazine* and guessed what they were saying. They had hit the ship's store of gunpowder!

The *Louisiana,* the smaller gunboat farther upriver, was drawing up its anchor, and a tight line of seamen, some of them dripping wet, were walking along the levee, pulling on a hawser. They were tugging the *Louisiana* by hand up the river, out of the range of the British guns!

The *Carolina* was sinking. Marie-Thérèse clenched her fists, watching as more men scrambled off the burning ship. Damn war, she thought, tears rolling down her cheeks. Damn all wars!

Was Jacques safe, or had he walked into something like this on that vessel on Lake Borgne? Where were Papa and Hébert? Would any of them survive this madness?

New Year's Day came and went unnoticed, with no sign of Jacques, and no message. Marie-Thérèse felt abandoned—utterly alone.

On the next night she was awakened by a light tap at her window. Her heart leapt and began drumming against her ribs. He had returned, as he had promised!

Doula rose up on her pallet. *"Ma'mselle?"*

"Wait!" She had barred the wooden jalousie shutters before closing and locking her windows, but he had apparently been able to slip a knife through the crack in the shutters and lift the wooden bar, because he was tapping on a glass pane of the floor-to-ceiling window.

Marie-Thérèse stepped over Doula's pallet and padded to the window. "Who is it?" she asked in a low voice.

"Roland Bacon."

Fear sharpened her voice. "I have retired, *monsieur.*"

"But I must speak with you, *mademoiselle.*"

"I will speak with you in the morning, *monsieur le lieutenant.*"

"Please," he coaxed. "There is never any opportunity to speak to you alone, and this is very important."

She hesitated. Could Jacques have sent a message through the golden-haired Briton? It did not seem likely.

"Tell me what you want," she ordered.

"You cannot expect me to say what I have to say through a damned window!" he protested. "I want to see your face when I speak to you."

She did not like his tone. He had had too much wine, she thought fearfully, and said firmly, "Good night, *monsieur.*" She went back to bed, but she lay tense and still and did not relax until she heard his retreating steps.

She wished the general would return to Petit Bois. He was a strict commander, but he had been kind to her. He did not come, but the next day his aide, Major Ashley, returned from the new encampment and took the general's chair. The major was charmingly attentive to her, and Marie-Thérèse was glad to be free of Lieutenant Bacon's persistent attentions.

The following night she was wakened again by someone at the window, and again her heart leapt in anticipation. But she soon saw that the man on the *galerie* had again managed to lift the bar on her shutters and was now using some tool—his knife?—to force the lock on her window.

Jacques would not do that!

She could not keep herself from remembering that dreadful night when mad Gama had chopped his way into her chamber and she had wakened to see his machete raised above her mosquito *barre.* Her heart began racing in panic. Jacques was not here to come to her aid now.

She yelled loudly, "Go away!" Although she had tried to keep her tone steady, her voice trembled.

"Hush! Do you want to wake everyone?" She recognized the lieutenant's voice.

"Shall I run and waken the general's aide, *ma'mselle?*" Doula asked.

"No," Marie-Thérèse said. Major Ashley had been exceedingly polite, but she was not sure she trusted him, either. Her heart was beating against her rib cage, and her thoughts raced frantically for something that would dissuade the lieutenant. Or, if that was not possible, something that would protect her.

"Send your maid away," the lieutenant ordered, "and open your window so that I can speak to you privately."

"But I don't wish to speak with you privately, *monsieur*. Please go away," Marie-Thérèse said, "or I shall have to wake someone."

"If you do, I will say that you invited me to your chamber."

Would he be believed?

She shivered. What could she do?

"You should listen to me, *mademoiselle*. I will have an important position when we have taken New Orleans."

"You will not take New Orleans!" she cried, striking out in her terror. "You are in your cups again, *monsieur!* Go to bed."

"I'm not asking you to become my mistress, Mademoiselle Dufret." His tone was defensive. "I am willing to marry you. A Creole wife will be a great help to an English government official in this colony."

Willing to marry her? Because it would help him advance in his position? She took a deep breath, her panic mixed with pure hatred. "Colony!" she exclaimed. "We are one of the United States! And our government officials are elected! Who in New Orleans would vote for you?"

"My king has already appointed one of my superior officers as the governor-general for the colony of French Louisiana. My legion commander will be customs inspector, and I am to be his deputy. You should consider my offer, *mademoiselle*. You will have no place to go when my general moves his lady into Petit Bois, which he will do."

"You are lying!" she cried, stung into losing her rigid control.

"Am I? Why do you think he hung her portrait in the salon? She is even now awaiting the end of the campaign on his vessel at the entrance to Lake Borgne."

Marie-Thérèse had been living at a low boil during these days of subjugation to the British, and his words made the pot boil over. How dare they claim positions in the government of New Orleans as if they had already won the city! How dare they assume they would occupy the beautiful plantations along the river! How did they intend to dispose of the present owners?

He was working doggedly at the lock with the point of his knife. In minutes he could enter her chamber. Marie-Thérèse's unreasoning rage was stronger than her panic.

"Bring me the *pot de chambre*," she whispered to Doula. Her maid gave her one startled look, then ran into the withdrawing alcove and came back carrying the high white chamber pot.

"Help me," Marie-Thérèse whispered.

Doula's giggle made Marie-Thérèse suddenly giddy with recklessness. They waited, holding the pot between them, while Lieutenant Bacon worked on the lock. When he succeeded and pulled the windows wide, Marie-Thérèse said, between her teeth, "Now!" and they flung the contents of the pot in his face.

"You French bitch!" he cried, sputtering and cursing, while a telltale stink rose on the *galerie*. He felt blindly for a handkerchief, and, not finding one, began wiping his face with his hands. A mixture of French and English curses rolled off his tongue. Marie-Thérèse and Doula burst into hysterical laughter.

Windows opened on the *galerie*, and his fellow officers appeared out of adjoining rooms, some in their nightclothes and robes. They came from around the corner of the upper floor of the house and crowded around the sputtering intruder. Soon the two women and Lieutenant Bacon were being treated to a chorus of laughter and cheers by the Briton's hugely amused friends.

Marie-Thérèse laughed with them, then pulled both her windows and her shutters closed. She clapped her hands over her mouth and glanced guiltily at the portrait on the wall. It had been a most unladylike thing to do, and she shuddered to think what her mother would say. But the sheer outrageousness of what she had done had eased the rage that had been eating at her like acid.

Doula moved her pallet against the closed windows and lay down on it, pulling her blanket up over her. Marie-Thérèse lay stiffly in her bed until the laughter and conversation on the *galerie* died down and she heard the retreating footsteps of the officers. Then she relaxed, knowing she would sleep.

The next day, Lieutenant Bacon sat as far from Marie-Thérèse as he could at the dining table, and one of his friends offered to repair her lock.

A heavy fog obscured the early dawn when Jacques was brought to the outskirts of New Orleans. Jacques sat in a small canoe the Acadians called a *pirogue,* while the fisherman who had been hired by the British poled it silently through the swamp.

Jacques was dreaming of the incredible softness of Marie-Thérèse's skin and remembering with guilt the innocent passion with which she had received his love. He had taken her maidenhead and all but sworn fidelity, and the euphoric happiness it had brought him amazed him. For it could not last. There was no place in his life for a woman like Marie-Thérèse.

"There's a curfew," the fisherman said, breaking the silence in his Spanish-Creole patois, "and it's strictly enforced. Watch yourself."

Merci, mon ami."

"The whole city is alert."

"Don't worry," Jacques said. "I am Creole. My language will protect me."

They went over the arrangements again in low tones.

Jacques had told the British officers aboard the general's vessel at the mouth of Lake Borgne that he would have to travel into the bayous, probably in the LaFourche *intérieur,* to find Lafitte. "If I can get to Dominique You, he will tell me how to find him."

"And if you cannot?"

"I can get back to the general's headquarters on the river," Jacques had assured them. "You will hear from him what I have found."

They were approaching the shore where the bayou ended on the outskirts of New Orleans. "I will return here at this time tomorrow," he told the boatman. "If I don't appear by sunrise, you will know I cannot come."

The Spaniard nodded, took the coin Jacques offered him, and departed silently. Jacques walked out of the swampy woods and into the city. The smells he had always associated with New Orleans were intensified by the fog. The aroma of roasting coffee beans hung in the heavy air, powerful and wonderfully stimulating. It rose over the strong fishy odors from the market and the river smells of wet wood, canvas and rotting vegetation, but it did not crowd out that lingering whiff of sewage in the streets that identified the city.

Jacques bought a café au lait and a roll at the market, wishing the Acadian vendor a good morning and telling him he had come down the river from Baton Rouge to volunteer. While he ate and drank, he allowed himself to think of the extraordinary thing that had happened to him. He, who had thought he would live out his days as a confirmed solitary on his brigantine, taking love where he found it, had found a woman who could keep him enthralled forever.

He couldn't have said how he knew it, but he knew it was true. Her face rose before him in the clearing mist, eyes deepened and marvelously softened by love, mouth made sensuous by his insatiable kisses. Her mixture of proud spirit and melting compassion, wrapped up in an enchanting package of beauty and innocence, clutched at his heart. But where could he take her? Not to Grande-Terre, certainly. Could he ask Marie-Thérèse Dufret to give up her life in New Orleans society to live on his brigantine?

It was impossible.

He had to keep his thoughts on the task before him, lest he become lost in his emotions and grow careless.

Le bon dieu keep her safe until he could return to her!

After listening to detailed directions to the house where the garrulous vendor of coffee said that the governor's men were accepting volunteers for training, he left and walked across the place d'Armes, where a group of wild-looking mountain men were being assembled by an officer in the blue uniform of the Louisiana Brigade.

"Where are they from?" Jacques asked an elderly Creole who, like him, had stopped to have a look at the frontiersmen.

"Tennessee."

In their nondescript buckskin clothing and possum caps, with their long stringy hair falling to their shoulders, they were a strange-looking regiment. But their eyes were shrewd and farseeing, and they handled their muskets as if they were extensions of their bodies.

Jacques went on until he came to the blacksmith shop in the rue St. Philippe. It was not yet open, so he entered the courtyard by the garden gate from the street and knocked gently at a rear door. It was opened by a large, dark-skinned woman who greeted him warmly.

"Monsieur Bonnard!" she exclaimed in French with a Saint-Domingue accent.

"Bonjour, madame."

"Come in!" she invited. "Please be seated. You look as if you could take a glass of wine. Have you been ill, *monsieur?*"

"Oui, madame. With the fever."

"Ah, Pierre also. Have you heard? He was captured when the army raided on Grande-Terre, but escaped. Dominique spent several miserable weeks in jail."

"He is not now in jail?"

"No. General Jackson offered him and his men a pardon if they would volunteer in the militia. Naturally, they accepted."

"And Jean and Pierre?"

"They also are helping the American general, who values their familiarity with the bayous."

Jacques felt his tension slacken. "I was not able to deliver Monsieur Livingston's message, and now I find it is unnecessary. But I should like to speak with him. Can you let him know I am here?"

"Mais oui!" She called to Pierre's son and gave him instructions, then poured Jacques a glass of wine. "Ah, this fog, it is melancholy, no? I sometimes wonder if I will ever see my home again. Such wonderful nights we had in Saint-Domingue! Not like this cold mist."

She insisted that he eat something while he waited, and set a basket of rolls and butter and cold roasted fowl before him. "You are too thin, Monsieur Bonnard! Eat, eat!"

At last the dapper American who was Jean's lawyer and Andrew Jackson's friend arrived and grasped Jacques's hand in greeting. In a few minutes of conversation with Livingston, Jacques learned at last what had happened when he failed to rendezvous with Jean the night his horse pitched him into the river.

"After the raid of his headquarters at Grande-Terre, Jean risked coming to New Orleans secretly, and I arranged a meeting with the governor. Claiborne and I were able to persuade General Jackson that he should pardon Jean's Baratarians and accept their offer to help defend the city.

"Of course," Livingston added with a twinkle, "the news that Jean and Pierre had upwards of seven thousand flints cached in the bayous helped to convince the general that he should grant a pardon. Andrew Jackson is a practical man. He now has flints for his muskets and pistols, and he has stopped calling the Baratarians 'those hellish *banditti*.'" Livingston laughed. "You are now all 'gentlemen privateers'! Jackson needed those flints badly."

He refilled their wineglasses, and asked, "Where have you been hiding? Jean said you never returned. Why?"

But when Jacques began telling him where he had been, Livingston stopped him. "Sir, I think the governor should hear this. And General Jackson, too, if he is not out of the city inspecting one or another of his units of defense."

"Please send for a carriage, then," Jacques suggested. "I don't especially care to be seen with you."

When Livingston stared at him clearly offended, Jacques laughed and said, "I intend to return to Petit Bois."

"The devil you do! Are you serious?"

"I'm serious."

"Then you must think the British have spies in the city who could recognize you!" Livingston exclaimed.

"I know only that the British I have talked with seem to know a lot about the rampart Jackson is building, so they must have spies somewhere. And many have seen me at British headquarters at Petit Bois, as well as on the British vessel that I visited. They are very cocky."

"The bastards! You know that they planned to attack us from Lake Pontchartrain, do you? Until they found Lake Borgne and the passage through the rigolets too shallow for their frigates."

"Yes," Jacques said. "They came to Petit Bois in their shallow flatboats."

"They fought like demons in those flatboats, and defeated our gunboats on Lake Borgne. That's why Jackson had no intelligence of their movements for about ten days, until young Dufret reached us. You want a closed carriage, is that it, Bonnard?"

"If you please."

"Very well." Once again Pierre Lafitte's young son was sent on an errand. But Livingston asked, with a hint of suspicion, "Why is it necessary to return to Petit Bois? Won't you be at risk?"

"Not so much at risk as Mademoiselle Dufret, who was also captured when the British occupied the plantation."

"I heard about that," Livingston said with a sad shake of his head. "Her father is wild with grief and guilt for leaving her in the country."

"She was left to nurse me back to health, and she did. I intend to bring her through the lines before the coming battle."

"Good God! Is she all right, then?"

"She was still safe when I left. She was pressed into service as the housekeeper at British headquarters, with the promise that the British general and his aides would treat her with respect. I hope that is still true."

"I wish you luck," the lawyer said cynically. "I remember her as a charming young beauty. But you'd better advise her that her misadventure has probably ruined her reputation."

"Watch your tongue, Livingston!" Jacques growled.

"Don't fear *my* tongue, my friend. It is the Creole ladies she should fear. They have convinced themselves that the British intend to ravish them as soon as they have secured the city."

"I don't know about the ordinary redcoat, but the officers have their wives aboard their fleet, and they are mostly gentlemen. I was introduced to several British officials who plan to assume the governance of New Orleans after it is taken, so they will probably try to restrain their troops."

"The hell you say!" said Livingston, his face reddening with rage. "I hope and pray we can give them a rude shock! But you should see the ragtag army Jackson is putting together. The only brigade with proper uniforms is the Louisiana Blue, composed of our social leaders and some of the wealthier plantation owners."

"Can they fight?" Jacques asked.

"They are part of our militia, brave men who enjoy drilling and rattling their sabers. But I ask myself, can they prevail against the army that brought down Napoleon?"

Chapter Fourteen

When Marie-Thérèse awoke, it was still dark outside her window. She was too restless to stay in bed and wait for her breakfast tray. As soon as she opened her eyes, she felt the tension that gripped Petit Bois. The British were preparing for what might be a decisive confrontation, one that could change Louisiana forever. Her thoughts began circling in a painful maze of anxieties about what would happen to Jacques and Papa and her brother when hostilities broke out, and about her own uncertain future.

"Doula?"

"Ma'mselle?" Doula murmured, raising her head from her pallet.

"Light a candle, and find me a fresh morning dress."

"It be early," Doula protested sleepily.

"Not too early to start the day. I want you to come with me to the storeroom."

It was not yet dawn when they went quietly down the back stairs, Doula carrying the light ahead of Marie-Thérèse, who had attached her great ring of keys at her waist. They took the covered walk between the rear gallery and the kitchen. Désirée was not yet up, and the fires were not made.

"Every mornin' you up earlier," Doula grumbled. She took a large tray and loaded it with bowls of several sizes to take with them.

"It's something I've learned lately, Marie-Thérèse said. "If you can't sleep, go to work." She picked up the lamp and led the way.

The storeroom was a sturdy one-room building made of cypress and built virtually moisture-proof, with only one solid door and no windows. Like the kitchen, it was set on brick pillars that raised it three feet off the ground, with a short flight of wooden steps.

Marie-Thérèse unlocked the door and entered, setting her lamp down on a table in the center of the room. A heavy sweetness in the air from the hogsheads of sugar and molasses mingled with the tang of spice from the dried onions, chilis and garlic that hung from the rafters, and the dusty smell of grains and flour. There were also the supplies from the British vessels, caskets of tea and matches, and hogsheads that held meat and fish laid down in salt.

"Go and wake Désirée while I fill these bowls," she told Doula. "Tell her to come and help you carry the food to the kitchen after she makes the fires."

"She'll be cross, *ma'mselle.*"

"She should be up, and the fires already made," Marie-Thérèse said firmly. But she did not blame Désirée. The middle-aged cook had little help these days. The British had put everyone old enough to work helping them settle in and prepare for the strike at New Orleans. Marie-Thérèse began selecting those staples that Désirée would need for her menus for the day.

Doula had left the door open, and when it slammed shut, Marie-Thérèse turned with a start. When she saw Lieutenant Bacon standing with his back to the closed door, she was so startled that she dropped the wooden scoop back in the hogshead of sugar, and with it the bowl Doula had brought for it.

The lieutenant's golden hair was in disarray and his eyes were like blue fire in the glow of the candle. He was not in full uniform, but wore a white shirt still open at the throat; he had not yet shaved.

Fear quickened her pulse.

"I saw your light from my window," he said.

"What do you want?" she demanded.

He was breathing heavily, but when he spoke, she realized that the passion he displayed was not lust, but a blazing anger. "You're going to pay for humiliating me before my fellow officers and laughing at me, *mademoiselle*. I don't take that from anyone, and certainly not from a Creole bitch and her black maid!"

Her heart was suddenly beating so hard she feared he would hear it and sense her panic. She could not let that happen. She knew instinctively it would inflame him more.

"Have you been at my Papa's excellent wines already, *monsieur?*" she asked him, as coolly as she could manage. She moved unobtrusively, putting the table between them.

"I won't offer marriage again," he warned, coming closer. "That is something you'll beg for when I've had my way with you and no one else will want you."

"Do you threaten me, *monsieur?*"

Her thoughts were darting this way and that, seeking a way out of his trap. What could she do? Cry out for help? Her cry would not be heard beyond these tight walls, unless it was by Doula and Désirée. And what could they do to protect her?

She tried to speak with confidence. "Your general will punish you for this! He promised me respect."

"The general will believe whatever I tell him about you. When he hears how you've led me on, flaunting your feminine charms..." He took a step toward her.

"Will you tell him how I protected myself when you broke the lock on my window?"

Hot blood darkened his face. "You have presumed on your position here, Mademoiselle Dufret," he warned, "and you'll regret it."

Marie-Thérèse picked up the lamp with her two hands and blew out the candle.

With the heavy door closed and the lamp extinguished, the dark seemed absolute, but Marie-Thérèse was familiar with the storeroom and its contents. She could still see in her mind the placement of every hogshead. The Briton's unfamiliarity with the space might help her. Perhaps in his anger he had not been very observant.

Still holding the doused lamp—he would hear her if she set it down!—she edged quietly around the table. She felt it jar when he bumped into it. He swore, then stood still, listening. She stopped immediately. She tried to calm her breathing, but she knew it gave away her position because she could hear his short angry breaths and judge from them where he stood.

When he took a step she moved, as silently as she could, going toward the door but keeping the table between them. They stopped, listening, then moved again, the hunter and the hunted, neither speaking. He was circling the table toward her, apparently feeling his way around it, but all at once she became uncertain of his position. She stood motionless and listened tensely. Had he changed his direction?

She did not know whether he was approaching her from the right or the left. She was probably only three long steps from the door, but, gripped by confusion, she feared she would run right into his grasp.

While she hesitated, Lieutenant Bacon lunged for her. Although she could not see him, her other senses alerted her that he was coming. But he had miscalculated. He must have hit the corner of the table, for it overturned, and bowls of food slid off it with a great racket. Dried beans rattled across the floor, and flour dust filled the air. Marie-Thérèse cried out in pain as the table struck her leg a glancing blow.

Bacon swore and lunged again, catching her by one arm in a brutally painful grasp that almost brought her down. His other hand caught the material of her dress, and she heard her morning gown rip apart at the waist seam.

Pure instinct had tightened her grasp on the extinguished lamp she still held between her two hands, and she lifted it and brought it down blindly. She hoped to strike his head, but he was taller than she realized. She felt a crunch as the lamp apparently hit his face. His yell of pain and rage galvanized her.

The lamp dropped from her nerveless fingers with a tinkle of breaking glass. She turned, her feet sliding on the hard beans, and ran, but stumbled on her trailing skirt in her haste. She almost fell flat, but caught herself with one hand; it slid through the thick syrup of spilled molasses. In a panic, she staggered to her feet and reached for the heavy cypress door.

When she opened it, she looked behind her. In the dim light of early dawn she had let in, she saw Lieutenant Bacon standing with his hands over his face, momentarily stunned with pain. Dark blood streamed through his fingers and dripped splotches on his white shirt.

She pulled the door shut behind her and wiped her sticky hand on her bodice, then felt frantically through the keys on the large ring that hung at her waist, the same ring her mother had carried. Her trembling fingers knew each key by its shape, and she found the right one, plunged it into the wrought-iron lock and turned it.

Lifting her sagging skirt, she fled down the few wooden steps, her breath coming in sobs. Behind her, the lieutenant pounded on the storeroom door, then began cursing her.

Doula suddenly appeared out of the shadows. "*Ma'mselle!* What happen?" Light was streaming from the open kitchen door.

Marie-Thérèse looked down at herself. Her clothes were torn, flour-dusted and molasses-stained, her hair, which Doula had pinned up only minutes before, was falling down around her face.

"It's Lieutenant Bacon—I've locked him in," she gasped. "What shall I do now? What will they do to me? Oh, Doula, where can I hide?"

"Oh, *ma'mselle!*" her maid said. She put her arms around Marie-Thérèse and drew her into the kitchen, which was warmly lit with candles and a quick-flaming fire. Désirée made a shocked sound, then filled a basin with water and began washing Marie-Thérèse's face and hands, as if she were still a child. She clucked when she saw the angry red marks the lieutenant's hand had left on Marie-Thérèse's arm.

"I think I broke his nose. It was bleeding buckets! What shall I do?" Marie-Thérèse sobbed. "I can't leave him locked in the storeroom, and if I let him out he will kill me."

Estelle had come into the kitchen, still rubbing sleep from her eyes. In a whisper, Doula quickly told her what had happened.

"Where can I hide?" Marie-Thérèse asked her. She was trembling.

"Child, if that man's nose is broke, he hurting. He not goin' come after you now," Estelle said. Her slow, calming voice was utterly convincing. "He likely go down to Jumonville to the hospital. And come daylight, the general be expecting him to come to that big camp they make on Ma'mselle Annalise's plantation, where he go every day, *non?*"

"He got problems, too," Doula put in, clearly convinced by Estelle's logic. "He won't want his friends to hear about this. They laughed at him when we gave him the chamber pot."

"Doula be right," Estelle said. "We got time to think. *Ma'mselle,* I think you must tell his general about that man!"

"He will lie to the general about me," Marie-Thérèse sobbed.

"Doula, take *ma'mselle* to her room. I fix her breakfast now," Désirée said.

Outside the kitchen, they met Apollo. *"Ma'mselle,* I came to find you. M'sieu Jacques is here."

Marie-Thérèse drew in a deep steadying breath and stopped trembling. He was safe! And he had come back! She felt faint with relief. And then a great rush of energy filled her, and she knew what she must do.

She pulled up her keys and removed one from the ring. "Apollo, this is the key to the storeroom. Get M'sieu Boddy and help him take care of the lieutenant. He will want to see a doctor, and perhaps M'sieu Boddy can take him down to Jumonville, where the British have taken over the infirmary for their hospital."

"And Papa can see *Maman,*" Doula added. "She been down there ever since the enemy come."

Apollo's eyes widened in shock. *"M'sieu le lieutenant* is locked in the storeroom?"

"He attacked *ma'mselle!*"

"Yes," Marie-Thérèse said, and then she asked anxiously, "Will the guard hear him pounding?"

"*Non, ma'mselle.* He down on the levee road now."

The slaves knew where everyone was at all times. "Where is *m'sieu?*"

"He in his room now, *ma'mselle.* He come in sometime in the night."

"Go quickly, then, and bring M'sieu Boddy. Doula, you stay and help Désirée clean up the storeroom after they leave." She was still shaky, but she went up the dark back stair on winged feet. Jacques had come back! She sobbed again, this time with relief.

Jacques was wakened by a soft knock on his door. The house still held that hush that comes with the dawn. He had been asleep only a short time, and his body begged for rest, but the knock had been mysteriously discreet.

"Who is it?" he growled.

"*C'est moi,*" he heard the one voice that could bring him instantly awake say.

Seconds later, he was opening the door. She slipped through it and came into his arms. He encircled her slender form with his strength, pressed her against his sleep-warm body and kissed her hungrily.

"You came back!" she whispered against his mouth.

He felt her trembling, and in the next instant heard her sob. The knowledge that she was crying moved him unutterably. "My love, my sweet, what is it? Are you all right?"

"Yes, love. But no one must know where I am."

Her tears fell on his hands. He moved them over her, down her back to the sweet curve of her *derrière,* up to her bosom to cup her breasts lovingly. But he sensed that her trembling was not of passion but of fear. And then his hands encountered the stickiness on her bodice and, incredibly, he smelled molasses. He found the gap between her bodice and skirt. Her clothes were torn! He stilled, his mood suddenly dangerous.

"What happened?" he demanded.

"Lock the door and I will tell you." Her voice was unsteady. "Is your window locked? And your shutters barred?"

Had she been violated? He was seized by a rage like a hurricane, such fury that for a few seconds he could neither move nor see. His hands tightened possessively on her. "Who did this? I will kill him! Tell me his name!"

"I'm all right, truly, my love! If you can hide me here until after breakfast, they will all leave for the encampment up at the Bourgets'."

He left her to close and bar the shutters outside his window and lock the door that opened on the hall. He remembered what Livingston had said about her reputation, and his fury became a sick rage against fate, against her father, who had left her here, against the British popinjay who had done this to her.

He returned and lit the candle in the lamp beside his bed. That was when he saw the marks of a man's fingers in a darkening bruise on her upper arm.

"His name! It was Bacon, wasn't it? I've seen the way he looks at you. I will kill him for this!"

"Jacques, dearest one, I am all right. I was able to escape him. You must not kill anyone. You must not endanger yourself by doing something so rash. I will tell the general—"

"How did you escape him?"

"I broke his nose with my lamp and locked him in the storeroom."

"He's locked in the storeroom? *Mon dieu!*" He looked at her with respect. "*Bon!* I'll go and carve out his liver!"

"Jacques, listen to me! *I broke his nose!* Apollo and Boddy are taking him to the infirmary at Jumonville." She was still trembling, and his heart was breaking for her. "Please don't leave me," she begged.

His own fingers were trembling, but with rage, as he unbuttoned her bodice. But Bacon could wait. The ruined dress dropped to the floor. He laid her in his bed in her shift and lay down beside her, still wearing his nightshirt. He pulled the covers up over them to shut out the January chill, but that did not stop her shivering.

"Now tell me everything," he ordered.

In low tones she told him about the lieutenant's two visits to her *galerie* window, and the incident of the *pot de chambre,* which had so amused his friends and so angered him.

In spite of his fury—or because of it—a savage laughter bubbled up in Jacques. He choked it back and hugged her.

"This morning he followed me to the storeroom and swore revenge," she finished.

"But you bloodied his nose with your lamp and escaped." What a brave and resourceful woman she was! But, *mon dieu,* if he had not come back for her!

Her voice faltering, she said, "I don't know what he will do now. Perhaps he will lie to the general about me."

His wicked enjoyment of Bacon's discomfiture had cleared his head. Although his rage at the Briton remained, he saw things in perspective again. He had other priorities just now, and the first one was getting Marie-Thérèse away from here to some place where she would be safe.

"My sweet, he can do nothing. I came back to take you away from Petit Bois."

"Away?" He saw the flutter of her pulse in her white throat. "Where?"

"With me, my dearest love, to New Orleans."

"Through the lines? How can you do that? Unless you are truly—" Her voice broke.

He stiffened. "Truly what?" Was she going to say "a British spy" again? Did she still distrust him?

She said aloud, "Tell me where you have been."

"I was taken to a British vessel, and then put ashore near New Orleans."

"By the British?"

"Yes, love," he said reluctantly.

"And how did you get back to Petit Bois?"

"A Spanish fisherman brought me in a small boat."

She looked at him strangely. "Tell me..."

He caressed her cheek, smoothing back tendrils of her hair. "Do you love me, Marie-Thérèse?"

"I adore you," she said unsteadily. "If you had not come back, I, I couldn't—"

His heart turned over. "Can you trust me, my love? Someday I can tell you everything, everything."

Around them the sounds of doors slamming and footsteps on the stairs told him the officers were leaving their chambers for the dining room.

Jacques pulled her close. "Are you expected downstairs?" he whispered, lovingly smoothing her hair.

"I never go down for breakfast."

"I will go down and join them. When they leave for the bivouac, I will send your maid to tell you. You must go about your daily tasks as usual," Jacques told her, "so that no one will suspect you have any idea of leaving."

The thought of leaving Petit Bois with him was suddenly overwhelming. She thought of all she would leave behind her, and asked, "Can I take my mother's portrait with us? It is hanging on my bedroom wall. The general—" her lips trembled "—put a portrait of his wife in its place."

He tightened his mouth to repress the hot anger that boiled up in him again. "It's not possible. I'm sorry, Marie-Thérèse."

She said hesitantly, "What about Doula? Can I not take Doula with me?"

"No, love. You must not confide in anyone. It could mean our lives."

"What will become of Doula, and Désirée and Estelle? I'll be leaving them at the mercy of the enemy! How can I do that to them, Jacques?"

He heard the genuine anguish in her voice, and his heart was heavy. "The British need them, even more when you are gone, love. They have a better chance of survival than we do.

"I have a legitimate reason for leaving again so soon," he continued. "But it is imperative that no one guess you are going with me. I will have one of the smaller boats tied up near the last orange tree. Since the bivouac has been moved out of your garden, you will be able to get to the boat without being seen, if you are careful. Wear a dark cloak and soft shoes. It might be wise to hide a loaf of bread and a piece of a cheese under your cloak."

"Yes," she said, apprehensively. Had she once bragged about the excitement in her life to Annalise? At this moment she wished fervently for a safe, dull life!

"Watch for the guard who patrols along the canal. Every fifteen minutes he climbs the levee to inspect the river. When that happens, go through the trees to the boat. Lie down in it and cover yourself with your cloak. I will come alone, before midnight."

Marie-Thérèse tried to visualize going into the swamp at night. Her mind shied away from the image. Although New Orleans was surrounded by unmapped marshes, where cypress trees grew so thickly in stagnant water that no sunlight passed through the umbrella of their leaves, she had never penetrated that eerily menacing twilight. The thought of journeying deep into it in darkness was even more daunting.

"I will have to tell Doula something, Jacques. She sleeps in my chamber and will be alarmed if I disappear."

He was silent, thinking.

"She can help us, Jacques. She will lie for me if someone comes to my door."

"You are expecting someone to come?" he asked, his voice suddenly hard.

"Yes," she said simply. "Someone who wants revenge for a broken nose."

He put his hand on her arm, and his grip was strong and possessive. "Perhaps she can help." He paused. "We will have to trust her."

He kissed her. "Sleep if you can, love. We must be wakeful tonight."

She got up and locked the door after him, but it was impossible to sleep. Now that she was safe from Lieutenant Bacon's assault, her terror at what might have happened was even stronger. And she was frightened of what Jacques planned for them. Her future had once been assured, now it was dark and uncertain.

The only surety was her love for Jacques. She had to trust him, because she loved him.

Doula came upstairs later. "Everybody gone now," she reported.

Marie-Thérèse went to her own room, where Doula had brought a breakfast tray of café au lait and rolls. After she had eaten, Doula helped her into another morning dress and took the torn one to Sophie to launder and mend.

"It's good to have M'sieu Jacques back, *non?*" Doula asked, smiling.

"It's good, *oui,*" Marie-Thérèse said, and they smiled at each other. But her heart was filled with anxiety.

The day seemed interminable. She did not see Jacques again until the noon meal, which was sparsely attended. He was totally immersed in a long conversation in English with one of the British officers present. Marie-Thérèse heard little and understood none of it until they parted at the meal's end, when the Briton said, in French, "I will get word to the general, *m'sieu,*" which seemed to confirm all her doubts.

There was no comment when Lieutenant Bacon did not appear in the dining room. He often took his noon meal at the encampment, but Estelle whispered to her that he was back from Jumonville and had asked for a tray in his room. Marie-Thérèse was glad. She was not sure she could have hidden her anxiety from his sharp eyes.

In the afternoon, Marie-Thérèse sent Apollo to find the overseer and bring him to the rear gallery. "What of the cane, M'sieu Boddy?" she asked him.

His mouth twisted. "What cane, *mademoiselle?*"

"The crop is ruined?"

"I'm afraid so. I've not been in the fields since the British arrived. None of us have. We have been ordered to move the artillery and carry cannonballs and supplies. Some of my workers are on the Bourget plantation, where the enemy is now encamped."

She lowered her voice, "And Mattie?"

His voice dropped to a near whisper. "She is well, *ma'mselle*. She works very hard. She can get word to me with the men who carry the injured to her."

"And Lieutenant Bacon?" Marie-Thérèse murmured.

"Very uncomfortable, *ma'mselle*. The British doctor set the bone in his nose and stuffed it with cotton." His eyes twinkled. "It seems he went for an early ride this morning on one of M'sieu Dufret's stallions and the beast ran under a low branch and knocked him off."

"Indeed!"

"Will you tell the general what he did? He should be exposed for the scum he is!"

"I will, M'sieu Boddy. Thank you for your help. I hope that someday my father can express his appreciation for your loyalty."

She wished she could warn him that she was leaving, and place him in charge. But she simply had to trust his loyalty and his judgment. Later, she managed to secrete a loaf of bread and a piece of a cheese in her dark cloak, along with her brush and comb and a few other personal articles. She lay down for a rest—her last in her own bed—and for an hour communed with her mother's portrait, trying to memorize every brush stroke. Someday, she promised herself, it would grace its proper place again, and she prayed to Our Lady of Sorrows for its safekeeping.

She dressed carefully for her last dinner at Petit Bois, and was glad when she found her salon once more filled with red-coated officers. The general had returned from the bivouac on the next plantation with a small group of his aides for a conference and a night in their own beds. She felt the baleful gaze of Lieutenant Bacon before she encountered it. His nose was taped inside an ingenious little cage of wire, and he was obviously forced to breath through his mouth.

The general called to him in English, and the lieutenant answered him with a deprecating shrug. Another officer made a remark that set everyone to laughing, and a young Briton smiled at her and said, in French, "Bacon has bad luck with both women and horses, *n'est-ce pas?*" Someone said something about a *pot de chambre* that filled the salon with guffaws. Lieutenant Bacon tried to laugh with them, but he turned an angry red. He kept his gaze on the floor, and she knew it was to hide his fury.

"What's this, *mademoiselle?*" the general demanded, looking at Marie-Thérèse.

Her lips parted, and she drew a quick breath. But her gaze was drawn to Jacques, who was standing nearby, his dark eyes sending her an urgent warning. It said to her, as clearly as if he had spoken, *Say nothing, or the general will spend the night questioning you and your servants, and I will have to leave without you.*

She exhaled, and said, "It was nothing, *monsieur le général.* The lieutenant had too much of Papa's wine one night and came to the wrong chamber. My maid brought me the *pot de chambre,* and with her help I made a sober man of him."

The general laughed heartily. Jacques approached him, saying, "*Monsieur,* I have just returned from the flagship of the fleet, and bring a message from your lady."

"Then you shall sit at my right hand, *m'sieu.*" He offered his arm to Marie-Thérèse, and they led the way to the dining room.

Marie-Thérèse felt like brittle glass that would shatter at a touch. She tried to keep a smile on her face while Jacques answered the general's questions about his wife, but it was difficult to maintain her mother's ideal of grace and dignity when she was filled with fear and the unbearable anticipation of escape.

After the traditional bread pudding dessert, the general suggested a private conversation with Jacques over port in his study. Grateful, Marie-Thérèse escaped the dining room. In her chamber she asked Doula to help her out of her silk dress and into a dark linsey.

Doula looked at her in surprise. "You are going out again, *ma'mselle?*"

"Yes, Doula." The time had come, and it required courage and resolve. In these past weeks when Marie-Thérèse had been isolated from family and friends, Doula had become her close friend and confidante. It was heartbreaking to leave her behind.

"Tonight I am going away secretly with M'sieu Jacques:"

Doula looked troubled. "You did not say 'we going,' *ma'mselle.*"

"No. I asked him if I might take you, but he said his boat is small and he cannot hide us both. I am desolate that I must leave you, Doula. And I must ask you to protect me this first night, and if anyone should ask for me, say I am sleeping. But before dawn, you must leave this house and go to Mattie at Jumonville, where you will be safer."

"Where will you go, *ma'mselle?*"

"M'sieu Jacques says to New Orleans. I must be with him, Doula."

"Oui, ma'mselle." Doula's eyes were very soft.

Marie-Thérèse brought out the great ring of keys that had been her mother's and put it in Doula's hands. "I can tell no one else I am leaving. In the morning, you can tell Estelle and give her these keys. Tell her to keep my absence a secret as long as she can."

"You will come back, *ma'mselle?*"

"Who knows?" Marie-Thérèse said. "Who knows how this war will end?" She added, painfully, "Forgive me,

Doula, for locking you out that night M'sieu Jacques left. It was selfish of me."

"C'est rien, ma'mselle," Doula said. Tears gathered in her eyes, and they embraced.

Marie-Thérèse decided to leave the house as soon as it was dark. While the officers still lingered over their wine, she was less likely to encounter one of them taking the air in the garden. She posted Doula on the gallery to watch and warn her if she was seen and followed. Then she left the house and crept from shadow to shadow across the ruined garden toward the last orange tree on the canal.

She found the flat-bottomed pirogue and stepped into it, quickly crouching to still its rocking. A bird cry had warned of her approach, but there was no other sound except the buzzing of a few hardy mosquitoes and the discouraged scraping of the last cicadas, sounding at odds with the chilliness of the night. She stretched out on the bottom of the boat and covered herself with her cloak, prepared to wait. In the eerie stillness, her heartbeat sounded frighteningly loud.

Chapter Fifteen

A small wind moved the boat away from the bank and rocked it gently. Marie-Thérèse lay on her back and watched the clouds move across the sky. The patterns they made shifted constantly. Sometimes they revealed a patch of stars and a sliver of a winter moon. When that happened, the dark around her was full of recognizable shadows. But when the clouds closed ranks, the night became a deep darkness in which she could see nothing.

An illogical mingling of the scents of oranges and gunpowder was in the air. Now and then, from the direction of the bivouac upriver, the wind brought the sound of male voices. The British soldiers were singing barracks ballads around their fires, their strong voices carrying faintly through the copse. They sounded confident and in good spirits.

She kept her ears sharply attuned to the sounds of the night—the tiny splash when a mink dived, the twitter of a bird disturbed in its sleep—and she was instantly aware of the approach of careful footsteps.

It couldn't be midnight yet!

He was apparently coming alone, but she dared not raise her head. Suppose it was not Jacques but the picket, investigating? Moving her hand with infinite care, she pulled the dark material up to cover her face and imagined herself an empty cloak lying limply on the bottom of the shallow boat.

"*C'est moi*," Jacques said on a soft breath. "Stay down."

She conquered the almost irresistible urge to uncover her eyes and look up at him. Little sounds told her that Jacques was untying the line securing the boat to a tree on the bank, and seconds later the coil of rope dropped at her feet. The pirogue rocked as he stepped into it.

He laid something heavy on the edge of her cloak—a pistol?—and threw what must be a hat down on it. Then they were moving out on the canal, silently except for the faint sucking sound each time Jacques drew the pole up and pushed it down again into the bottom mud. She lowered the cloak and looked up at the dark figure towering above her, his silhouette in his caped greatcoat reminding her of a great black bat, and thought, *This can't be happening*.

Who would have believed it could happen? She was entrusting her life and her future to this man, not because she trusted him, and not because he was the only one who could help her. No, she was here because his hands and his lips could rouse her to ecstasy, because she could think of nothing else but the language of love he had taught her.

What will become of me?

The odors of the swamp, decadent and unmistakable, invaded her senses. The musky smells of the animals that inhabited it mingled with the stench of decaying wood and rotting leaves. She had a premonition of danger so strong that she could not lie still. Her body flinched involuntarily.

Jacques said softly, "You can sit up now, *chérie*. Take care you don't tip us into the soup."

She shivered. There were alligators living in holes hollowed out in the banks between the roots of overhanging trees. In the past she had seen their eyes glowing ruby red when a lantern was held about the canal after dark. She tried not to think of them, or of the water snakes that sometimes slithered up on the garden grass when the rains were heavy and the bayous overflowed their banks.

She pulled herself up and faced Jacques, her back to the bow of the boat. "It can't be midnight."

"No," Jacques said. "I couldn't stomach thinking of you waiting in the boat alone."

She was warmed by his concern and felt more confident. Jacques was silent and watchful, poling the boat forward while she sat quietly at his feet. The shape of the drainage canal soon disappeared into the watery wastes of the cypress swamp. She wondered how he could find his way in the maze of trees which they entered, zigzagging to miss the barely submerged cypress knees that could overturn the boat.

But now and then a glimpse of the crescent moon through streamers of moss proved that they were keeping a fairly consistent course.

This was another world, still and fetid and oozing fertility. Overhead, the canopy of leaves thinned, and for a brief time the moon shone boldly through the trees. In its pale light, a darker mound rose out of the black water ahead of them. It was an island in the swamp, thickly wooded, one of those heaps of shells Marie-Thérèse had been told had been left by a race even the Indians did not remember.

Over the centuries, the heaped shells of mollusks had collected and held the silt washed down the river by floods until they formed a solid hummock where oaks could take root. *Chênières,* they were called, places where oaks grew.

Jacques pushed the boat away from it into an opening in the trees.

Suddenly a black figure, darkened still more with black mud, leapt out of the shadows of the mound and splashed toward them. His expression was terrifying. Jacques pulled up his pole and raised it to strike, but before he could bring it down, the black man had seized their pirogue and over-turned it, pitching them both into the stagnant water.

Marie-Thérèse screamed and choked on the water that poured into her mouth. The opening in the thick-growing trees signaled the presence of a deep hole in the mostly shallow swamp. She had been pitched into it, and she knew an instant of pure panic as she sank into a greenish-brown murk where no light penetrated.

She fought to the surface and paddled toward the mound. When her feet touched a bottom made solid with shells, she stood and found herself with her head and shoulders above the surface. She looked for Jacques and froze in terror at what she saw.

He was struggling with the black man who had tipped over their boat. To her horror, she recognized the runaway slave who had tried to kill her with his machete. His wildly rolling eyes were those of a man gone mad.

He and Jacques were standing in water above their waists, locked in a test of strength. Apparently they were fighting for possession of the boat, which floated very near them, keel up and barely visible in the darkness. Gama's big frame was emaciated, but his madness and his desperation made him a dangerous opponent.

Her heart was thudding. Without a boat, the swamp was virtually impassable. They would be stranded—as Gama had been since running away. Was this where her life would end, and Jacques's? They would be at the mercy of alli-gators and snakes and the treacherous sucking mud of the bottom if they ventured away from the mound. They could die here without anyone knowing!

The two men wrestled in silence, scarcely splashing the water, the only sounds their grunts of exertion. She saw that Jacques's fist was clenched around the wrist of the other man's upraised arm. But Gama was slippery with mud, and Jacques's hands were wet. Marie-Thérèse thought with regret of Jacques's pistol, which he had laid on her cloak in the pirogue. It was somewhere on the bottom now, along with her mother's silver-backed comb and brush and the few other personal articles she had brought with her. And the cheese and bread she had brought for their food.

She could not see whether Gama was armed or not until a moving cloud again cleared the slice of moon and a faint reflection glanced off something in his raised hand.

She screamed, "He's got a cane knife!"

But of course Jacques had seen the ugly curved blade long before she had. That was why he was trying desperately to hold Gama's arm!

She sobbed in pure terror.

Jacques cursed his carelessness in leaving his pistol lying in the bottom of the boat. He should have worn it stuffed in his belt. He had obtained a dagger, which was tucked into his boot, but he could not risk loosening his grip on Gama's slippery wrist to reach for it. The big canecutter needed only one second to bring down his ugly blade and slash off Jacques's head.

It was a contest of strength in the gloom, agonizingly slow because the water hampered their movements, and Jacques's boots slipped often on the shells on the bottom. Gama was most certainly barefoot, and he had the strength of madness. Jacques read murder in his eyes.

He could not allow himself to tire first, for that would leave Marie-Thérèse at the mercy of the rebel slave.

Where was the pole? He risked a glance and saw it floating not too far away. From the corner of his eye, he saw Marie-Thérèse paddling toward it.

"Go back!" he shouted.

But Marie-Thérèse continued paddling until she seized the pole. She backed into shallower water, where she could find a footing, and raised the pole above them.

Mon dieu! Jacques thought. She was as likely to strike him as the maddened slave, and that would give Gama the second he needed to strike with his deadly weapon. Praying his strategy would succeed, he gave Gama a great push away from him. To his immense relief, Marie-Thérèse reacted as he had hoped she would and brought the pole down on Gama's head.

It seemed to have no effect on him. Jacques saw the machete splash down where he had been. He threw himself on his back and kicked away from Gama.

"Give me the pole!" he cried, rolling over in the water, and Marie-Thérèse pushed it toward him. He took two strong strokes toward it. Gama came after him, slashing murderously at the water with his cane knife.

"Get out of the way, *chérie!*" Jacques shouted, and Marie-Thérèse obeyed, scrambling up the mound.

While she watched, eyes wide with terror, Jacques seized the pole and swung it up and then brought it down. Gama ducked, and the tip of the pole struck his shoulder. He tried to grab it but missed, his arm movements apparently slowed by Jacques's paralyzing blow. Jacques swung the pole up again, but Gama kicked himself close under it and raised his knife.

He was only three feet away, and the ten-foot pole was unwieldy at that distance. Gama would be on him before he could raise it high enough to have any force. With a strength born of desperation, Jacques swung it in a semi-circle.

Marie-Thérèse had never felt so helpless. *I can't watch this,* she thought. Her eyes were closed for only an instant, but she heard the sickening crack when the pole struck Gama's head, and turned to see the poor mad man sink below the surface, his knife going under with him. Jacques backed up a few steps, breathing hard, then turned and splashed toward the mound, pushing the long pole ahead of him up on dry ground.

He staggered up after it and collapsed beside Marie-Thérèse, who sat shivering uncontrollably.

The moon was covered now by a gray cloud that looked as if it were full of rain. It cast a dull shadow over the already dim scene. There was no sign of Gama anywhere. They sat in the darkness until their breathing quieted.

"Is he dead?" she asked, and the haunting cry of a night bird answered her.

"It had to be one of us," Jacques said wearily. He added, "I'm sorry you had to see that, *chérie.*"

"I know, love." Her heart was beating hard. It seemed to be saying, *Jacques is alive!* But she felt nothing but a great numbness and a chilling cold. The night was going to be frosty.

After a long moment, he said, "I'd better get the pirogue," and went back into the water. She waited, trembling and praying.

When he came back, he brought both her cloak and his greatcoat. "They were floating," he said. "Not quite soaked through, but almost."

Her teeth were chattering. He threw down the cloak and, sitting on it, pulled her into his arms.

"I was so afraid for you," she said.

He hugged her close. "I might have gone down into the mud with him if we had not had the shell bottom to stand on."

She thought of the murky hole and shuddered, but she said, "Poor soul. What he must have been through these weeks since he left Petit Bois! I wouldn't have guessed he could survive that long."

"He found some shelter on the mound," Jacques said. "And he had a knife. He caught small game, no doubt. But I can't feel your charity for him, *chérie*, after what he tried to do to you."

"They said he took a boat the night he left. I wonder what happened to it?"

"A big alligator can destroy a small boat, if it attacks."

Marie-Thérèse shuddered. He pulled her closer, and she felt the warmth of his body through his soaked clothing. "I'm so cold," she said.

"Come, love, let's find a drier spot."

He took the dagger out of his boot and cut off some brush to cover the pirogue, and then they climbed the mound. From its top they could see the entire hummock. It was soon obvious that Gama had been alone here. They saw a log that the slave had tried to hollow out, perhaps to make a canoe. There was no sign that any other human being had ever set foot on the place.

Near the summit, they found a large oak with leaves and moss so thick the carpet of deciduous debris beneath it was almost dry. Enclosed by a filigree of hanging moss, the space seemed like a private chamber. Near the trunk was a pile of flattened bush.

"This is where he sheltered," Jacques said. "But he didn't have any flints. There are no ashes."

"Do you have a flint?"

"Yes," he said. "In my pistol. I imagine it's pretty wet by now." He shrugged. "If I lit a fire, the British would find us. You may have been missed by now."

He spread her cloak on the ground. "We should take off these wet clothes, love. It's fairly dry here beneath the oak."

She began pulling down streamers of fresh moss.

"What are you doing?"

"I will make us a bed," she said. "Every year, right after the candle-making, I have my women gather fresh moss to stuff our mattresses. We'll have to sleep on it as it comes from the tree, but it will make a fine bed."

"Of course it will." Smiling for the first time since they had been set upon by Gama, Jacques cut the gray streamers down for her. They arranged them in the shape of a bed and spread her cloak over them. Then he cut more moss and piled it beside her cloak. He began unbuttoning her bodice, and the light brush of his knuckles against her breasts as he struggled with the tiny buttons sent a singing warmth through her.

He wrung out the excess water from their clothes and spread them over some low palmettos. "There's not a chance our clothes will dry," he said. "We can keep warmer tonight without them." He pushed her bodice off her shoulders with a caress. When he unfastened the tie at her waist, her dress dropped to her feet, and she stood before him in her clinging wet shift.

Jacques looked at her small sweet body, outlined by the wet underclothing, and felt an overwhelming tenderness. He thought, with a certainty that surprised him, *I want her for my own woman, my only woman. I can never let her go.*

It was something he realized he should have known before. The thought had been there, lying in the dark recesses of his mind, for weeks, waiting for his acknowledgment. It completely changed his priorities, and it would change his life forever. But it was something he could not deny, and it meant he had to tell her the truth. To deceive her indefinitely was not only undesirable, but impossible.

Would she be able to accept the truth, to love him for himself?

"I'm so cold," she said through chattering teeth.

"I'll keep you warm, love." He pulled the wet shift over her head and flung it over a small palmetto, then quickly took off his wet clothing and draped it over another shrub.

He lowered her onto the bed they had made, then covered her with his greatcoat. Over it he spread a thick layer of moss. He slipped in between the two cloaks and wrapped his body around hers. It was a surprisingly warm nest.

She snuggled close to him, accepting his warmth. His skin tingled wherever their bodies touched, and he felt himself rise in response, not with urgency, but with a deep caring.

He murmured into her wet hair, "I never thought I would love a woman the way I love you, *chérie*. Does every lover feel that his love is more important than life itself? If anything should happen to you—"

"I know, love," she said. "When Gama raised his knife, I wanted to die with you."

It was said so simply, with such innocent candor, that he felt a blessed peace. She loved and trusted him. He could tell her who he was now—*what* he was. Confess that he had once thought to seduce her for his own selfish need, for her help in escaping from Petit Bois. Confess the deeds that had caused her suspicions.

In spite of them, she had loved him enough to trust him. He vowed he would never betray that trust. He would never again lie to her. He would protect her with his life, because his life would be nothing without her.

"Dearest love," he whispered.

Her long, dark lashes, lying against her ivory cheeks, did not quiver. She was falling asleep. And no wonder, after the emotional strains she had suffered that day. He ran his hand down her slight form, fitted so sweetly to his, lingering on each curve with an exquisite tenderness, fixing it forever in his memory.

Rest, my darling.

Tomorrow, he thought, relaxing in exhaustion, gratefully closing his own eyes against the cursed swamp and the haunting eyes of the poor crazed slave he had sent to his Maker. *Tomorrow we will talk about the future....*

He slept, with her precious weight on his shoulder and his body sheltering hers.

Chapter Sixteen

Marie-Thérèse wakened in Jacques's arms, aware of his warmth even though she felt chilled through. They were lying curled up and fitted together like two spoons under his damp coat with its covering of moss. She opened her eyes and saw in the leaves above her head a feral little face with two bright eyes peering down at her through a black mask.

She gave a startled scream, and in the instant that Jacques awoke and leapt to his feet she saw that it had only been a curious raccoon whose territory they had invaded. Quick as a flash of gunpowder, it disappeared among the quivering leaves.

Jacques burst into laughter. "What a rude awakening!"

She looked up at him, straight and manly, broad of shoulder but still pale-skinned from his lengthy illness, and felt weak with love. She did not remember when he had shed his wet clothes, and she found the fact that they had slept like Adam and Eve in Eden enormously exciting. Somewhere beyond the canopy that had kept them almost dry, the sun was coming up behind a gray cloud cover. The air was damp and all around her was the smell of their bed of layers of fallen leaves and moss.

Pop, pop! Pop! Pop, pop, pop! It was the sound of distant muskets.

"The battle has begun!" Marie-Thérèse exclaimed.

"It's just a skirmish. You don't hear fife and drum, do you?"

"We're too far away."

They're not firing the artillery," he pointed out. He bent and pulled her to her feet and kissed her. She put her arms around his neck and clung to him while he rubbed some warmth into her bare back. The hairs on his chest tickled her breasts. Their nakedness in the chill air sent shivers of warmth through her wherever they touched.

"I am shameless, Jacques. I want you to love me."

Her words were the sweetest he had ever heard. His longing for her was suddenly unbearable. He cupped her breasts in his hands and bent to kiss first one, then the other. When she put her hands on his cheeks and pulled his head toward her and kissed him, his hunger for her exploded.

He cupped her head in his big hands and kissed her deeply. Heat flamed between them. "*Mon dieu,* but I've missed you, *chérie!*"

Still kissing her, Jacques lowered her down on her cloak. He caressed her throat and her breasts and moved his lips down her exquisite body, kissing her everywhere and murmuring endearments until she began moaning, "Please love me, Jacques, please, *please—*"

He moved with the urgency of need. A night bird cawed and flew out of the branches arching over them as Jacques quickly knelt above her. In seconds she was receiving the fullness of his love with a feeling of intense gratification that was more than pleasure. She felt a conviction that loving him was as necessary to her as breathing.

The canopy of oak leaves above them partially protected them when the clouds, which had changed direction with the wind now moving up from the Gulf, opened to splatter them with large drops of moisture. Rain fell softly on them, feeling pleasantly warm after the chill of the past week, and washed away the smell of the bayou. Their bodies glistened and shone. Diamonds of moisture lay in their hair. They moved in the age-old rhythm until Marie-Thérèse began shuddering in ecstasy and Jacques bowed his head to stifle his cry against her breasts. She whispered his name into his wet hair, her arms holding his head to her breast.

When they kissed again, Marie-Thérèse licked the fresh, sweet rain from Jacques's lips. *I've never been so completely without the comforts of life, and I've never been happier. How strange is life—and love. . .* she thought.

After a few moments of utter relaxation, they returned to reality. Jacques hugged her close, and said, "Can you put on wet clothes, love? The faster we move, the sooner I can see you warm your hands around a café au lait."

Privately, he was eager to get as far as possible from the route the British flatboats were taking through the swamp to their headquarters at Petit Bois. He picked up his clothing and left her in the privacy of their mossy chamber to make her toilette.

When he returned, she was struggling with the small buttons of her damp bodice, and he helped her with a patient tenderness that was new to him. When they were finished, he said, "I'll race you to the boat!" and they went sliding in zigzag fashion down the mound between the trees to where he had hidden the pirogue and its pole.

Jacques felt a relief to find the boat still there. He had not been able to dispel an unconscious fear that Gama would rise again from the swamp and carry the boat off. Now that he knew Gama was no longer a threat, he looked at Marie-Thérèse with a full heart.

She was warm and flushed by the time she had helped him push out the flatboat and stepped into it. With her hair in damp braids, with curling tendrils around her face and her wrinkled dress clinging to her slight figure, she still looked lovely to him.

He poled them out from the mound into the black, leaf-strewn water. Marie-Thérèse looked uneasily over her shoulder, and he knew she was remembering the maddened slave's attack. He vowed that he would devote the rest of his days to keeping her safe and making her happy.

He had never imagined himself loving another human being as he loved her, and he could never have imagined the happiness of having his love returned. It was a miracle that humbled him and made him feel blessed beyond anything he deserved. As he poled, Jacques watched her. Her hair fell in tangled tendrils around her face and her damp dress clung to her small breasts, outlining them deliciously, and her liquid dark eyes raised now and then to regard him with shining love.

Once they were away from the mound and moving silently and easily with the long pushes of his pole, he said, "If I say 'duck,' lie down in the bottom of the boat immediately and cover your face with your cloak. It will mean we have encountered a British supply boat going to Petit Bois."

She nodded, shivering with the damp cold but still warmed inside by the knowledge of his love.

Pop, pop! Pop!

Jacques had turned northwest and was following a course parallel to the edge of the swamp when the sound of muskets firing came clearly through the cypress trees. In his mind he saw the arrangement of the riverside plantations along the wide, level plain between the river and the swamp. The scattered musket shots told him they were nearing the plantations that separated the two encampments, the region that would likely be the battlefield when the British were ready to attack.

He had to keep close enough to the edge of the swamp to know when he had reached the canal that led to General Jackson's headquarters in the de la Ronde house, yet stay far enough in the swamp to be concealed.

He knew he was risking being mistaken for a British scout. If they were lucky, they would be captured by the Americans and taken to the general. If unlucky, they might be shot before they had an opportunity to identify themselves. *Le bon dieu* couldn't allow that to happen now, when he had found his reason for living. It would be too cruel.

But it could happen, and he was filled with an urgent need to tell Marie-Thérèse what was in his heart and soul before they met that final challenge. He must reveal himself and his love for her while there was still time.

He pushed the boat into a small space between close-grown cypress trees and plunged his pole through a noose in the boat's line and into the mud of the bottom. The boat swung around its primitive anchor and lay still. He sat down, facing her.

The cloud cover broke, and for a few minutes, rays of dappled sunlight struck brilliance from the water. Marie-Thérèse looked at him with a question in her liquid eyes. A glint of sun made her wet locks shine like jet.

"Do you know how much I love you, *chérie?*"

"As much as I love you?" she asked softly, and his heart turned over.

"More than my life," he said, and her eyes filled with tears. "But that life could end at any time, my dearest love, and there are things I must say to you while I still have breath to say them. I thought I could love you and let you go. But I can't. If I live through this battle for New Orleans that is coming very soon, I will fight for your love. I want to keep you with me always."

"That is what I want," she said, her voice low but firm.

"Before you can decide that, you must know who I am—and what I am."

"I know what you are," she said confidently. She sat erect in the boat, which swayed slightly, and looked up at him with grave eyes. Disheveled though she was, she still had an aura of dignity and feminine pride.

"I know you are brave and strong and resourceful, and—" her voice trembled with feeling "—a tender lover...."

He interrupted her. "I have lied to you, my sweet."

"You pretended you had lost your memory," she said, a tiny smile curving her lips. "Do you think I believed that? Not for a moment!"

"At first I plotted quite selfishly to seduce you in order to get your help in escaping Petit Bois," he confessed.

"I suspected that," she said.

"And yet you didn't shun me. I vow by all that's holy that I will never lie to you again."

"Can I rely on that?" she teased.

"There must be no more secrets between us. I want to tell you where I was going when my horse pitched me into the river and you found me and saved my life." He leaned toward her, his smile rueful. "You saw through me, love. But you have still wondered sometimes if I am not a British spy. Isn't it so?"

She flushed.

"I've told you how I was orphaned in Haiti. You know that my childhood friend dragged me away from my burning house. Our fortunes have been linked ever since then....

"It was that friend I was riding to meet, carrying an important message, when I found myself unexpectedly in the river. My friend had been offered a great deal of money and a commission in the British navy if he would throw in his considerable resources with the British in their attack on New Orleans. My friend was not inclined to help the British, but unfortunately he was considered an outlaw by the Americans.''

Marie-Thérèse frowned. "An outlaw?"

"He sent me to offer his help to General Jackson if those charges against him could be dropped. And because a great horned owl spooked my horse, I failed to take him the general's answer, which, by the way, was an insulting rejection.''

Marie-Thérèse's eyes were fixed on him with a fierce intensity. "So he turned traitor?" *And you, Jacques?*

"No, indeed. Fortunately, he was able to reach the general without my help. And this time the general accepted his resources.''

"What resources does he have?"

Jacques drew a deep breath. He felt uneasy now, wishing he did not have to continue. But he had to tell her. "Ships and ammunition. Soldiers.''

Marie-Thérèse stiffened. "Ships?"

"My friend and his brother own fast little sloops, which they used in ferrying émigrés from the troubled West Indies to New Orleans, and later in running the British blockade. I had a small inheritance from my parents that survived the flames of rebellion. My friend and his brothers helped me get my brigantine and my master's papers. There were times when Britain would have hanged either one of us had we been caught. But my friend grew powerful and very wealthy.''

Her face was white. "By importing slaves?"

"He sometimes attacked a ship that carried slaves and seized them as part of the cargo. I wouldn't stoop to that. If I suspected a ship carried slaves, I left it alone."

She regarded him with disbelief. "You attacked ships?"

"Enemy ships," he admitted. "Sometimes they attacked us, because we were running the blockade with contraband goods—"

"You are *pirates?*"

"Gentlemen privateers," he corrected her.

"Privateers," she repeated contemptuously.

"Yes, love. We attacked the British, and sometimes the ships of her ally, Spain, with the sanction of the American government. Although not Louisianians by birth, we are Creole, like you. New Orleans is now my friend's home, and America his country, as it is mine. When the British asked for his help in capturing New Orleans, he delayed answering them in order to give me time to carry his offer of our help to Governor Claiborne. I was on my way back with the news of the governor's rejection when my horse tossed me into your life.

"I deceived you about who I am, love, and now I am deceiving the British in order to take you away from them. They think I'm going into the deep bayous where the man they tried to bribe is hiding from the United States Army. But he is out of hiding and is now on General Jackson's staff of advisers."

"Who is this man?" she asked through bloodless lips, although she had a dreadful certainty that she already knew.

"His name is Jean Lafitte."

The pirate Jean Lafitte. One of the beasts who were responsible for the deaths of *Maman* and Adoré—and who perhaps had ravished them, too?

Oh, Mon Dieu, Mon Dieu!

Nausea rose in her throat. Her empty stomach churned, and her head felt curiously light. *A pirate!* Jacques was one of those animals in man's likeness whose brutal attack had devastated the happy family at Petit Bois.

She remembered her first impression of Jacques, when she had seen him lying half-drowned on the bank. A dangerous man, she had thought. Her instincts had been sound.

How many vessels had he captured, how many women passengers had he ravished before stealing their gold and their jewels to bring to New Orleans? She remembered *Maman's* lovely aquamarine necklace, which Papa had found among the jewelry confiscated when Lafitte's headquarters on Grande-Terre had been raided by the United States Army, and she could no longer fight her nausea. She leaned over the gunwale and emptied her churning stomach into the bayou.

"Chérie!"

Jacques knelt in the bottom of the pirogue and held her forehead and caressed her back. Marie-Thérèse wanted to shake his hands away, but she was too ill. She could only lean against the edge, tipping the little boat dangerously, and suffer his hands supporting her head and stroking her hair.

When she thought of their lovemaking that morning on the mattress of moss she had constructed under the oak tree, she was sick again, and more violently. She felt sullied by her response to his passion. How could she have given herself to a man who was not only one of Jean Lafitte's despoilers, but also his close friend?

Jacques dipped his hand into the water and bathed her face. With his cupped hand he offered her water to rinse her mouth, and she took it. But when he would have put his arms around her to pull her wet face against his shoulder and comfort her, she drew away from him in horror and revulsion.

"I can no longer bear the touch of your hands," she said.

Jacques sucked in his breath. For a dizzied moment, he thought he would be ill, too, and he stared, unseeing, down at his feet, struggling for control. When he could lift his head, he saw that Marie-Thérèse lay back in the boat, looking white and spent. He wanted to take her in his arms and comfort her, but when he stretched out his hand, she flinched.

The pain that tiny movement brought him was almost more than he could bear. He had known he was taking the chance of losing her by telling her the truth, but he had not foreseen the despair he would feel when she recoiled from him and he saw sick revulsion replace the love in her eyes.

With a set face, he stood up to raise the pole from the bottom and toss the line back into the boat. Then he began doggedly poling it through the cypress swamp again.

The morning sun filtering down through the canopy of leaves caused a mist to rise from the surface of the water, and it swirled through the trees, enveloping the boat in a world of grayness. The low-hanging fog muffled the sporadic musket fire that Jacques kept on their left, for he had no other landmarks now. The sounds of skirmishing grew louder for a time and then began to diminish.

He told himself he could not have concealed his true identity from her much longer, and that there could be no future for them unless it was based on truth. He had had to tell her. He had gambled and lost, but he had not known how much it would hurt.

He had thought nothing could ever again hurt him as deeply as seeing his mother and father struck down as they fled their burning house, and yet he was once again almost paralyzed by pain.

He had to make a decision, and yet he could only feel this deadening despair. His intention had been to take Marie-Thérèse to Pierre's woman and ask her to keep his darling hidden from the British should they capture the city. Clearly, he now had to deliver her to her father, who would be somewhere in the American encampment. Perhaps he could place her in the care of General Jackson.

After that, well…after that it didn't matter what he did. His own future stretched before him like a desolate, uninhabited plain. He would join Dominique You and that old pirate's band of smugglers on the battlefield. Now there was no one to care whether he survived the coming conflict or not. He did not much care himself.

He could no longer hear the occasional firing of muskets. Judging his position by the rising sun, he headed northwest, moving ever closer to the swamp that concealed the line of plantations along the river. When he caught sight of the beginnings of a man-made drainage canal on his left, he suspected he had reached the plantation that Livingston had told him was General Jackson's headquarters.

He had barely entered the canal when he was hailed in a gruff voice: "Halt or be shot!"

"Is that you, Redbeard?" he called, recognizing the voice.

"Jacques? What the devil—?"

Marie-Thérèse raised her head and stared in alarm at the rough-looking man pointing his musket down the embankment at them.

"I've come to join your regiment," Jacques said. "I have with me Mademoiselle Dufret, General Dufret's daughter, who has been held prisoner by the British. As have I."

"Well, damme! Old Dominique will be pleased to see ye," said Redbeard. He shouldered his musket and came sliding down the embankment toward them.

Marie-Thérèse looked at the man with the heavy red beard and the gold ring in one ear and shuddered. His appearance fitted her idea of a brutal pirate so exactly that she felt a return of the nausea that had overcome her.

She looked from him to Jacques, standing in the boat, and saw a man at once intimately familiar and yet a stranger. His unshaven face was darkened by a two-day stubble against which the scar running from the corner of one eye down his cheek to his jawline stood out palely. She had grown so accustomed to his scar that she had almost forgotten it. Now, in his unshaven and disheveled condition, it could not be ignored, and it made him look as sinister as he had seemed when she found him lying unconscious on the river's bank.

She shuddered as she remembered exploring that scar with a loving finger as she lay in his arms. The feel of his stubble of a beard against her sensitive skin, and other sensual memories rushed into her consciousness, and she recoiled from them with disbelief.

Her actions of the past weeks had been contrary to all her religious and social training. Even though she suspected he was a British spy, that had not kept her from loving him.

But a pirate! One of Lafitte's men, on his way to the smuggler's bayou lair!

He had bewitched her!

The red-bearded pirate put two fingers in his mouth and whistled. Within a few minutes, a third ruffian appeared at the top of the levee and pointed his musket at them. He, too, wore a gold hoop in one ear. A heavy black beard concealed most of his face, and his left eye socket was empty and hideously scarred. His long hair was braided into a pigtail that hung down his back, and on his head was a red scarf tied into a rough cap.

"Jacques Bonnard, by God!" he exclaimed, lowering his barrel.

"This is Mademoiselle Dufret, General Dufret's daughter," Redbeard said. "Escort *mademoiselle* to General Jackson's headquarters, then bring Jacques to Dominique's tent. Dominique will be pleased to have you with us, Jacques."

Dominique! Dominique You! Marie-Thérèse shivered with horror. It was a name gossip had linked with piracy and the Lafitte gang.

The one-eyed man stepped into the small boat, and his added weight brought the level of water almost to the gunwale of the shallow canoe. He took the pole from Jacques, who sat down facing her. Marie-Thérèse drew her knees up under her skirt in an unconsciously fastidious gesture.

Poling powerfully, their new captor turned the pirogue about and followed the narrow canal, going due west.

Marie-Thérèse was sunk in misery. The voices of the men discussing the coming encounter with the British came to her ears as from a great distance.

Gradually they emerged from the swamp. The trees changed from cypress thrusting up out of the water to reeds and then to scattered oaks. Soon there was cane stubble on both sides of the canal and the buildings of the de la Ronde plantation came into view. Another sentry, this one in the familiar uniform of the Louisiana militia, halted them.

Their escort poled them to the bank and stepped out to secure the boat. Dimly Marie-Thérèse heard him explain who she was and say she should be taken to General Jackson.

Marie-Thérèse lifted her head and looked at Jacques, who sat facing her, and their gazes locked with a painful intensity. She saw a big, gaunt man with a growth of dark beard, disheveled hair and quelling dark eyes that were eloquent with a strong emotion.

Neither spoke.

Then Jacques leaned toward her and said, "If ever you need me—"

She shook her head slightly in an instinctive rejection.

He began to speak, but his voice faltered. Under his breath he said, "God help me, I will never love another woman as I loved you."

Loved, he had said. Marie-Thérèse felt a stabbing pain at the thought of what they had lost. Tears sprang to her eyes, but she could not reply. Her throat seemed frozen. Ignoring his outstretched hand, she got to her feet and allowed the soldier in blue to help her step on the bank.

Chapter Seventeen

With the soldier supporting her, Marie-Thérèse climbed the bank without looking back and walked in her ruined shoes the short distance to the de la Ronde mansion. The lower floor and *galerie* were crowded, a beehive of activity, with men in a variety of odd costumes coming and going.

In her confusion, still suffering from shock and still feeling ill, she wondered if the scene before her eyes could be real. There were men wearing deerskin trousers and coats and fur hats, looking like frontiersmen from Tennessee or Kentucky. Here and there she glimpsed an Indian in a bizarre combination of deerskin and cloth garments. Acadian fishermen from the bayous in nondescript clothes with no military trappings milled about with officers in the tailored blue uniform of the militia.

They merged in a weird patchwork of color in her vision as they tramped in and out of the de la Ronde mansion, much as the British officers had at Petit Bois.

She must look as oddly garbed to them, she thought, in her wet and ragged dress and with her hair in disarray. Some of them glanced curiously at her as servants took her to the service stairs. She was led to a luxurious chamber where they brought her a warm bath and a change of clothing.

The beautiful black girl who helped her dress and then brought her a tea tray reminded her of Doula. Was she safe with her mother at Jumonville?

In spite of her anxiety about Doula and the other house servants, the events of the past weeks seemed already years distant. As she sat upon a small damask-and-cherry-wood settee with a silver tray containing tea and sandwiches on the small table before her, Marie-Thérèse thought she must have awakened from a dream.

She was back in her own world, surrounded by a luxury she had, until very recently, taken for granted. It was as if these past weeks at Petit Bois after the British invaded, and the incredible two days in the swamp, had not been real.

The very room in which she sat was not unfamiliar to her. She had attended weekend house parties at many of the river plantations, including this one. Looking at the high carved bed, with its matching canopy and coverlet of blue velvet, the pastel flowery rug on which it sat, and the elaborate gold frames of the pictures on the damask-covered walls, Marie-Thérèse could easily imagine that she had dreamed those weeks that she had been in the custody of the enemy— except for the presence of the soldiers she had seen on the lower floor, and the ache in her breast whenever she thought of Jacques Bonnard.

There was a light tap on the door.

"Enter," she said.

When she saw her father, she leapt to her feet, crying, "Papa!" and flung herself at him. A deep sob escaped her as she was pulled into a fierce embrace.

"Are you all right, *ma fille?*" he asked in a broken voice she had not heard since they were given the terrible news about *Maman* and Adorée.

"I'm all right now that you're here, Papa." She drew back and looked at him. There seemed to be more white in his luxuriant hair, and there were little lines of weariness and anxiety that she had never before seen around his eyes.

"And Hébert?" she asked fearfully.

"He was wounded, but he got the news of the British invasion to us in spite of that. He is still basking in the glow of being hailed as a hero. Right now he's convalescing in the convent of the Ursulines, and chafing to be on the battlefield with me."

Marie-Thérèse laughed shakily. "*Cher* Hébert! I'll go to him as soon as I reach the city."

He looked at her searchingly. "You are truly all right?"

Her lips felt stiff. Would she ever be "all right" again? But she said, firmly, "Yes, Papa. I've not been harmed."

He sighed with relief. "There is someone with me," he said, and went to open the door. The man who stood there looked very handsome in his blue uniform, but slightly uncomfortable.

"Gabriel," Marie-Thérèse said faintly. She had not thought of him in weeks, but the last time she had seen him was suddenly fresh in her memory. She had refused to consider his proposal of marriage until after the British were routed.

"*Mademoiselle,*" he said, bowing. He advanced into the room and took the hand she extended, bringing it formally to his lips.

"I must return to my duties, *chérie,*" Papa said. "I'll leave you two to have a little chat."

"Papa—" Marie-Thérèse protested, her heart beating faster in apprehension.

"It was fortunate the messenger found me, and that I happened to have Gabriel with me. We are engaged in retreating to the McCarty plantation, which is behind the line of defense General Jackson has chosen. I have arranged for the messenger who delivers dispatches to Governor Claiborne to take you with him to New Orleans on his next trip," he said. "He will carry my note to the governor asking if Madame Claiborne will offer you sanctuary in their home for the present."

"Papa, can I not go home to rue St. Pierre?"

"The house has not been opened. The servants are all at Petit Bois, as you know."

"I can find someone, Papa!"

"I must remain with my regiment, and I have no time to see about getting a chaperon for you."

"But there's Hébert. I can bring him home and care for him there."

"With no staff? Besides, when the nuns release Hébert, he will return to my regiment." He said, with finality, "You will be safe with Madame Claiborne, who has been kind enough to invite you to stay. It will relieve my mind to know that you are among friends."

"All right, Papa."

He kissed her on the forehead and said, "I'll send you word from time to time when it's possible." He left her with Gabriel, who had stood silently by, listening.

Papa closed the door behind him. That signaled a trust in Gabriel that seemed ominous to her. She remained standing, forcing Gabriel to stand, also.

He wasted no time. "*Mademoiselle,* when last I saw you, I offered you my hand in marriage."

He was so formal! This was a Gabriel she did not know. "Yes, Gabriel." After their last meeting, she had tucked his long love poem into her pocket and returned to Jacques, who was burning with fever. She had never read the poem, she recalled guiltily.

Gabriel said, "I want you to know that I am prepared to honor that offer in spite of..." He hesitated.

She stared at him. "In spite of what?" she asked with dangerous calm.

"In spite of any, any dishonor you may have suffered in these past dreadful weeks at the hands of the enemy," he said stiffly. "I'm prepared to stand by my offer—"

"How noble of you!" Marie-Thérèse interrupted in icy fury.

"I suggest an immediate posting of the banns," he said, "and a wedding as soon as it can be arranged. Of course, those arrangements will depend somewhat on the course of the war."

"Oh, indeed!" she said. "And why, pray, Gabriel, do you imagine that an immediate announcement of the banns is necessary?"

He flushed. "I should think that would be obvious, *mademoiselle*. You must know there has been, ah, speculation among our friends—"

"Gossip, you mean? I appreciate your concern, *cher* Gabriel, but I assure you that it is not necessary to sacrifice your good name for mine. My answer to both your questions is no."

"Both?" he repeated uncertainly.

"No, I will not marry you, and no, the British officers did not fall upon me like slavering beasts."

His face reddened still more, and there was a trace of anger in his eyes. "*Chère mademoiselle,* you have been living in your house with a dozen or so of the enemy for several weeks, have you not? Unchaperoned, except by your slaves. What are people to think?"

"That is their problem, not mine. Actually, I shared Petit Bois with *eighteen* high-ranking officers," she said, and saw his face grow pale. "I was allowed a certain amount of freedom, in return for managing the household. And I was treated with respect, except for one man whom I shamed before his fellow officers. I am not entirely helpless, Gabriel.''

He was looking at her strangely, and she could not help flushing as she wondered if her lovemaking with Jacques had left a telltale imprint. She knew those hours of ecstasy in her lover's arms had changed her forever—but did it show?

"It is difficult to believe—'' he began, but stopped when he saw her expression. "However,'' he said, stubbornly, "I have assured your father that if I survive this war I will make you my wife, and that I will challenge any man who insults you.''

"That is generous of you,'' she said ironically, "but I cannot accept your sacrifice, Gabriel.'' She walked to the door and opened it. She had to be alone, to sort out her painful emotions.

"I assure you that I have every intention of keeping my word, *mademoiselle.*''

"Adieu, mon ami,'' she said coolly.

When she had closed the door behind him, she realized that she was trembling. The thought of marrying anyone was abhorrent to her. No man would ever be given the love and affection she had once felt for Jacques Bonnard, the pirate. . . . Dear God, what if she was carrying his child?

She had been too besotted to think about that! Was that what was in Gabriel's mind, that she might be pregnant?

She put her hands to her temples, trying not to think of that possibility. The very idea brought back a host of sensual memories—the soft warmth of Jacques's coaxing lips with the taste of rain on them, and the magic warmth of his naked body lying against hers in their mossy bed. The smell of the swamp came back so strongly with the memory of his caresses that she lost her appetite, and when the servant came in answer to her jerk of the bellpull, she said, "Take the tea things away. I cannot eat!" even though she'd had little food since leaving Petit Bois.

Later in the day, a servant brought word that a horse was saddled to take her to the city, and the same girl who had helped her dress brought her a riding habit, only two sizes too large, that belonged to the absent mistress of the plantation.

The house had become strangely quiet since the morning, and the messenger who was her escort told her why as they began their ride to New Orleans. "We are withdrawing. The men are building a rampart on a line General Jackson has chosen," he confided, "where he will make his stand."

They were following the levee road to the city, and they were soon behind a regiment of the United States Army retreating to the new encampment, which slowed their progress considerably. After they passed the old Rodriguez canal, now drained, where the volunteers were throwing up Jackson's bulwarks on the north bank, their progress was faster. But it was over two hours before they had covered the nine miles to the outskirts of New Orleans.

Marie-Thérèse looked around her at the streets that were so familiar to her and found them strange. At first she did not realize why everything seemed different. But as they clattered down the cobbled streets past the market to the place d'Armes, she realized they were oddly empty.

There were no street hawkers, crying their wares of ginger cakes or fresh oysters, no shoppers at the market except for a few servants wearing the obligatory colorful turban, no women gossiping with their neighbors on the balconies overhanging the narrow streets. The balconies were empty, the windows shuttered.

"Where are all the men?" she asked the messenger.

"With the army," he said, in surprise. "Only the very old and the very young are left in the city, and the women are all fearful."

He took her first to the governor's office, where they waited with others there to see him. When the governor read her father's note, he penned one of his own to his wife and sent them to his home in the garden district.

Madame Claiborne was from a prominent New Orleans family, an attractive woman who brought Creole charm to her American husband's office. *"Pauvre fille!"* she exclaimed, embracing Marie-Thérèse. "Your father has been beside himself with worry! Were you very badly treated, my dear?"

"Not really," Marie-Thérèse said. "I was made a glorified servant of the British general. That is, I was given the choice of acting as his housekeeper and managing the servants or remaining bound as a prisoner."

"Really? His housekeeper?" Madame Claiborne repeated oddly. She looked very grave. "You must tell me frankly, *chérie,* if I am to help you. Did he force his attentions on you?"

"He did not!" Marie-Thérèse chose her words deliberately. "The general has other things on his mind than dalliance, madame. His wife is on a vessel in the British fleet on Lake Borgne, waiting until she can move into Petit Bois as our new governor's lady."

Shock altered Madame Claiborne's expression. "Is this so?" she exclaimed.

"So I was told, *madame.* But he is a gentleman who commanded his officers to respect me."

She thought the governor's lady's dark eyes held doubt, as well as shock, but Madame Claiborne said cordially, "My husband says you were forced to leave your *femme de chambre* at Petit Bois, so I have asked Betté to look after you." She indicated a young black woman standing by in the foyer. "She will show you to your chamber. You have brought no clothing with you?"

"It was not possible, *madame*. This is a borrowed habit," Marie-Thérèse admitted. "But I have some clothes at our house in the rue St. Pierre. Perhaps Betté could go with me to bring some gowns here?"

"Certainly, my dear." Madame Claiborne hesitated, then said, "The ladies of the city are coming here tomorrow, as they have been doing daily, to roll bandages and make necessary articles for our wounded. Perhaps you would care to join us?"

"Of course. But first I must go to the convent and find my brother."

"You may take my carriage, *mademoiselle*, and take Betté with you. I shall be occupied here the rest of the day."

After a brief rest, Marie-Thérèse set out for the convent of the Ursuline nuns, with Betté sitting on the high seat of the carriage beside Madame Claiborne's groom.

The convent was in the *quartier*, the oldest part of the city, near the barracks of the Louisiana militia, a short distance from the levee. She and Adorée had spent their school years here, and the gray stone building, with its spacious walled garden, held many precious memories of her sister. Here they had often looked from their dormitory window at the soldiers going through their drills in their trim uniforms. It was somehow ominous to see the parade ground deserted.

The nun who answered her ring of the bell at the gate was Sister Mathilde, a middle-aged nun with a plain face that shone with an inner light. She gave Marie-Thérèse a welcoming hug with tears in her eyes.

"We prayed for your safety, dear child," she said, "and *le bon dieu* has answered our prayers."

"*Merci,*" Marie-Thérèse said humbly. "How is my brother?"

"Ah, Hébert!" Sister Mathilde laughed. "He is well enough to help us prepare to take more wounded. We have sent all our students home and are turning the convent into a hospital. At present we have a few men in the dormitory."

Men in the dormitory where she and Adorée had lain in bed and speculated on the true nature of the opposite sex? How her sister would have enjoyed that irony!

"Hébert is directing the placement of borrowed cots. We will need many volunteer nurses, dear child. Perhaps you—?"

"Of course, I will help in any way I can," Marie-Thérèse promised. Waves of pain suddenly rolled through her as she remembered the nights of hovering over Jacques while they had battled his fever.

"Come, then, let us find Hébert. He is begging the doctor to discharge him. We shall miss him when he returns to his regiment."

They found Hébert in one of the larger classrooms, supervising a few very old men in the placement of cots around the walls.

"Our last student left yesterday. We are putting beds everywhere—in the classrooms, even in the halls."

Marie-Thérèse scarcely listened to Sister Mathilde's explanations, her gaze eagerly seeking her brother. He looked pale but unchanged, except for the sling supporting his right arm, and a certain stiffness in the way he held his shoulder.

"The ball struck his collarbone," said the nun, "but young bones heal quickly. He will soon be released to his regiment."

Hébert saw her then and exclaimed, "Marie-Thérèse!" They met in the center of the room and embraced. He held her tightly. "You escaped!"

"Yes."

"I hated to leave you behind, but it was imperative that Papa be told that the British had arrived."

"But they wounded you!" she cried. "I was afraid of that. I was so afraid they had killed you."

"They nearly did. I got to the Bourget plantation and found everyone gone, of course, but the Bourget's overseer rowed me across the river, where I was able to get a horse."

"With a broken bone? Oh, Hébert!"

"I arrived in New Orleans half out of my mind with pain. And when General Jackson decided on an immediate attack, even the laudanum Dr. Boudreau gave me could not help me sleep for worrying about you. Tell me what happened. Tell me everything!"

Sister Mathilde left them alone, beckoning to Hébert's aged helpers to follow her.

"There was great confusion that night," Marie-Thérèse said, experiencing again the feel of Jacques's arms encircling her from behind as they watched. "The enemy was caught unprepared. But, oh, Hébert, there are so many of them, and more keep coming! The garden is ruined, and so is the cane!" she said mournfully. "They have lit their cooking fires everywhere. They use everything, our slaves, our horses, our food supplies and all our possessions, as if they own them. The general in command plans to move his family into Petit Bois after they capture the city."

"The devil he does! We'll see about that! And you, dear sister? Did they use you, as well? *Par dieu,* I'll bayonet as many of them as I can reach!"

"They used me only as their housekeeper," she said. "In return their general promised me protection, and that he would find you and bring you to his physician if you were alive."

Hébert caught and pressed her hand. "And what of the British spy?"

Marie-Thérèse voice faltered. She could not tell him that Jacques had been her lover! No one must ever know—unless ... What if there was a child? She suppressed a shiver of fear and thought, *I'll face that when and if it becomes necessary.*

"It was he who brought me out through the swamp."

"He is not their man, then?"

"No. He is one of Jean Lafitte's band of pirates. He was on his way to them when his horse tossed him into the river."

Hébert gave a snorting exclamation. "A *pirate?* I'll be damned! So what do you think of your precious patient now?"

Chapter Eighteen

"Marie-Thérèse!" Annalise Bourget and Sister Mathilde stood side by side in the doorway, Annalise's bright silk dress, coat and little hat, with its waving plume, making her look like a fabled bird of paradise beside the nun's sober habit.

Annalise's welcoming cry was ecstatic. She ran to Marie-Thérèse and embraced her. Sister Mathilde smiled and turned away, leaving them.

"Annalise, it's so wonderful to see you!" Marie-Thérèse said. "Did Madame Claiborne tell you where I was?"

Annalise turned to Hébert with a wide smile and offered him a small package. "Actually, I came to bring Hébert some of those ginger cakes he likes. Sister Mathilde told me you were with him."

Marie-Thérèse looked at her brother, who was grinning fatuously. She turned back to Annalise, feeling left out. What about the fiancé in Paris? she thought indignantly.

Annalise quickly changed the subject. "It's so wonderful that you have escaped the enemy, *chérie!* Tell me, is it true that my father's plantation is also occupied?"

"Yes. The officers remain at Petit Bois, but the encampment has been moved upriver. Much of it is in your father's cane fields right now. Our crop is ruined, and I expect yours looks just like it.''

"Oh!" Annalise moaned.

"They are using all the horses in both stables, including my sweet Beauté, to move their heavy artillery, which they drag over the young cane shoots."

"Poor Beauté!" Annalise said. "But you are safe! I am so glad to see you, *chérie!* You must tell me every single thing that happened to you. Tell me about your handsome spy!"

Hébert snorted, but Annalise rushed on, "Did he fall in love with you?"

It was a typical Annalise remark, and it meant nothing, but Marie-Thérèse felt such pain that she could not answer.

Annalise seemed not to notice. She asked, "What did he do when the British came?"

"Yes," Hébert said. "Tell us what happened."

Marie-Thérèse moistened her dry lips. "He was captured, too."

Annalise exclaimed, "But wasn't he one of them?"

Marie-Thérèse continued, before Annalise could think of more questions, "Hébert, I was proud of you. You knew immediately what you had to do, and you did it. I picked up your musket, and would have shot the first officer who entered the house, but Jacques—*M'sieu* Jacques—stopped me. It was just as well. Had I fired, the British would have killed us both. He knew that and grabbed the musket from me."

Annalise gasped. "He *was* their spy, then? Did he lead the British to Petit Bois?"

Hébert gave another little snort. "He was no spy, Annalise. He is a Baratarian."

Annalise looked at her friend's stricken expression and said, "But he rescued you, didn't he? How romantic! Do you care for him, *chérie?*"

"A pirate?" Marie-Thérèse exclaimed. "It makes me ill to think of such a thing!" She closed her lips tightly. She would say no more about her weeks in captivity.

As for the night in the swamp, she could never speak of it, not even to her brother or her best friend. She wanted to think of it as a bad dream. She wanted to deny that it had ever happened, any of it, the terrible fight with Gama and the joyous lovemaking that had followed.

But it could not be denied. She knew that night would always be in her memory to bewitch and haunt her.

She said, "I'm staying with Madame Claiborne, and I have her carriage. I must go."

"Then I will see you there tomorrow," Annalise said cheerfully.

"I'll return," Marie-Thérèse promised Hébert.

"I'll be joining Papa on the battlefield any day," he told her, unwrapping the package of cakes her friend had brought him.

"May *le bon Dieu* keep you safe," Annalise said softly, reaching out to help him with the package.

Marie-Thérèse left them, feeling very much alone.

The next morning, Marie-Thérèse descended the stairs to find Madame Claiborne's salon filled with a twittering congregation of women dressed in fashionable morning gowns, drinking coffee from small china cups and tearing cotton fabric into strips that they rolled up for use as bandages. They chattered as they worked, their tongues as busy as their fingers, and their soft, high voices made a kind of musical obligato that came to an abrupt end when Marie-Thérèse hesitated in the doorway.

All conversation ceased, and a hush fell over the salon. She knew most of the women present. They were the wives and daughters of the most prominent citizens of New Orleans, and she had entertained many of them at Petit Bois.

"You all know Mademoiselle Dufret." Madame Claiborne said. "Her brother, although wounded, heroically brought us word of the British landing. How is your brother, my dear?"

"He is recovering, *merci, madame.*"

"I am so glad. What a brave young man! *Mademoiselle* has escaped from the British, who occupied Petit Bois," she explained to her guests. "Her servants are still at the plantation and she will be my guest while her father and brother are fighting with the brigade."

All eyes were on her, and for a long moment no one said anything. Marie-Thérèse could feel the strain in the room. Then a woman asked, "Is it true that the British have occupied other plantations downriver beside Petit Bois?"

"*Oui, madame.* They are encamped on both of the plantations that adjoin my father's land." Marie-Thérèse told her. "They have enlarged the Jumonville plantation infirmary to take care of their wounded and have moved their bivouac upriver, where they have installed heavy artillery."

"Cannons!" a fearful voice said.

"Did you see the burning of the *Carolina?*" another guest wanted to know.

"Indeed I did, but not before I thought I would be killed by her cannons. Many cannonballs sailed over my house and fell on our cane fields."

A shocked murmur rippled through the room.

"And what can you tell us of the British men?" Madame Roquefort, a small, dark woman with a rather homely face, asked. The question was so pointed as to be subtly insulting.

"There are a great many of them," Marie-Thérèse answered. "And more keep coming through the swamp from the British fleet. They are also bringing in very large guns from their ships."

Madame Roquefort persisted. "But what kind of men are they?"

"I know only the high-ranking officers who made Petit Bois their headquarters, and I do not speak English. But they seem to be well-educated gentlemen, and many of them speak French as well as we do—"

"Gentlemen!" exclaimed one of Madame Roquefort's friends. "Is it a gentleman who promises his soldiers 'booty and beauty' if they capture New Orleans?" A murmur of agreement spread through the women listening. "I have it on good authority that this is the British army's slogan. If they capture the city, none of us will be safe!"

A young woman across the room cried dramatically, "I carry a small dagger in my reticule. I will kill myself before I will submit to being ravished by the British beasts!"

A kind of hysteria ran through the salon in the wake of her words.

"I am sure they intend to empty our warehouses of every last hogshead of sugar and every last bale of cotton," Marie-Thérèse said bitterly, "and I am certain that they will help themselves to everything we own. The general who occupied Petit Bois helped himself to my father's wines and stores, and anything else that caught his fancy. He admitted that British ladies, who remain on a vessel of the fleet, look forward to moving into the river plantation houses they have heard so much about."

Indignant exclamations broke from many lips.

Marie-Thérèse continued, "But I never heard anyone boast of the women he would ravish. Nor did I hear any officer use that slogan."

"I have it on the best authority," the woman insisted.

"The general respected my position as his hostess and a member of a Creole family," Marie-Thérèse said stiffly.

"Are you asking us to believe that you spent weeks with all those British soldiers and escaped being molested—you, one of New Orleans's loveliest young women?"

"Merci, madame," Marie-Thérèse said, with irony. "I did not say I was not molested. One night a young officer who had indulged too freely in my father's port came to the window of my chamber and began picking the lock. I sent my maid, who slept in my room, for the *pot de chambre,* and when he finally managed to open the window, we threw its contents in his face."

There was a startled gasp from several women, then some titters.

"You should have heard him!" Marie-Thérèse continued with spirit. "His curses woke his fellow officers, who came pouring out of their chambers onto the *galerie,* and when they realized what had happened, they laughed so hard that he slunk off like a whipped dog." Marie-Thérèse's infectious laugh rang out, full of the satisfaction of that moment, and soon the roomful of women joined her in gales of laughter.

The strain she had felt in the salon was dissipated in their frank enjoyment of the British officer's discomfiture. For the first time Marie-Thérèse felt welcome, and the women seated nearest her began showing her how they were rolling the bandages. Madame Claiborne gave her a tiny smile of encouragement and returned to her task of distributing squares of muslin to the workers.

A few moments later, Annalise arrived and shrieked her delight at seeing Marie-Thérèse again. She immediately began peppering her with more questions, but in her enthusiasm gave Marie-Thérèse little opportunity to answer them, and Marie-Thérèse was grateful.

Later, after the older women had left, Annalise accompanied her to her chamber, where she made herself comfortable, propped up against the pillows on the bed. "Now, tell me all about that fascinating pirate!"

With a pang in her breast, Marie-Thérèse lied to her friend. "There is nothing to tell."

Annalise looked both wise and mischievous. "I think you're in love with him, *chérie.*"

Her friend knew her too well. But she could not admit her feeling for a man who attacked and stole from innocent passengers aboard merchant ships. Marie-Thérèse seized the offensive. "What do you know about love?" she demanded. "I thought you were engaged to be married. Why are you carrying cakes to my brother?"

"Because he is a hero," Annalise said, laughing. "Hébert knows it means nothing."

"I hope so, Annalise. He is very young and impressionable."

"And very sweet," her friend said.

Annalise left to go home soon after that, and Marie-Thérèse walked downstairs with her. Madame Claiborne was in the deserted salon with one of her maids, who was gathering up the supplies and putting them away for tomorrow's workers.

Annalise asked, slyly, "Has Marie-Thérèse told you, *madame,* that the British spy she was left behind to nurse is not a spy at all, but one of Monsieur Lafitte's band? Isn't that exciting?"

"Indeed?" Madame Claiborne exclaimed. "Then I am not surprised that he helped her escape the British. The Baratarians are well versed in stealth and cunning. After all, where would we have been these past years without the goods they have smuggled through the blockade for us?"

"Exactly!" Annalise said, laughing.

"They are patriots, too," Madame Claiborne said. "Monsieur Lafitte himself is now attached to General Jackson's advisory staff, and my husband is very happy that the Baratarians are helping in the defense of the city. He says their supplies of ammunition and their experience in warfare could make the difference in whether we can fight off the British attack."

"How can the governor join up with *pirates?*" Marie-Thérèse asked passionately. "A man like Jean Lafitte is beyond the pale!"

"Perhaps," Annalise admitted, "but wouldn't you rather have his fighting men on our side than face them in the British ranks?"

"Ah, yes," Madame Claiborne said. She added, with a slight flush, "I once met Monsieur Lafitte. He is a charming man."

"You met the pirate Lafitte?" Marie-Thérèse exclaimed, disbelieving. "How could that happen, *madame?* Surely you did not visit that place in the bayous where he offers his smuggled goods for sale?"

"And slaves," Annalise put in.

"The place they call the Temple? No, although some of my friends have seen it. No, I was visiting at a plantation downriver from New Orleans, and a strange man who was traveling the bayou stopped in and asked for my host's hospitality. His boat had suffered some misfortune, which I have forgotten. Anyway, he was invited to spend the night. He introduced himself as Monsieur Clement, or some such name, and I found him to be a delightful dinner partner, much traveled and a great conversationalist, with the most polished manners. It was only later that I was told I had gone in to dinner with the notorious Jean Lafitte.''

''I cannot believe that you would do that!'' Marie-Thérèse said. She was deeply disturbed.

Madame Claiborne said gently, ''Life demands many compromises of us, *ma chère.* Monsieur Lafitte may be a dangerous man to his enemies, but that is all the more reason for having him as a friend at a time like this.''

''A friend,'' Marie-Thérèse cried, ''who is the murderer of my mother and my sister!''

''I am sorry for you, *chérie.* But you do not know that for certain, do you?''

Marie-Thérèse said stiffly, ''Forgive me, *madame,* but I cannot discuss this subject. Will you excuse me, please?'

''*Au revoir,* dear Marie-Thérèse,'' Annalise said sadly, but Marie-Thérèse had already turned and was running up the stairs.

That night the nightmare returned. She saw the schooner being boarded by swarthy pirates who slashed the crew with their swords, forcing them over the rail. Blood ran everywhere. Adorée ran screaming from a black-bearded ruffian who chased her to the stern of the ship and grabbed her. But Adorée slipped out of his grasp and climbed the rail. With a terrible shriek, she jumped into the bloody sea.

''Adorée!'' Marie-Thérèse wailed.

''*Chérie!* Wake up, my dear! Wake up!'' Madame Claiborne, wrapped in a blue silk robe, was bending over her, gently pressing her shoulder. ''What is it, child? What is the matter?''

Marie-Thérèse came fully awake and became aware of a familiar stickiness between her legs. She sighed deeply and said, ''Nothing is the matter.''

There was no child. She could forget Jacques completely. Irrationally, she felt a deep sense of loss.

"If I can help you—" Madame Claiborne said, with loving concern.

"It was a nightmare, *madame*. I was dreaming of my sister."

"Ah, *ma pauvre petite*. You know you can tell me anything. If you want to talk about it..."

"There is nothing to tell," Marie-Thérèse insisted wearily, "because I know nothing. I'm sorry I wakened you, *madame*."

Madame Claiborne bent and kissed her hair, caressing her with soothing words for a few moments, then left her. Marie-Thérèse stared bleakly into the darkness of her room.

In the morning she went to the Ursuline convent and offered her services as a volunteer nurse. Hébert had left to report to General Jackson's headquarters. Sister Mathilde thanked her and said she would welcome her help when the British attacked and the defenders began sending more wounded men to the city.

There was no need, she said, for her to come now.

Reluctantly Marie-Thérèse went back to the governor's residence to roll bandages and wait.

Chapter Nineteen

The British marched at dawn the next morning, in a heavy fog. Bugles called, drums tapped a *rat-a-tat* and fifes played as they marched toward the American line. When they were within range, the Americans fired.

Behind the barricade Jacques reloaded his musket and sighted along its barrel. The scene before him was like something out of hell. Smoke and fog obscured the battlefield, but it was a smoke lit lividly by flashes from the big guns firing death and destruction into the advancing ranks of British redcoats.

They came in waves, marching in ranks into the deadly cannon fire with what Jacques thought was a sublime but incredibly foolish bravery. General Jackson had ordered all the buildings on the Chalmette plantation dynamited so that the British would have no place to hide from his army's deadly fire. But the British made little attempt to seek cover. They came marching across the destroyed fields in arrogant self-confidence.

Jacques held his fire, as the riflemen had been ordered to do, for the straggling survivors of the cannon fire. Few of them reached the American barricade.

On each side of Jacques were members of the Lafitte organization, their position central in the line. Some of them were firing cannons the Baratarians had brought. A little distance away, to the right, were cannons manned by men in the blue uniform of the Louisiana Brigade.

As Jacques glanced that way, he saw a burly redcoat break ranks and race toward the American barricade. Incredibly, he reached and clambered up it in a desperate attempt to silence a big gun. He had a bayonet affixed to his musket, and he charged a Louisiana artilleryman who carried only a pistol at his belt.

A second Louisianian, a youth, used his musket like a fencing sword to thrust the bayonet up, and the gunner scrambled away. The British soldier brought his weapon down on the second Creole's arms, causing him to drop his musket, which tumbled into the ditch at the base of the rampart. The youth grabbed the redcoat's weapon, trying to wrest it out of his hands, and Jacques held his fire as they struggled in hand-to-hand combat.

The redcoat held on to the weapon for his life, dragging the young Creole over the barricade. They both fell into the ditch. With cannonballs screaming over them, the redcoat got to his feet first and raised his bayonet over the prone soldier in blue.

As he aimed his musket, Jacques recognized the youth who was about to be run through. He was Hébert Dufret, Marie-Thérèse's brother. Jacques fired, and the redcoat fell on Dufret. Without stopping to consider the risk, Jacques threw down his musket and leapt from the barricade into the ditch. Stooping, he ran under the barrage of cannonballs to the fallen youth.

He rolled the redcoat off Dufret and dragged Hébert up and over the barricade to safety. It was only after he picked up his musket that he thought, *And this is the young fop whose sister warned me was looking for an excuse to kill me!*

Dufret was in shock and still panting from the exertion of his struggle with the redcoat. When he looked up and recognized Jacques, he said, "You?"

"*Oui, c'est moi,*" Jacques said, drily.

"*Merci beaucoup, monsieur.*" His words were heartfelt.

Jacques looked at the youth, who had lost most of his arrogance and was still pale from his close encounter with death. His resemblance to Marie-Thérèse was startling. "I did it for your sister, Dufret," Jacques said roughly.

Hébert grimaced and said, "I won't forget this, *monsieur.*"

Jacques was hearing her voice saying, *I can no longer bear the touch of your hands.* Nothing had ever hurt him as much as those few words had, coming at a time when his body still throbbed with the feel of her soft warmth, and when for the first time his heart had made a commitment.

He said harshly, "I'm afraid you've lost your musket, Dufret. I'd advise you to take better care if they issue you another." He stalked off.

When the cannonade began at dawn on the eighth of January, the roar of the big guns could clearly be heard in the city, nine miles away. In twos and threes, the Creole ladies and a few American friends arrived at Madame Claiborne's to tear and roll bandages, as usual. One who had driven by St. Louis Cathedral reported that it was crowded with frightened women and children and old men, gathered to take part in a mass for victory. Everyone seemed to sense that this was the big push that the British had been preparing for.

The house rattled and shook from the constant explosions, and Marie-Thérèse who had seen the destruction the big guns could wreak, shuddered each time she heard one. She prayed for Papa and for Hébert, and she could not help wondering about Jacques, who must also be in the thick of the battle. Had she saved his life only to have him lose it on the battlefield?

He was a pirate, she reminded herself, who had himself caused death and untold grief. Why should she mourn for him? But the thought of his death was intolerable.

She prayed for his life, and for the strength to stop loving him.

At first, everyone in Madame Claiborne's salon flinched at the sounds of explosive cannon fire, but as the day advanced and the sounds of battle continued unabated, some of the women sat silent, touching their rosaries and praying as they worked. Rolling bandages was all they could do while downriver, on the ruined plantations, men were dying.

Others wept while they worked, and some were crying so hard they could scarcely whisper their prayers for their loved ones. All had sons or husbands or fathers and brothers in the battle, and the longer the cannonade went on, the more their fears increased.

Fears for themselves fueled hysteria in some; fear of fire and death, or worse, at the hands of the enemy. The great guns roared until late afternoon, when there was an ominous silence. Madame Claiborne's ladies waited in numb terror for the British to overrun the city.

Then a messenger arrived, and Madame Claiborne took his message in the foyer. When she came back into the salon, bright roses in her cheeks, her voice crackled with excitement.

"The British have asked for a truce," she said, "to allow both sides to pick up their wounded. General Jackson requests that all available carts and carriages come to the battlefield to carry the injured soldiers back to the convent and the other hospital sites."

"He is asking us to come to the battlefield?" the young woman, who had revealed that she carried a dagger, asked in horror.

Madame Claiborne's dark eyes flashed. "There is a truce, *mesdames!* Are you not willing to go for your loved ones? I shall take my groom and my carriage," she declared, "and make as many trips as are necessary to bring our brave soldiers here where we can help them recover from their injuries."

Inspired by her courage, each woman with a waiting carriage volunteered to follow her example. Marie-Thérèse and Annalise set off on foot for the convent to offer their help there.

They walked quickly through the deserted streets with Betté following a step behind. When they reached the convent, wounded soldiers were already being carried in from a bloody wagon. Many were unconscious, but some screamed with pain as they were lifted out. Marie-Thérèse's throat tightened. What if Jacques was one of those inert bodies? Or Papa or Hébert? She looked from them to Annalise, who had blanched. They hurried up the walk from the convent gate, following a trail of blood dripping from the man being carried ahead of them.

Once inside the convent doors, their ears were assailed by a horrendous noise. All around them men were moaning and weeping and groaning. Some screamed as the nuns and the women helping them bend over the beds, trying to undress them and stanch their bleeding. Sister Mathilde looked up from a bed with a pair of bloody scissors in her hand and saw them.

"Thank you for coming. You can help us get the men into the beds." Her hands were bloody and her habit was stained, but her voice was steady and calm. "You'll have to get them out of their uniforms so that the doctor can see their injuries. Pick up a pair of scissors from the table there, and some alcohol to clean the wounds."

There was blood everywhere. Marie-Thérèse was glad she'd had nursing training from Mattie on the plantation. Annalise was deathly pale and her widened eyes looked sick.

"Sit down and put your head on your knees," Marie-Thérèse ordered, literally forcing her friend to take a chair.

"I'm so ashamed," Annalise whispered, her eyes tightly closed. "It's . . . the blood . . ."

"It's the first shock of seeing it," Marie-Thérèse said. "You just have to ignore it. You can do it."

There was no time to stay longer with her. More wounded were arriving, and the nuns were almost running ahead of the litters to turn down the beds. Marie-Thérèse picked up a pair of scissors, poured alcohol on a bandage and went to work. When she glanced back a few minutes later, she saw Annalise get to her feet and pick up scissors and bandages and advance cautiously across the floor, which was now slippery with blood.

Every time new wounded were brought in, Marie-Thérèse looked for Jacques, certain that he would be among them sooner or later. She wondered if she could bear it. All through the long night her anxiety built. At dawn, exhausted, she threw a blanket down where volunteers had cleaned the stone floor and fell instantly asleep, while the work of the doctors and nurses went on around her.

She slept for two hours, then rose and joined them again.

The big guns were still quiet. She did not see Papa or Hébert among the wounded, nor Jacques, although they might have been brought in while she slept. She wished she could search through the convent for them, but there were too many who needed immediate attention.

A weak voice said, *"Mademoiselle?"* and Marie-Thérèse looked across several cots to find the speaker.

He looked very different out of his red coat, but she could not fail to recognize the golden hair and those intense blue eyes. She went to his side and said. "A British soldier here?"

"My own army left me for dead," Lieutenant Roland Bacon muttered. "I wish I were."

"Nonsense!" Marie-Thérèse said briskly. She pulled down the sheet and looked at the bandage on his side. It was not bloody. "You've been patched up. You'll be all right." She hoped it was true. At least his wound was not yet infected.

"Nothing will ever be right again," he said, looking at her in despair. "I saw the Royal Highland Fusiliers, our finest regiment, mown down. The other regiments, experienced fighting men who defeated Napoleon all decimated. We marched abreast across the fields into that cannon fire, and we fell like a picket fence in a high wind. The battlefield was littered with dead, all British."

"You mustn't talk," Marie-Thérèse told him. "Rest now."

"The Americans never left their barricade," he said bitterly. "They stayed where they were protected and picked us off one by one if we survived the artillery blasts.... My general is dead."

"The general?" she said, shaken in spite of herself.

"I saw him ... fall." His voice faltered.

"Don't try to talk," Marie-Thérèse said gently. "Your task now is to get well."

His gaze fastened on her. "You don't hold a grudge against me, *mademoiselle?*" he asked.

"Not if you don't hold one against me."

He smiled faintly, but despair lay deep in his eyes. "My general rode into the artillery fire at the head of our regiment. We were staggering back from the terrible barrage, and he tried to rally the troops. His horse was hit, too, and it fell on him. They carried him off the field, but I was near enough to see . . . he was mortally wounded."

Marie-Thérèse thought of the woman who had worn long white gloves to have her portrait painted and was now awaiting the general with the British fleet, expecting to become the new mistress of Petit Bois. "Rest now," she said gently.

He closed his eyes and said in a flat voice, "You have defeated England's finest."

"The battle is over?" Marie-Thérèse exclaimed, hope leaping in her breast.

His blue eyes opened, but the distant look in them told her that what he was saying was not for her. It was something he had to put into words for his own understanding.

"It couldn't happen, but it did. We brought fifteen thousand trained fighting men from England, and a handful of backwoodsmen, fishermen and pirates defeated us with their underhanded Indian ways."

"Pirates?" Marie-Thérèse whispered. Had Jacques survived?

"Incredible marksmen," he whispered, looking suddenly faint with exhaustion. "Like the Kentuckians. Not a wasted musket ball."

"You are fortunate you survived," she said firmly. "I pray my father and my brother were as lucky." *And Jacques.*

"I'm sure they were . . . luckier," he said. "I am . . . a prisoner of war."

"You must be still, *monsieur,* so that your wound can heal." She poured a spoonful of laudanum for him, which he took without protest, and left him to attend to a soldier nearby who was begging for water.

When she saw Sister Mathilde a few minutes later, she asked, "Is it true that we have won the battle?"

"It has not been confirmed," the nun said, her fingers going to her rosary, "but we have been told that the British have suffered great losses. They are still removing their wounded and dead from the battlefield."

"Have you seen Papa, or my brother?"

"No, Marie-Thérèse, but they could have been taken to the barracks or one of the chapels, you know."

"I want to pray for them, Sister, but there is no time—"

"Your work here is a prayer God hears, my child."

Jacques. His name was a prayer on her breath. Pirate or not, he must not die.

A dozen times as she moved among the cots in the convent, Marie-Thérèse saw a shock of overlong black hair and the strong line of a jaw that made her heart leap to her throat. But when she looked for the thin line of a scar running down his cheek, or the way his eyebrow tilted upward with secret laughter, she was always disappointed. It was never Jacques.

It was an odd thing, but the nightmares that had begun again after she came to Madame Claiborne's had changed. Over and over she lived through the terrible attack on *Maman*'s ship, but the pirates were not the swarthy brutes she had imagined before. They were handsome men with a thin curve of a scar on one cheek who looked at her with a bold sidelong glance that held a hint of laughter.

One night she dreamed Jacques was dead, and she woke up sobbing. When she slept again, she dreamed she was back in her room at Petit Bois, wrapped in his arms, enjoying the mysterious delights of love, and she awakened filled with shame.

She wouldn't love him. She couldn't!

At odd times, as she worked, an image would flash before her eyes. She would see that dark, dangerous look that had first challenged her and wonder how she could have given such a man her heart. Then she would remember the incredible sweetness of his lips. Would she ever forget?

Annalise found her in the refectory when she stopped for some lunch. "I have some great news for you!" Annalise's eyes were glowing, and Marie-Thérèse's heart skipped a beat.

"Papa and Hébert?" she cried. Who could tell her whether or not Jacques had survived? Would she ever know?

"Well, no. That is, I don't know," Annalise said, regretfully. "But your Gabriel is safe."

"He is not my Gabriel!" Marie-Thérèse snapped, but Annalise ignored her protest.

"He has been helping bring the wounded in." Her brow clouded. "But he had sad news, Marie-Thérèse. Darling Etienne Picou was killed instantly by a musket ball."

"Oh, no!" Marie-Thérèse cried. Etienne, so merry, such an outrageous flirt, so much fun—dead?

She embraced Annalise, and they shed a tear for their friend, then returned to work in their separate rooms in the convent.

That evening the big guns were still silent, but a rumor ran through the convent that the American forces under Captain Morgan had been forced to withdraw. If the reports were true, this was a victory for the British.

At nightfall, Sister Mathilde told Annalise and Marie-Thérèse to go home and get a good night's sleep and come back in the morning. While Betté prepared her bath, Madame Claiborne told her she had received news that her father and Hébert were uninjured, and Marie-Thérèse went to bed feeling much relieved.

But she had scarcely closed her eyes in exhausted sleep when they flew open again. She had heard the rumble of Jacques's deep laugh as clearly as if her head were laid against his chest the way it had been the night she told him about Lieutenant Bacon. As angry as he was, he had been able to laugh at the way she and Doula defeated the Briton. She felt a surprising pang of love.

But to feel love for him was to betray her mother and her sister. She could not love such a man. The very thought sickened her.

The next day, rumors of a British withdrawal ran through the convent, unbelievable at first. It was too good to be true! Then she looked up from a grizzled Tennessee rifleman who had taken a ball in his shoulder to see her father, looking grand in his uniform, standing beside her. "Papa!" she cried, tears of relief flooding her eyes. "Oh, I have been so worried!"

He embraced her tenderly. "Are you well, *ma fille?*"

"Yes, Papa."

"I'm proud of what you are doing," he said.

"Hébert?" she asked anxiously.

"I don't know how he managed it, but he has come through without a scratch."

"Thank God," she breathed. But who could she ask about Jacques Bonnard? "Is it true that we won the battle, Papa?"

"It's true that the British largely decamped in the night. But General Jackson expects them to attack from another direction. In fact, several of their gunboats have come up the river and are now attacking Fort Philip. My regiment has been deployed to Chef Menteur to guard that entrance to the city. Lake Borgne is too shallow for their vessels. That is why they made the incredible trip through the swamps to Petit Bois, a folly that cost them the battle.... I have little time, *ma fille,* but I had to assure myself you were well."

"Give my love to Hébert, Papa."

He kissed her and left.

The next day, the bells of St. Louis Cathedral began a joyous pealing. Soon the vessels in port joined in the clamor, blowing their whistles and tooting their horns. Word passed like a swift wind through the convent: The British had lost three of their top commanders on the battlefield and were engaged in transporting their wounded back through the swamp to their fleet. In spite of General Jackson's warnings, many believed it meant the British were abandoning their attempt to take the city and then move up the Mississippi.

Later Marie-Thérèse encountered Dr. Boudreau as he was leaving the convent. He greeted her kindly, saying, "I was distressed to hear you were still at Petit Bois when the British invaded. Was it bad for you, *mademoiselle?*"

"It could have been worse," she said. "I was not harmed."

"I'm glad to hear that. I've been ordered to take charge of the hospital at Jumonville, where the British have left about seventy of their wounded instead of trying to take them back to their ships."

"They are being cared for," Marie-Thérèse said. "Mattie and her daughter, Doula, are at Jumonville. Please tell them you have seen me and that I am well."

"It will be my pleasure, *mademoiselle.*"

Some friends were with Madame Claiborne when Marie-Thérèse brought Annalise home with her from the convent that evening. The women were full of excited admiration for their hero, General Jackson.

"Annalise!" one of them cried. "You're the very person we want to see!"

"Me, *madame?*"

"Yes, you. The abbé is going to conduct a mass to give thanks for our victory, and we want to honor General Jackson. A triumphal arch will be erected in the place d'Armes—"

"A temporary one," one of her friends put in.

"In his honor. He insists that it is premature to speak of victory, and that he will not celebrate until the British have left Louisiana, but we have to make our plans, don't we?"

"This is what we have planned." Her friend took over the recital. "The Louisiana Brigade will furnish an honor guard to form a double line from the landing to the triumphal arch. From there to the cathedral our loveliest Creole maidens, each one representing a state of the union, will form another double line."

"They will wear white, with blue veils hanging from flower wreaths on their hair," the first woman said.

"Behind each *jeune fille* will be a standard bearing a shield with the coat of arms of her state," another put in.

"The general will walk between the honor guards to the arch, where he will be crowned with the laurel wreath of victory—by some children, I think. Cherubs. Then Miss Louisiana will give the speech to express our appreciation."

"Then General Jackson will walk between the young women to the cathedral, where the abbé will give another speech and escort him in to hear the mass."

"And that evening," her friend cried, "there will be a victory ball at the French Exchange, with dancing in the ballroom upstairs and supper downstairs. It will be a ball to remember, that one!''

While Annalise and Marie-Thérèse regarded her questioningly, she finished. ''We have chosen you, Annalise, to represent Louisiana at the cathedral.''

Annalise looked at her in shock. ''Me? Give a speech? Oh, no, *madame,* not I! Marie-Thérèse is better suited—She is more accustomed—''

''The housekeeper to an enemy general?'' The gentle question came from Madame Duvallier, Gabriel's mother. ''I think not, *chérie.*'' She looked at Marie-Thérèse and said kindly, ''I'm sure you did what you had to do to survive, *chère* Marie-Thérèse, but surely you realize that you are not the proper person to express our profound admiration to General Jackson.''

Marie-Thérèse's cheeks flushed. *If we were men, I could call you out for this!* she thought. She would have said it aloud, had not Annalise spoken first in acute embarrassment.

''*Madame,* I cannot believe you mean that!'' her friend exclaimed. ''Marie-Thérèse was a prisoner of war! She deserves a heroine's reward. No one is more fit—''

Marie-Thérèse met Madame Duvallier's implacable black gaze and could feel her heart beating hard with fear and rage. ''What Annalise means to ask, *madame,* is who is more fit than I to salute General Jackson, who has had to defend his lady's reputation—with duels, no less!—against just such slander?''

Madame Duvallier gasped. ''It is not slander! Everyone knows that the general married a divorced woman, and her divorce not yet final! I, for one, will not recognize her.''

''Madame Jackson will not be taking part in the presentation in the place d'Armes,'' the governor's wife said in a conciliatory tone. "We do not yet know whether *monsieur* will accept for the ball."

Marie-Thérèse turned to her friend and said firmly, "Of course you must give the speech, Annalise. You will do it perfectly." She curtsied to Madame Claiborne. "Good night, *madame*," she said, then turned to the others. "Good night, *mesdames*." She left the salon and ran up the stairs.

Alone in her room, she allowed her rage full rein. She was a proud young woman, proud of her position as her father's daughter. The unpleasant truth was that her reputation had been tarnished by the things that had happened to her, just as Rachel Jackson's good name had been tarnished because she left an alcoholic husband who mistreated her for a brilliant general who loved her enough to fight for her. Everyone knew the story.

Before the British had captured her, Madame Duvallier would have been overjoyed to hear Marie-Thérèse had accepted Gabriel's proposal. Today, Gabriel's mother had made it clear she would not willingly welcome her as a daughter-in-law.

Marie-Thérèse had once been the most sought-after heiress in New Orleans. She had known it without really caring about it. She had not been interested in getting married. But now?

She tried to control her emotions and assess her situation. She was reasonably sure that she was still an heiress, even though Petit Bois had been damaged by the British occupation. But she was no longer above reproach, although not for the reasons the gossips imagined. It was a chastening, indeed humiliating, realization to one who had taken her impeccable position in society for granted.

Gabriel would stand by his marriage proposal, she knew. It infuriated her to admit that marrying him was probably a necessity if she hoped to regain respectability! She paced her room, burning with helpless anger.

"Never!" she raged. "Never!" She would never marry for such a reason.

Oh, Jacques, Jacques, I gave you my love....

Chapter Twenty

Although the British army had withdrawn from the battlefield, rumors were rife that they would attack by other routes to the city. General Jackson held his troops battle-ready and moved more regiments to the forts and the pass at Chef Menteur.

But the city was euphoric over the general's success at Chalmette, and the plans for a mass of thanksgiving and a victory ball were readied for the day when the British force would have completely withdrawn from Louisiana. Marie-Thérèse and Annalise, like the other Creole women, dug lengths of silk out of trunks and armoires and engaged *modistes* to make new gowns. Officers of the army and their aides were promised leave, and word went through the city that General Jackson and his lady would attend. The women who came to Madame Claiborne's to plan the ball talked of nothing else.

"Will he really bring her?"

"But of course he will bring her! He defends her fiercely."

"Well, I, for one, will not recognize her!" It was Madame Duvallier speaking.

"You may be challenged to a duel, *madame,*" Marie-Thérèse could not resist saying wickedly.

"I trust you will not presume to be so rude to our guest of honor's lady!" Madame Claiborne chided Gabriel's mother, with a hint of steel beneath her ever-gracious manner. "At this ball to honor our heroes, there may be many whom you would not invite to your home."

"I dare say," Madame Duvallier sniffed, and Marie-Thérèse felt the snub as if it were personally addressed to her.

But on the day word came that the last of the British forces had departed from Louisiana and the date of the special mass and victory ball was set, Marie-Thérèse received a message from her father saying that Gabriel had been granted leave to attend the ball and would escort her, together with Hébert and Annalise. Papa's own carriage would be in use, because he was inviting his good friend, Madame Serbin, to accompany him. Regrettably, there would not be room for the young people.

"Just like that, he assigns me an escort!" Marie-Thérèse fumed to her friend as they worked side by side in the convent, where a few patients remained. "I don't want to go to the ball with Gabriel!"

"Why ever not?" Annalise asked her. They were preparing food trays for other volunteer nurses to carry to the patients.

"Because he will talk about marriage again, and I don't intend to encourage him, even if Papa does favor his suit."

"*Mon Dieu*, Marie-Thérèse! You don't have to accept him just because he escorts you to the ball! This is one you surely don't want to miss. It's an historic social event, *chérie,* one we will tell our grandchildren about. What does it matter how we get there?"

"I know, Annalise. It would be a pity to miss it." But Marie-Thérèse sighed.

Annalise looked at her with concern. "As for marriage," she said thoughtfully, "you could do worse than Gabriel."

"Annalise, you saw how hateful his mother was to me! She acts as if I were tainted by my imprisonment by the enemy."

"Well, fortunately for you, Gabriel is not a man who is under his mother's thumb."

"But why should I marry at all?" Marie-Thérèse argued. Her insides churned at the thought. "You know I'm happy at Petit Bois, looking after Hébert and Papa."

"Hébert will bring home a wife before many more years. She will be mistress of Petit Bois, because he is the heir."

"Papa will still need me. " Hébert's wife will be young and unused to his ways." Marie-Thérèse thought about Jacques and felt a knifing pain. "I expect to grow old looking after Papa."

"What if your father should marry Madame Serbin? Wouldn't she expect to assume the management of his household? And be his hostess?"

Marie-Thérèse looked aghast. "Surely you're not seriously suggesting—"

"She is an extremely attractive widow, and she would bring some property with her. You know it could happen."

Marie-Thérèse glared at her. She did not even want to talk about the possibility of her father remarrying. The very idea dulled her anticipation of pleasure at the ball.

The dress Marie-Thérèse's *modiste* was making for her was a deep rose silk with tiny puff sleeves above a square *décolletage* that ended just below where the gentle swell of her bosom began. The long, slender lines of the skirt ended in a froth of ruffles that fanned out gently when she whirled in a dance step.

"It is very becoming, *mademoiselle*," the *modiste* said at the final fitting, adding, not without envy, "You will have a wonderful evening."

"*Merci, madame,*" Marie-Thérèse said, but she did not expect the evening to be wonderful. Not with Gabriel.

Betté helped her dress and had just finished recombing her hair when Madame Claiborne knocked at her door. "You look lovely, *ma chère,*" she said. "The governor and I are leaving now to call for General and Madame Jackson. I have instructed Roman to serve wine when your friends arrive."

"*Merci, madame.*"

A few minutes after they left, Gabriel's carriage entered the drive. He had Hébert and Annalise with him, and they all came into the house and were offered wine by Madame Claiborne's servant. Annalise exclaimed over Marie-Thérèse's gown. She herself was wearing a creamy buttercup satin that brought out highlights in her brown hair, and the two young men were sleek and trim in the dress uniforms of their rank.

Gabriel raised his goblet of wine. "To our two lovely *mesdemoiselles!*"

"I'll drink to that," Hébert said.

Gabriel lifted his glass again, this time tilting it toward Hébert. "And to our closer relationship, Dufret!"

Marie-Thérèse raised an eyebrow at Annalise, who gave her an encouraging smile.

Gabriel said, "*Chère* Marie-Thérèse, you look like a dewy rosebud in that gown. I think I am beginning to compose a poem. But it won't do you justice. You *are* a poem this evening."

Annalise rolled her eyes comically, and Marie-Thérèse struggled to keep from laughing. But she could not prevent herself from tapping her foot in irritation.

Hébert noticed and said, "Old fellow, our ladies are more interested in the ball than in chatting with us," then finished his wine in a single gulp. He was feeling very adult, Marie-Thérèse saw, in the company of Gabriel and Annalise.

"Exactly," Gabriel said. Betté came forward with Marie-Thérèse's cape and threw it over her shoulders.

She clutched it around her and preceded Gabriel out of the door, which Betté held for them, wishing them a pleasant evening.

It was going to be a long one, Marie-Thérèse thought. She should have defied her father and refused to come with Gabriel. But if she had done that, not only Papa, but Hébert and Annalise, as well, would have been upset with her.

It had been too long since anyone had given a ball. She was determined to enjoy it in spite of everything. But tonight she must make it clear to Gabriel that she could not marry him, even if it was her father's wish. She could not marry anyone as long as she was so obsessed with Jacques Bonnard that she dreamed of him nightly. And she could tell no one why.

It looked as if all of New Orleans society, dressed in its finest, were gathered in the spacious hall. Never before had Marie-Thérèse seen such a varied array of guests.

She stood between Gabriel and her father, exchanging pleasantries with Madame Serbin as they surveyed the crowded ballroom. Hébert and Annalise were nearby.

Many of the men present were in the dress regalia of their regiment and rank, and the bewildering variety of their uniforms ranged from the magnificent to the bizarre. Some vied with the women in both the color and the richness of their costumes, but not a few represented volunteer regiments that had no official uniform, and they were as un-pretentious as the homespun they wore.

The musicians were playing, but they were drowned out by the animated conversation. The hall was ablaze with candles, but no one was dancing. All were watching the wide doorway, awaiting the entrance of General Jackson and his lady.

Through the door came the sound of footsteps on the stair, and the waiting guests tensed with anticipation. The president of the ball strode to the doorway and paused, arm raised to silence the room. When he brought his arm down sharply, it was a cue for the musicians. A drum roll sounded.

As General Jackson and his lady entered the hall, fol-lowed by Governor and Madame Claiborne, the level of noise rose. Like many other women there, Marie-Thérèse stood on tiptoe to get a glimpse of the general's Rachel. She saw a woman considerably shorter than her husband, a lit-tle plump, looking subdued in her simple gown beside his magnificent uniform, with its fringed gold epaulettes.

The sibilant whispers of the women were lost in the cheers that erupted.

"Vive Jackson! Vive le général!"

"Vive Claiborne!"

"Jackson!" the Americans shouted. "Long live the general!"

The president of the ball bowed and began a flowery speech of welcome. When it ended and General Jackson cleared his throat to respond, the hall grew very quiet.

"Ladies and gentlemen, *messieurs et mesdames,"* he said, "you do me a great honor. And I honor you for your support and your bravery in battle. I wish to thank all of you who volunteered your help in the defense of your city and America. Together we have faced great odds and won a stirring victory. The war is not yet over, but with your continued perseverance and God's help, we will prevail. Thank you.''

Again the hall erupted in shouts and whistles and clapping. After the enthusiastic response to General Jackson's words died away, the president of the ball said, "*Monsieur le général,* will you please choose the couples you would like to join you and *madame* in the first set, which will open our festivities?''

General Jackson's gaze wandered over the hall, and those who were not as tall as he craned to see whom he would choose.

"The governor, and Monsieur Livingston, of course," Monsieur Dufret said, observing the general's choices. "And who is that?''

All around her, Marie-Thérèse was hearing the murmurs—Lafitte. "Jean Lafitte?''

"It's him, all right. The pirate."

"Are you sure?''

"I guarantee it."

"I never thought to see the blackguard in this company!''

"No one knows our bayous like Lafitte. We should be glad he was with us and not the British.''

Like the others, Marie-Thérèse craned her neck to see the notorious Lafitte, a slender dark-haired man elegantly turned out. Beside her, her father said, "*Mon Dieu!* That looks like—''

It was! Marie-Thérèse felt a jolt like a blow, and her heart seemed to stop. It was indeed Jacques, standing beside his infamous friend—and General Jackson was approaching them.

Her heart was pounding. Jacques was alive and well! She crossed herself and begged forgiveness of her mother and

Adorée for her relief. He looked stunningly handsome in close-fitting cream trousers and a royal blue tailcoat over an embroidered cream waistcoat. She experienced a wave of longing so intense it was painful.

"But who's that with him?" she heard voices around her asking. "That's not Lafitte's brother."

"One of his lieutenants, no doubt."

One of his lieutenants. Lafitte, murderer of women and children. Jacques's friend. She felt an equally painful despair.

How could she destroy this exotic love that Jacques had planted in her heart? It grew like a rank weed, crowding out everything else. Nothing could kill it. She was doomed to love a man she despised.

The guest of honor was speaking again. "I wish to introduce a man whose help was very important to me in this campaign, the man who brought us seven thousand flints for the muskets you were issued. Ladies and gentlemen, the privateer Jean Lafitte."

The murmuring in the hall rose to a crescendo. A man murmured, "He's no longer a hellish bandit, eh?"

"*Mon Dieu*, he's a hero tonight!"

The general raised his voice. "And his friend, one of many brave fighters he brought us, one who I'm told made a daring rescue at great risk to himself that fateful day we turned the British back. Jacques Bonnard, will you do me the honor of joining out set?"

"I have no partner," Jacques muttered as the general turned to make another choice.

"Choose one, dolt!" Jean said before turning to address a young matron who had been eyeing him with a fascinated curiosity.

Jacques had seen Marie-Thérèse Dufret arrive with another young woman and two young dandies in the uniform of the Louisiana Brigade. She was a vision in rose silk, slender yet curvaceous, so beautiful she took his breath away. Her gown fell almost straight from just below her enchanting bosom, which swelled provocatively above her *décolletage*. Her midnight-dark hair was pulled up into a Psyche knot, which displayed the beautiful heart shape of her beloved face.

His eyes sought her out now. He felt both a pain and an immediate physical response to her beauty, and an angry red tide flowed before his eyes. She was smiling. She looked as if she were enjoying herself, and it infuriated him that she could make him suffer so keenly and be untouched herself. Who was the fop with her? Jacques had a primitive desire to smash that arrogant face.

How was he going to live without her?

He started across the room with such resolute purpose that the watching guests melted out of his way. Questioning murmurs followed him, swelling as he passed.

Marie-Thérèse watched him come in helpless terror. He looked incredibly elegant as he strode toward her. His dark hair had been trimmed, but it was still unruly, and he looked powerful and dangerous beside Hébert and Gabriel, who were both youthfully lean. He was a man to be reckoned with, a man who would be dangerous to cross.

The buzz of conversation heightened around them. "Who is she?" she heard.

"Not Marie-Thérèse Dufret!"

"*Oui!* It's Marie-Thérèse."

"The Dufret girl, who was captured by the enemy? *Non!*"

"*Mais oui!*"

He stood before her. His eyes had that look of danger that had intrigued and excited her the first time they looked on her, but they were full of something much more disturbing now.

The look that pierced her now was an accusation. It said bitterly, *You told me you loved me, but you are faithless.*

Jacques bowed before her and held out his hand, his eyes challenging her. She could not refuse him, not when he was obeying General Jackson's request and everyone was watching them. She extended nerveless fingers, feeling unreal, and he led her toward the center of the hall, where the spectators had cleared a space for their set.

The musicians launched into a minuet, and she moved in an automatic response. His gaze on her smoldered with a deep emotion as they circled in the stately dance, only their fingertips touching. He wanted her. She knew it with a thrill that shot through her body, further weakening her. He still wanted her, even if he was angry.

And hurt.

She must have hurt him deeply when she'd shrunk from him in revulsion. For the first time she was able to understand what she had done to him, at a time when he was most vulnerable, after they had been so close that night in the swamp. Closer than she had thought a man and a woman could ever be. Until he had revealed himself to be a pirate...

She burned where his fingers clasped hers, and her cheeks felt hot. As they circled each other and bowed, she tried to avoid his gaze, but she could look at no one else, and each time their eyes met she felt the force of his emotion. Yet, whatever else he felt, she knew he desired her, and that knowledge fueled her own passion for him.

As the set ended, some officers of the Tennessee regiment began calling for a jig. "No more of this la-de-da stuff!" one of them shouted. "Give us some real mountain music! After all, our general is a Tennessean!"

The musician who played the fiddle understood him, and played a few bars.

"No, no!" the Tennessean yelled. "Give us 'Possum up de Gum Tree'!"

The musician shook his head in confusion, whereupon the officer from Tennessee jumped up on the stage and said, "Give me your fiddle!" He seized it and began scraping it in a lively and, Marie-Thérèse thought, impossibly fast tempo. "Show them how to dance a jig, Old Hickory!" the fiddler cried, and the Americans cheered.

Marie-Thérèse was trapped at Jacques's side by the crowding spectators. She was fighting a flush of desire, stirred by his nearness in the warm, perfumed air. To have encountered him here in these surroundings, dressed in such elegance—it was not fair. Oh, but he was devilishly handsome!

After a shaky start, the other musicians took up the tune, and General and Madame Jackson did a jig, which, after the initial shock at seeing the tall, gaunt and usually dignified general and his plump little wife hopping up and down, so amused the Creoles that they could not help laughing at the spectacle.

Marie-Thérèse escaped Jacques's side as soon as the crowd began to form sets for a pavane, but Jacques followed her to where Hébert was talking to her father and Madame Serbin. To her consternation, Monsieur Lafitte followed Jacques, who was greeted warmly by Hébert and her father. She looked frantically for Gabriel and saw that he and Annalise had already joined a set.

Jacques was introduced to Madame Serbin, whose eyes danced with excitement as he introduced his friend. Marie-Thérèse curled her fingers into fists with tension as her father said, "Monsieur Lafitte, my children. Marie-Thérèse and Hébert."

Lafitte and Hébert bowed. Marie-Thérèse glared at her father. She would not curtsy to a pirate! But Madame Serbin was obviously enjoying the encounter.

Her father did not appear to notice Marie-Thérèse's rudeness. He began eagerly questioning Jacques about the condition of his plantation. He listened closely to what Jacques said, but he refused to be downcast.

"I believe, *messieurs,* that the United States government will reimburse those of us whose crops were destroyed by this invasion. We have all fought the enemy, but a few of us have contributed our entire profits for this year, and possibly the next."

"I hope you're right," Monsieur Lafitte said dryly. "I would like to recover some of the property that was taken when the United States Army raided my headquarters on Grande-Terre."

Marie-Thérèse was outraged, thinking of her mother's beautiful aquamarines, recovered in that raid. She would never be able to bring herself to wear those stones. Had Papa *forgotten?*

With a smoldering glance at her, Jacques said, "I can sympathize with you, Monsieur Dufret. My brigantine was one of the ships impounded by the United States government. I hope it can soon be returned to me."

When he will sail out of my life, Marie-Thérèse thought.

Madame Serbin smiled at Jacques. "You might consider going into business as an importer, *monsieur,*" she said archly. "After all, we will no longer need smugglers—is that the right word?—to bring in our supplies once a peace treaty is signed."

"The word is *privateers,*" Monsieur Lafitte said smoothly.

Jacques regarded Madame Serbin narrowly. "An interesting suggestion, *madame,* but one that would require some capital."

"See my banker," Lafitte advised, looking amused.

"Or I can introduce you to mine," Papa offered.

Marie-Thérèse gasped.

"That is generous of you, *monsieur,*" Jacques said.

"Not at all," Monsieur Dufret responded. "Thanks in part to you and your friends, we are still a democracy. That should gladden the heart of every American of French blood!"

"True!" Jacques and Lafitte said, almost together, and Hébert echoed them, "True!"

Marie-Thérèse heard them in astonishment. How could Papa talk so amiably to these pirates? And Hébert! His friendliness toward the man he had resented at Petit Bois was a complete turnabout.

She understood a moment later, when Hébert burst out, "Papa, you heard what General Jackson said about Monsieur Bonnard's bravery? It was my life that he saved at great risk to his own!"

Lafitte glanced quizzically at Jacques, but he was looking at Marie-Thérèse, his handsome head tilted to one side. She bit her lower lip to keep it from quivering. It was obvious that he hated her. Just as she should hate him, but could not.

"Is that true?" her father asked Hébert.

"It is, indeed." Hébert described in detail how Jacques had shot the redcoat who had dragged him over the barricade, and then jumped into the line of fire himself to pull Hébert back to safety. "In another instant, the Briton would have run me through with his bayonet."

Papa turned to Jacques and said, "I am forever in your debt, *monsieur*. First you bring my daughter safely through the British lines, and now you have saved my son!"

"Any one of us who saw what was happening would have fired at the redcoat," Jacques said.

"But not just anyone would have leapt into the fray to pull me to safety," Hébert said warmly.

"I shall be eternally grateful," his father repeated, with deep emotion.

Marie-Thérèse listened with growing agitation. She was confused in her feelings, grateful for what Jacques had done, but thinking angrily, "What of *Maman* and Adorée?" How could Papa forget that, and become so familiar with their murderers?

She could not. Would not!

"Will you dance again, *mademoiselle?*" A set was forming almost at her elbow, as Jacques's eyes dared her to refuse. She looked around for Gabriel, but he and Annalise had joined another set.

She said desperately, "I have promised this turn to Hébert."

"And I relinquish it to your former patient," Hébert said with a bow.

Jacques looked wickedly amused as he took her hand. "You are kind to grant me another opportunity," he said mockingly.

"My impetuous brother has left me no choice. He is awash with hero worship."

"How about a waltz?" Jacques shouted to the musicians.

"A waltz!" Marie-Thérèse gasped as Jacques put his arm around her waist.

She could protest no more, since he was already whirling her around the floor, the musicians having immediately obliged. They were more familiar with waltzes than with jigs, obviously. But the waltz was still somewhat scandalous in Marie-Thérèse's circle, because it allowed a man to put his arm around a woman so intimately.

Jacques grinned down at her, his eyes telling her he knew exactly what she was feeling. Her hand was on his shoulder, and she was resisting the strong impulse to slide it around his neck in a caress.

They circled the floor in dizzying turns. Marie-Thérèse was so disoriented that she did not realize, until he captured her lips, that Jacques had whirled her behind a bank of greenery that concealed a hall leading to the withdrawing rooms. She moaned a protest that might have been a sound of pleasure. Pure fire cascaded through her veins and memories of his intimate exploration of her body flooded her mind. Her breasts ached for his touch, and a yearning she could not control possessed her. Her remembering hands crept up without her volition to twist her fingers in the curls of hair at his nape.

With a growl of pleasure, he pulled her closer. They clung together, the kiss deepening, until Jacques suddenly lifted his head and looked down at her with blazing eyes. "Can you still claim that you can't bear my touch?" he demanded, holding her so close that she could feel his fierce arousal.

She was appalled at how she had revealed her desire for him when all her reason recoiled from it. In a panic, she tore out of his arms and returned to the dance floor, enduring the stares of two ladies on their way to the withdrawing room. Her face felt cold, and she knew she must have paled. A short distance away, Gabriel awaited her, his eyes burning with suspicion. Jacques had caught up with her, and she introduced the two men, scarcely able to hear her own voice for the thundering of her heart. They bowed stiffly to each other.

Jacques stared Gabriel up and down and gave her a look of contempt that infuriated her, then excused himself. Gabriel was obviously angry, but he said nothing, only pursing his lips as he offered Marie-Thérèse his hand.

From the corner of her eye as she began following the steps of the dance, she watched Jacques walk away. He went straight to Madame Serbin, and invited her to join him in a set. Papa politely excused her, but looked after the handsome widow with regret and admiration. Marie-Thérèse felt a fluttering of alarm. Surely, surely not...

"This Monsieur Bonnard, who is on such intimate terms with the notorious Lafitte," Gabriel asked coldly, "is he the man your father left you to nurse at Petit Bois?"

"We thought he was a British spy. The army wanted to question him."

"A serious misjudgment, was it not?"

She refused to answer.

"He seems to have captivated all of the Dufrets. You most of all."

"He is a Baratarian! I despise him."

"Prove it," he challenged her as he circled her in measured steps. "Let me tell our families tonight that you have consented to our betrothal."

"I'm sorry, Gabriel. I can't marry you."

"You're in love with him!" Gabriel's eyes glittered with suppressed emotion. She had a chilling feeling that the emotion was rage.

"That's ridiculous!"

"Is it? Then why won't you give me your promise?"

"Please forgive me, Gabriel, but I don't wish to marry anyone."

"Has my mother said something to offend you?"

So Madame Duvallier had spoken to him against her. "Of course not!" she lied, but her flush defeated her attempt to deceive him.

"She doesn't control my fortune, Marie-Thérèse. She can do nothing to prevent me from making you my wife. Listen to me, *chère!* You can stop all their wagging tongues by marrying me. They have always been envious of you. Once you are my wife, they will soon be fawning over you again."

The prospect struck her as horrendous. "But I will not marry you, Gabriel."

"I think you will, my darling. You are not a fool."

She kept a smile on her face as they went through the stiffly formal movements of the minuet, and resolutely kept her eyes from following Jacques and the beautiful widow who had charmed Papa.

But Marie-Thérèse had never been more unhappy.

Chapter Twenty-One

Why couldn't she forget him?

Because she loved him. Because there was no other man in the world for her, and never would be. That was the horrifying truth.

The morning after the ball, she was back in the convent. She went from bed to bed, parrying the compliments and laughing at the jokes of the men who were recovering, and doing what she could for those who were still very ill. But beneath the surface of her composure she was fighting the memory of Jacques's stolen kiss at the ball and the shameful way she had responded to it. She was remembering the accusation of fickleness in his smoldering eyes, and something rebellious and wicked in her was exulting that he still wanted her.

Oh, how mysterious and confusing love was! Why couldn't she feel the way she should?

Hébert came by the convent to say goodbye before leaving the city to rejoin his regiment. "Things are not going well between you and Gabriel, are they?"

"How did you know?"

"How could I not? I don't think you spoke two words to him in the carriage on the way home from the ball! Tell me,

Marie-Thérèse, do you still have a *tendresse* for our pris-
oner-patient?"

"Hébert!" She flushed hotly. "How can you say—"

"Don't try to deny it, Marie-Thérèse. I was there."

"I hate him for what he is. I can't understand how you
and Papa can forget what happened to *Maman* and Adorée!"

"Monsieur Bonnard was not responsible for that!" Hébert said indignantly.

"He is a Baratarian! And we know it was a Baratarian
who set them adrift in a small boat in rough weather. Didn't
Papa find *Maman*'s necklace among the jewels seized in the
raid on Grande-Terre? Isn't that enough?"

"It isn't evidence against Monsieur Bonnard. Many privateers used Lafitte's headquarters as a warehouse.
Granted, some were guilty of piracy. But aren't you judging him rather harshly? What would we have done during
the long blockade without the privateers who smuggled
goods to us?"

"You have certainly changed your tune, haven't you?
The pirates are all heroes now!" she said scornfully. "Is it
because they know how to kill?"

"Monsieur Bonnard saved my life. Does that mean
nothing to you?"

She was momentarily silenced, feeling shame as she remembered how Jacques had struggled with the mad Gama
to save her, not once but twice! But the shame of loving him
was greater. "Of course it does, Hébert. But how many
others has he robbed and killed aboard the vessels he captured?"

"Why don't you ask him?" Hébert said angrily. "He
didn't save me out of any love for me, you know. He let me
know that soon enough when I tried to thank him. Said he

did it for you." Surprisingly, he grinned. "Now I know why."

She stared at him as he turned to go. Then he paused and said, "The Baratarian unit is still at the encampment where we fought the British."

Marie-Thérèse fumed as she returned to her wounded soldiers. Was Hébert actually suggesting that she go to the battlefield in search of Jacques?

Never!

Sister Mathilde found her and said, "Some soldiers are coming for our Lieutenant Bacon this morning. See if you can help him get ready to leave."

She found Lieutenant Bacon sitting glumly on his bed, dressed in some clothing that had been donated to replace his ruined uniform. He looked up at her. "I am going to prison, *mademoiselle*. Will you visit me there?"

Two American soldiers walked up to the bed. The first one examined a piece of paper in his hand, and said, "House arrest, lieutenant. We are to take you to the residence of a Monsieur Touré."

Hearing the name, Marie-Thérèse could guess what the American had said. "You'll be all right, *monsieur le lieutenant*. You'll likely be sent back to England when the peace treaty is signed."

"I'll be happy to leave this mosquito heaven!" he muttered, but his face had brightened.

"For shame!" she said. "You were fortunate to be left behind by your companions. If they had tried to take you with them, you wouldn't have survived."

He grinned sheepishly. "You may be right, *mademoiselle*."

For the first time she felt a sympathy for him. *"Bonne chance!"* she told him, handing him the little package of his belongings.

A little of his cockiness returned as he walked away between the two American soldiers.

When she went to the refectory for coffee, she found her father there, talking with Sister Mathilde. Like Hébert, he was on his way back to his regiment and had come to say goodbye.

He saw Marie-Thérèse and got to his feet. The nun rose, too, and said, "I will leave you with your daughter, Monsieur Dufret. We have been happy to have her help, but we can spare her now."

"What's this, Papa?"

"I have something to ask of you, and I wanted to make sure Sister Mathilde doesn't need you more than I do. She says many of your patients have now been sent home to their families. After talking with Monsieur Bonnard, I am very curious to know what condition the British left my property in, but neither Hébert nor I can get away from the army long enough to visit the plantation until General Jackson releases the volunteers."

"What is it you want to know, Papa?"

"I want you to hire a carriage and go down to Petit Bois. Don't go alone—ask Madame Claiborne to send one of her grooms with you. Find out if any of our horses remain and if they are being cared for. Ask Boddy to tell you the condition of the fields. If Beauté is still there, ride over the plantation with him."

"Oh, I hope I find Beauté there! I have missed her so."

"I also want to know the condition of the house. You may bring the staff back with you and instruct them to make ready the house in the city so that we can move into it as soon as we receive official word that the war is over. General Jackson seems determined to keep us all battle-ready until then, damn him!"

"You will supervise this with your usual efficiency, Marie-Thérèse, but I wish you to remain at Madame Claiborne's until I return. Did you have a good time at the ball, *chérie?*"

"Of course, Papa."

"I couldn't help but notice that Gabriel did not take you to his mother, although she was present."

"Madame Duvallier is not speaking to me, Papa. Like Rachel Jackson, I am tainted goods."

Her father's face flushed with sudden anger. "And I would have left you with that stupid woman if I had taken a musket ball! What if Gabriel had taken one, as well? I'm sorry I encouraged his suit." His eyes sharpened on her face. "You haven't accepted him?"

"No, Papa."

"There are other men, you know."

"Yes, Papa."

"Shall I tell Gabriel when I get back to the regiment that you have refused his offer?"

She smiled. "*Merci.* Papa...his poems are incredibly banal."

He laughed and hugged her. Then he stood back and studied her shrewdly. She felt suddenly as if he knew much more than she had told him.

"The war has changed many things, eh, *ma fille?*" he said at last, and then he left her to return to his regiment.

Marie-Thérèse was glad to have something to do. Jacques had rejected her, the nuns no longer needed her help, and social life in the city was, as Annalise complained, largely nonexistent. All the men of young or middle age still manned the forts and General Jackson's defense encampments. But she had mixed emotions about returning to Petit Bois and its painful memories.

On a mild February day, when the sky was blue with only a scattering of white clouds, she set off for the plantation. Her borrowed groom rode up beside the hired driver.

Sitting alone in the carriage as it bounced along the levee road, she let her thoughts return to the tumultuous days of her house arrest by the British, and she grew more depressed as the miles were covered. She passed the McCarty house, which was now General Jackson's headquarters, and soon after that, the encampment where Jacques was posted, an army of tents and campfires. Almost immediately she was passing the torn and muddy battlefield, still strewn with rubble thrown up by the cannonballs and with the debris left behind by wounded and dying men. The spasmodic heavy rains that had fallen since the battle had left it a sea of mud. When she passed Annalise's former home, she regarded it sorrowfully. A cannonball had pierced the roof, and already the house looked like an abandoned relic.

But when she came in sight of Petit Bois, her tears began to flow. It's pillars marched around the two-level *galerie,* shining white in the sun and reflected in the many-paned windows. The house looked forlorn amid its ruined gardens and felled trees, but smoke was rising from the chimneys.

When the carriage drew up before the steps, Estelle and Sophie and Apollo came running out to meet her, and soon Désirée came stumbling forward from the kitchen, followed by her girls, calling excited greetings and full of news and questions. The two older women embraced Marie-Thérèse emotionally. Soon Boddy came out of the office to greet her. They entered the house, and Désirée prepared food for her and fed her driver and groom in the kitchen.

Then Marie-Thérèse took her father's overseer into the library and asked for the accounting her father had requested.

"There will be no crop this year," Boddy said, "and there is much work to be done. But the land is still here, and most of the slaves remain. Two have disappeared, and two others I have sent to the hospital in Jumonville because there was no one here to treat them."

"How are Mattie and Doula?"

"They are well, but working very hard, caring for the British soldiers left behind."

"I want to ride over there to see them when we inspect the fields," Marie-Thérèse said. "Do we still have horses?"

"We lost some, but the British didn't try to take any mounts with them. Your Beauté is still here."

Marie-Thérèse cried, "She is all right? Oh, I am so glad."

"The British left in such a hurry that they didn't loot the house, either. There may be a few small things missing, but they left the furniture and carpets in fair condition."

"I want to check on things here this afternoon. Tomorrow morning, early, we will ride over the plantation and down to Jumonville.

After Boddy left her, Marie-Thérèse and Estelle went through the house. In the salon, she stopped short when she saw the empty space above the mantel where the portrait of the British general's lady had hung. Even in the tragic duty of returning the general's body to his vessel they had not forgotten to return the portrait to the new widow.

"Have my mother's portrait brought to its proper place immediately," Marie-Thérèse said to Estelle.

"*Oui, ma'mselle!*" Estelle was obviously mortified that she had not done it before.

Papa and Hébert would not have to see that space vacant.

That night, Marie-Thérèse retired to her own bed in her own chamber, with its repaired locks and painful memories. But she could not sleep. That wicked part of her mind that insisted on loving a pirate kept reminding her that Jacques had risked terrible odds in order to save Hébert, and after Hébert had all but killed him at Petit Bois when he struck him down and reopened his wound!

Her mended mosquito *barre* reminded her of the night Jacques had saved her from Gama's machete. He had come to her rescue when he was still almost too weak to stand.

She remembered how Jacques had prevented her from firing Hébert's musket when the British took possession of Petit Bois, probably saving both their lives. And how lovingly he had held her in the lee of a protective pillar while they watched the confusion of the British soldiers during the Americans' surprise attack.

That had been her first taste of the horrible reality of war, the screams and curses and the terror of the disorganized British soldiers who were forced to face gunfire without their weapons. It had prepared her for the bloody hell of suffering and dying men she would encounter in the convent hospital. Jacques had held her and comforted her, and that night he had made love to her.

As the memories of his loving came crowding back, she put her hands over her ears and told herself, "Stop this!"

But, oh, he had loved her so tenderly, so wonderfully, that she could not imagine ever accepting any other man's love.

Here at Petit Bois she was helpless against her memories. She relived Jacques's fight in the swamp with the crazed Gama, when she had feared for his life. Oh, she had been wild with anxiety! But she had been anxious before that. How she had brooded over his fever after Hébert had struck him down in the stable! Even then she had loved him.

Sleep would not come. It was almost as if he were there beside her. He had confessed that he had once thought to seduce her into helping him escape from Petit Bois. *I thought I could love you and let you go. But I can't.* He had escaped the British and then had come back for her.

He loved her....

Marie-Thérèse set off with Boddy early the next morning. Her eyes were still wet from her emotional reunion with Beauté, who had snuffled into her hand and tossed her head with pleasure. When they rode down the lane between the slave cabins, the children playing in the yards ran after Beauté, crying *"Ma'mselle! Ma'mselle!"* and their mothers appeared in the doorways, smiling and waving.

"Everyone is glad to see the soldiers go, and that you are back," Boddy observed.

But when they reached the cane fields, Marie-Thérèse viewed the damage with a profound gloom, and each mile they covered added to her depression. The stench of fermented cane stalks hung over everything. There was no green of young shoots showing. The only color in the ruined landscape came from the faded shirts and bandannas and straw hats of the field workers, who were filling up cannonball craters and plowing furrows.

"We should have been laying in the cane eyes for the new crop last month," Boddy said. "Instead, all my workers were unloading cannons and cannonballs and furnishing game and fish for the British army."

"Is it too late to plant now, M'sieu Boddy?"

"We're getting the ground ready, as you can see, but we'll have to buy the eyes of the cane from some place that harvests later than Louisiana. Ours have fermented, lying out in the weather all this time. Fortunately, our winter was cold, so they weren't all lost, but if we plant now there's scarcely time for the crop to ripen before we harvest. If we have one this year, it will be very small."

"I see," she said, feeling even more discouraged.

"In my birthplace, Saint-Domingue, sugarcane is an eighteen-month crop. Here we're trying to grow a tropical plant in a country that's only semitropical. We have to harvest it before it's completely ripe, in order not to lose it to a killing frost. You know how our canecutters lop off the top joints of the cane?"

She nodded. Cane harvest was the most exciting time of the year. Everyone on the plantation celebrated, the field workers, as well as the servants in the big house. In spite of the hard work, it was a time of parties and feasting. Growing up, she had watched every phase of it, enjoying the molasses treats along with the other children, stringing pecans on a thread and dipping them into the boiling syrup to make a delicious candy.

"The top's the part of the stalk that hasn't ripened yet and so has little sugar," Boddy was explaining. "They'll be lopping off half the stalk next fall."

That sounded ominous. "Papa won't be happy to hear this."

"No, *ma'mselle.*"

She had seen enough, and the odor of fermented cane was sickening her. They headed for Jumonville. There the picture was no less depressing. The once-neat landscape surrounding the mansion was littered with cast-off red coats left by the retreating army. The British had enlarged the plantation infirmary, and the guards patrolling it pointed up its function as a prison, as well as a hospital.

Inside the building, men wearing bandages and splints and using crude crutches lounged in a large room, four of them around a whist table. They looked on curiously when Doula ran to greet the visitors at the door, crying, "*Ma'mselle!* You came back!"

Marie-Thérèse embraced her and felt her ribs. "Yes, M'sieu Jacques took me to my father. You're very thin, Doula!"

"I'm fine, *ma'mselle.*" There was a question in Doula's dark eyes as they looked deep and saw the misery Marie-Thérèse was suffering, but she did not ask it. "I came just as you told me, and *Maman* put me to work. *Bonjour*, Papa." She hugged Boddy and said, "I'll go tell *Maman* you here."

But Mattie came in from the ward just then, her heavy round face alight with pleasure. "*Ma'mselle*, I knew it were you soon as you spoke! Is your papa well? And Hébert?"

"Papa and Hébert both came through the battle without injuries, Mattie."

"Then *le bon Dieu* heard my prayers!" Mattie looked tired, but she was obviously happy to see them. She turned to her husband and pecked his cheek. "You bought us a nice surprise today, Boddy."

"Mattie!" It was Dr. Boudreau's voice, calling her from the ward.

"Oui, m'sieu!"

Marie-Thérèse walked into the ward with her. It was a room full of cots, most of them occupied. A sheet had been pinned up around several of them. Dr. Boudreau emerged from behind one of them, saying wearily, "I need you here, Mattie." Then he saw Marie-Thérèse and said, *"Mademoiselle! Bonjour."*

"Bonjour, monsieur le docteur. How are you?"

"We're all exhausted here. Excuse me, *mademoiselle*. I'll be free in a few minutes."

Mattie followed him behind the screen of sheets, and Marie-Thérèse returned to the lounge to tell Doula that she wanted to take her back to New Orleans with her.

Doula's eyes gleamed, but tears welled up in them. "I be needed here, *ma'mselle*," she said. "*Maman* and Dr. Boudreau, they need me."

"We'll find someone who can do the work you do here," Marie-Thérèse promised.

Later she discussed Doula's leaving with the doctor and with both of Doula's parents. The doctor was reluctant to see her go but said it was Doula's choice. Boddy said, "She is a free woman. She must be free to come and go. I will be looking for a good husband for her."

Mattie told Doula, "There are many free families of color in the city. You will meet people like us."

"Remember that you are free," Doula's father told her. "That means that you can come home to your *maman* and me whenever you want."

"I'll take good care of her," Marie-Thérèse promised.

So it was decided, to Doula's delight. When Marie-Thérèse returned to Petit Bois, her young *femme de chambre* rode behind her father on his horse. A few days later they set off, with Doula in the carriage with Marie-Thérèse and the entire household staff in one of the wagons the British had left in good condition. It would follow leisurely, with Apollo at the reins and Beauté trotting behind it at the end of a rope.

When they passed the battlefield, Doula put her head out of the carriage window to see the barricade the British soldiers had stormed, where many of them had received the wounds she had bound. But Marie-Thérèse was looking for the encampment where the Americans awaited another attack that might never come, and wondered which tent was Jacques's.

That night, back in Madame Claiborne's guest chamber, she spent another sleepless night. Hébert's angry words kept repeating themselves in her head.

Aren't you judging him rather harshly?
Why don't you ask him?

Hébert had matured considerably during the past weeks since his entry into the militia. Living through the terrible battle with others dying all around him, and facing death himself, had made him grow up quickly.

Was he right about Jacques?

Jacques had looked so wonderful at the ball—a man who stood out among men. But General Jackson was keeping his army on the alert, and that meant that Jacques was detained at the encampment at the battlefield. If she wanted to see him, she would have to go to him.

Before morning she had come to a decision. She would do as Hébert had suggested. She would ask Jacques to tell her the uncensored truth about his past as a privateer and about any atrocities he might have committed. And if he told her that he had not ravished or murdered the women aboard the ships he had captured, she would believe him. Because she loved him.

She did not think she could have fallen so deeply in love with a man who would put women adrift in a small boat, let alone ravish them first! Wouldn't her heart know? If she told her he was not guilty of such crimes, she would believe.

A few days later, Marie-Thérèse mounted Beauté and, with her groom following her, set off down the levee road.

Spring was in the air that early February day, and she did not feel the cold. She would not let herself imagine what Jacques might say, because she feared that she would lose her courage. She rode along the river below the levee, listening to the birds singing in the trees beside the road, thinking how normal everything looked.

When she reached the McCarty plantation, she dismounted and gave her reins to the groom. A low picket fence ran around the house and garden. She went through the gate and up the path to the steps. A guard carrying a musket stood before the door.

"This is General Jackson's headquarters, *mademoiselle.* Do you have business here?"

"I have a message for the Baratarian Monsieur Jacques Bonnard," she said. "Will I find him here?"

"No. But you may give me the message," the guard said, "and it will be delivered to him."

"I can't do that," Marie-Thérèse said. "I must deliver it personally."

"Then wait here," the guard said, "and I will send for him. Who shall I say wants him?"

"Just say a messenger, *monsieur.*"

"Very well." He went inside.

She took a chair on the *galerie* and prepared to wait.

Chapter Twenty-Two

The scene she looked on was pastoral, with only the presence of uniformed men to suggest that a terrible battle had been waged a short distance away less than a month before. Across the road was a tremendous old oak tree dripping with gray moss that moved gently in the breeze coming off the river. Birds darted to and fro in its branches, hunting insects. Behind it, the mast of a gunboat with its sails reefed rose above the grassy levee.

The guard returned and took up his post beside the door.

Marie-Thérèse could feel her nerves tightening. What was she going to say when Jacques came? What if he didn't come?

After what seemed an interminable wait, she saw him walking upriver along the levee road. Her heart leapt when she recognized his familiar figure, wide-shouldered, with unruly hair lifted by the breeze. Her heart pounded. When he was fifty feet away, he saw her sitting on the *galerie* and for a moment stopped dead.

Obviously he had not expected to see her. After a pause, he came on.

She stood and walked down the steps to meet him at the gate. *"Bonjour,"* she said, her mouth dry. She could find no other words.

His gaze took in every detail of her appearance hungrily, but there was some dark emotion buried deep in it, something he was holding back. *"Bonjour, mademoiselle,"* he said. And then he added unbelievingly, *"You* have brought me a message?"

"Yes." She moistened her lips and came through the gate, closing it behind her. She was aware of the armed guard on the *galerie* watching them curiously. "Will you walk with me?"

He did not reply, but stood waiting, so she started across the road toward the big oak tree. After a moment he followed her. She walked around the tree to where the slope of the levee began and climbed a few steps until the upper branches of the mossy oak hid the house and the curious guard. There she turned to him.

"If I ask you a question, will you answer me truthfully? No matter what I ask?"

A spark flashed in his eyes, and she remembered that he had sworn never to lie to her again. "I have no reason to lie to you now."

"No," she agreed, and after a painful pause, asked, "Please, what is the difference between a privateer and a pirate?"

One eyebrow slanted upward, and his lips tightened. "Is that your question?"

"No. But I—I need to know."

"A privateer carries papers from a government authorizing him to stop and seize merchant vessels of an official enemy who may be carrying supplies. A pirate captures vessels of any country and lines his own pockets with their cargo."

She could barely form the words. "And you—?"

"As I have told you," he said stiffly, "I am a privateer with papers from a country sympathetic to the United States government. Does that answer your question?"

She flushed. "The, the passengers aboard the ships you captured—"

He said levelly, "It was my practice to put them ashore at the nearest port."

She moistened her lips, fighting the pain of the tragedy that had changed all their lives at Petit Bois. "I promise you that I will believe what you tell me, no matter what your answer." Drawing a deep breath, she spoke very fast. "I've been told that...that it's common...that the pirates who captured the ship my mother and sister were on p-probably ravished the women who were unfortunate enough to be passengers, and that some were m-murdered." She stopped, seeing his eyes harden.

"I have never struck a woman. And I have never had to force a woman I wanted. Does *that* answer your question?"

She lowered her eyes. "Yes."

"And you have no message for me?"

She looked up, her eyes brimming with tears. "I believe you," she said.

Jacques's gaze darkened with overwhelming emotion. He said nothing, regarding her with his jaw clenched until the thin scar on his cheek stood out whitely. He raised his arms and then pulled her into his embrace and kissed her with hard hunger.

She melted into the heaven of his arms, dizzy with joy at his nearness, glorying in the overwhelming strength of his desire. Her passion leapt to meet it. She felt as if she were melting into him, bones and all. His devastating strength seemed to be feeding on hers, which seemed to be flowing out of her. She clung to him, fearing she could not stand alone.

He lowered her to the grass, and for a moment she thought he would take her there, concealed only by the levee and the mossy branches of the oak, and her heart began racing.

But instead he leaned over her and looked deep into her eyes. "I can't live without you, Marie-Thérèse."

"Nor I you," she whispered, and a great peace settled in her heart as she admitted it. "There can never be anyone else for me."

He kissed her again, putting his hand on her breast in an infinitely tender caress. "I want you for always. Can we be married, do you think? Or must I steal you?"

Her heart leapt. "It would be heaven to be your wife."

"Will your father try to prevent it?"

"He will ask you how we will live."

He gently opened her bodice and looked at her breasts. She looked at his lips, curved with tenderness, and longed for his kiss.

He said, "You heard what Madame Serbin said at the ball? Jean can arrange financing for me to open an importing business in New Orleans after the treaty has been signed. He has great influence right now. Besides, his banker has always had an interest in Jean's business, so he will be favorably inclined. But your father is very influential, too. Damme, if I had my brigantine, I'd be tempted to simply carry you away! But I want to do this right. Because you are my love, my only love, and I want to spend the rest of my life loving you."

"Oh, Jacques, I will marry you gladly! What heaven it will be!" She reached up and touched his cheek, then ran her fingers lightly over his lips. She was remembering what her father had said when he had asked her to go to Petit Bois for him, and she told Jacques now, "I think Papa likes you, Jacques. As he said, the war has brought us many changes."

He held her tenderly, and they clung together, devouring each other with kisses, until he suddenly jumped up and pulled her to her feet. "I've got to go back to the encampment before I lose my head and end up in the brig! When the peace treaty is signed, I'll come to you. And I swear it, I'll never leave you again!"

With a groan of regret in his throat, he pushed away from her. Jumping down the slope, he went swiftly down the road.

In the suddenness of his leaving her, she staggered and sank to her knees on the grass, dazed by happiness and the tumultuous emotions aroused by his kisses. After a while, she was roused by a whinny from Beauté. She got to her feet and walked down to where her groom waited with her mount. He helped her into the saddle, and she began the long ride back to New Orleans, filled with ecstatic dreams.

She had not gone to confession since Jacques had rescued her from the British, but she would go now and confess her sins and her love for Jacques. And perhaps she would ask the priest about posting the banns when the peace treaty was signed.

In March General Jackson announced that he had received official word that a peace treaty had been signed in Ghent on the twenty-fourth of December, two weeks before the battle that had driven the British out of Louisiana!

Papa and Hébert came home, and Marie-Thérèse returned with them to the town house in the *quartier,* with its wrought-iron balcony railings and curved stair leading from its charming brick-paved patio to an inner *galerie* onto which their bedchambers opened. Marie-Thérèse came out of her chamber one afternoon and looked down to see Jacques standing in that patio, looking wonderfully fit and happy. She ran down the stair and flew into his arms.

"I've come to speak to your father," he said.

Monsieur Dufret greeted him warmly and ordered port brought to his study. They were closeted in there for a very long time, and then Marie-Thérèse was summoned.

"Monsieur Bonnard has asked for your hand, *ma fille.* Is this your desire?" He did not seem surprised.

"Yes, Papa." She looked at Jacques with all her love shining in her eyes.

"I do not know anyone who has more right to become one of our family," Monsieur Dufret said. "I shall have the banns posted, and you may plan a wedding. Ask Madame Serbin to help you. I expect to leave immediately for Petit Bois to discover what is left of my fortunes."

Six weeks later, Marie-Thérèse and Jacques exchanged their vows and were united in wedding rites in St. Louis Cathedral, at a ceremony attended by a large congregation, all curious to see the privateer who had won the most eligible heiress in New Orleans. But the happy bride and groom pledging their love had eyes only for each other.

* * * * *

Author's Note

Jean Lafitte has become a legend in accounts of the Battle of New Orleans, and I have drawn on both legend and fact in my fictional story. The British offer for his help in their Louisiana campaign has been established as fact, but I have telescoped the dates somewhat in the interests of my plot.

The peace treaty between England and America ending the War of 1812 was signed in Ghent, in the Netherlands, on December 24, 1814, but word of the signing did not reach either the British or the Americans until March of 1815. The Battle of New Orleans was fought on January 8, 1815, and the following night the defeated British began pulling out of Louisiana. On January 23rd, General Andrew Jackson was honored as a hero in the place d'Armes, which was later named Jackson Square in his honor.

The shared defense of New Orleans brought the Creoles of the new state, who had looked to Europe for their culture and their way of life, a better understanding of their fellow American citizens—and the Americans more respect for the Creoles.

ROMANCE IS A YEARLONG EVENT!

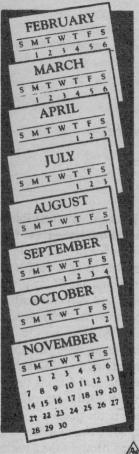

Celebrate the most romantic day of the year with MY VALENTINE! (February)

CRYSTAL CREEK
When you come for a visit Texas-style, you won't want to leave! (March)

Celebrate the joy, excitement and adjustment that comes with being JUST MARRIED! (April)

Go back in time and discover the West as it was meant to be . . . UNTAMED—Maverick Hearts! (July)

LINGERING SHADOWS
New York Times bestselling author Penny Jordan brings you her latest blockbuster. Don't miss it! (August)

BACK BY POPULAR DEMAND!!!
Calloway Corners, involving stories of four sisters coping with family, business and romance! (September)

FRIENDS, FAMILIES, LOVERS
Join us for these heartwarming love stories that evoke memories of family and friends. (October)

Capture the magic and romance of Christmas past with HARLEQUIN HISTORICAL CHRISTMAS STORIES! (November)

WATCH FOR FURTHER DETAILS IN ALL HARLEQUIN BOOKS!

CALEND

THREE UNFORGETTABLE KNIGHTS

First there was Ruarke, born leader and renowned warrior, who faced an altogether different field of battle when he took a willful wife in *Knight Dreams* (Harlequin Historicals #141, a September 1992 release). Now, brooding widower and heir Gareth must choose between family duty and the only true love he's ever known in *Knight's Lady* (Harlequin Historicals #162, a February 1993 release). And coming later in 1993, Alexander, bold adventurer and breaker of many a maiden's heart, meets the one woman he can't lay claim to in *Knight's Honor,* the dramatic conclusion of Suzanne Barclay's Sommerville Brothers trilogy.

If you're in need of a champion, let Harlequin Historicals take you back to the days when a knight in shining armor wasn't just a fantasy. Sir Ruarke, Sir Gareth and Sir Alex won't disappoint you!

IN FEBRUARY LOOK FOR *KNIGHT'S LADY* AVAILABLE WHEREVER HARLEQUIN BOOKS ARE SOLD

*O*nce upon a time...

There was the best romance series
in all the land—Temptation.

You loved the heroes of REBELS & ROGUES.
Now discover the magic and fantasy of romance. Pygmalion, Cinderella and Beauty and
the Beast have an enduring appeal—and are the
inspiration for Temptation's exciting new
yearlong miniseries, LOVERS & LEGENDS.
Bestselling authors including Gina Wilkins,
Glenda Sanders, JoAnn Ross and Tiffany White
reweave these classic tales—with lots of sizzle!
One book a month, LOVERS & LEGENDS con-
tinues in March 1993 with:

#433 THE MISSING HEIR
Leandra Logan
(Rumpelstiltskin)

Live the fantasy....

LL3

HARLEQUIN®

my Valentine

1993

The most romantic day of the year is here! Escape into the exquisite world of love with MY VALENTINE 1993. What better way to celebrate Valentine's Day than with this very romantic, sensuous collection of four original short stories, written by some of Harlequin's most popular authors.

**ANNE STUART
JUDITH ARNOLD
ANNE McALLISTER
LINDA RANDALL WISDOM**

**THIS VALENTINE'S DAY, DISCOVER ROMANCE
WITH MY VALENTINE 1993**

Available in February wherever Harlequin Books are sold.   VAL93